SORCERER'S FEUD

SORCERER'S FEUD

Katharine Kerr

OSEL BOOKS
San Rafael

Cover design by Laila Parsi.

ISBN: 978-1-940121-02-4

Osel Books
Published by Urtext Media LLC
San Rafael, CA 94901
www.urtext.us

Printed in the United States of America

In Memoriam

Barbara Ramsey Jenkins

1938 — 2013

AUTHOR'S NOTE

These days, many readers depend on genre labels when they're looking for something to read. Those who classify books—booksellers, librarians, and reviewers—have typed this book and its predecessor, *Sorcerer's Luck,* as Urban Fantasy. Neither book, however, fits particularly well into that subgenre, which, like all subgenres, has rules of its own. The "Runemaster" books actually fall into the category of "occult novels" or perhaps "fantasy noir."

CHAPTER 1

Late afternoon sun spilled across the living room carpet, a promise of warmth and fresh air. I turned off the hyperactive air conditioning in our second-story flat and opened the windows to let in the breeze. It carried with it the scent of our neighbor's roses mingled with the dry grass of early fall. My laptop and a cup of coffee waited for me on the coffee table. I sat down on the leather couch and managed to control my shaking hands enough to boot up the laptop and hit the Internet. The coffee sloshed in my mug when I picked it up. I held it in both hands and tried a cautious sip.

"Sweetheart?" Tor said. "What are you doing?"

I set the coffee down and turned to look at him. He was standing just behind me and staring over my shoulder at the screen.

"Hunting for news," I said. "Like you probably knew already."

"Maya!" He walked around the couch and sat down next to me. "It's been two weeks. The police have no idea that you—"

"I know that. It's not the police thing that bothers me. I just can't forget what happened as easily as you can."

Tor sighed and turned sideways so he could look at me. I waited for him to go on, but he stayed silent and considered me with a little frown.

Two weeks earlier, at the beginning of September, I'd killed a man by draining him of his élan vital, his life force, his chi—different names but the same mysterious energy. I have a disease that you could call vampirism, not that I'm undead like the vampires in the movies. I just can't regenerate my élan like normal people do, so as a child I learned how to steal it from others, just a little bit here and there, not enough to harm anyone. But I used it to kill when Tor's uncle, Nils Halvarsson, attacked me.

"Look," Tor said. "It was self-defense."

"I know, but—"

"There isn't any but. He put your brother in the hospital. He was trying to kill me. He would have killed you, too, if he'd dragged you off somewhere." His voice dropped to a growl of rage. "And shit, who knows what he would have done to you first?"

Revulsion rose in my throat with the taste of vomit. "I know all that! But I killed someone, Tor. After I swore to God and my father that I never would."

For a moment he blinked at me. "Okay," he said at last. "Breaking an oath, that's hard."

I felt like screaming at him, but anger only wastes élan. I'd learned that lesson, too, how to keep every shred of it inside. The guilt, though, lay beyond my control. At times it made me tremble. Tor said nothing further, just watched me surf the Net until curiosity got the better of him.

"Find anything?" he said.

"What about this? You've got a cousin you didn't know you had, and he's out here now, dealing with his dad's death."

That revelation made Tor wince.

"He totally looks like you," I pointed at the photo on the webpage.

Tor studied the image of another tall, lean guy with sandy brown hair and brown eyes. They shared the same strong jaw and broad hands.

"Joel Halvarsson," Tor said. "I guess his family decided against naming him the old way. He should be Nilsson, and Joel isn't a Nordic name."

"You would think of that." I tried to smile.

Tor reached over, took my hand, and kissed my fingers

before he went on. "Look, brooding about it is only going to make it worse."

"If I could stop, I would." I let my voice trail away, because I'd spotted an important point in the web article. "I guess Joel's not all torn up over this. Thank god for that!"

The reporter quoted him as saying, "My father was an odd, distant man. I didn't know him well at all. He divorced my mother when I was just a kid, and I only saw him a couple of times a year." When the interviewer asked why he was handling his father's estate, Joel answered, "I'm the oldest son." Nothing more.

"Oldest son, huh?" Tor said. "He must have brothers, then."

"Nils was married a couple of times at least. Maybe he had kids in each marriage."

"That's a possibility, sure."

"Do you think Joel knows that his father was a vitki? Or that you are?"

"I'm more interested in whether he's a sorcerer himself. Run that video, will you? Maybe I can pick up something about him."

I clicked on the arrow in the video window. Joel and the reporter basically repeated the interchange in the text. Joel spoke crisply, a little fast, but you could tell that he'd planned out every word. He ended the interview with a firm statement, "I've got an appointment with my father's lawyer in an hour. That's all I'm going to say at this time." I stopped the video.

"The talent's skipped him," Tor said. "I'm pretty sure of it, anyway. That's a relief."

"Why?"

"I'm hoping he won't carry on his father's feud with me. Joel's going to send us something. What he sends should tell me what's going on with him."

"What? When did he say that?"

Tor grinned at me. Sorcery. I don't know why I bothered to ask.

For the rest of the evening, I managed to put the killing

out of my mind, but it caught up with me again. I'd been sleeping badly ever since it happened, and that night I kept waking up from pieces of bad dreams. I finally dragged myself out of bed at eight in the morning. I set up the laptop on the breakfast bar that separated our living room from the kitchen. While I ate some yogurt, I surfed for news.

Tor came yawning into the kitchen a few minutes later.

"You look tired," he said. "Do you need élan?"

"Yeah, maybe that will help."

"Help what? You're not still beating yourself up over Nils, are you?" Tor caught my hand between both of his. "Sweetheart," he said, "you really didn't have any choice."

I wanted to believe it, for his sake as well as mine. "Okay. You'll have to help me forget it."

"I'll do everything I can. You should know that by now."

I leaned over and kissed him. "I do know. I love you."

"I love you too." He took another kiss. "That's better. You—" ،

The front door, downstairs at street level, buzzed as loudly as a snarling animal. The laptop screen flashed and switched automatically to the security system. I saw a grayscale shot of a FedEx man with one of their cardboard document envelopes tucked under one arm.

"I'll go get it," Tor said.

The documents in the envelope turned out be from Joel Halvarsson. Tor read through the cover letter, then handed it to me while he looked over some legal size papers. The letter was addressed to Torvald E. Thorlaksson, Tor's full name.

"In a recent codicil to his will my father requested that you receive a box of various notebooks and papers, which are, as far as I can tell, written in Icelandic. I have no idea what they are, but the instructions implied that you're capable of reading them. The docs accompanying this letter list them. He also wanted you to have a portrait of our mutual grandfather, Halvar Svansson. I've deposited this material at the lawyer's office, where you can sign for it. His address and phone number are on the copies of the legal listings. You'll need to show a picture ID. There's been an incident. Yours, Joel Halvarsson."

"Cold," I said.

"He probably didn't know I existed until he read the will." Tor laid the papers down on the breakfast bar. "What do you say to a cousin you've never met?"

"And what do you think means by incident?"

"No idea!" He shrugged. "Nils hated me. Why's he leaving me family papers?"

"Do you think they're poisoned?"

"No." He grinned at me. "Cursed, more like it. I'll do a banishing over the box before I bring it into the house, don't worry."

"Can't we just burn it?"

"I'm too curious." He tapped the list with one finger. "Some of these papers come from Grandfather Halvar. His journals. A magical record. I've got to see them."

I felt dread, an icy cold twist in the pit of my stomach. "It's dangerous. Something's wrong with the stuff at the lawyer's. I can feel it."

"Of course there is! I'm not arguing with you. I'm going to exorcise it. Don't worry, Maya! I won't bring it inside till I've worked it over. Look, could Nils ever beat me? With magic, I mean."

"No. That's why he got violent."

"Okay. I know a little about the runes, don't I?"

A little! The rituals I'd seen him work and the power he could summon! More than a little, for sure.

"Okay," I said. "It's just that everything scares me these days."

"I know. Let me feed you. You'll feel better."

I fell in love with Tor before I realized he could help me with my disease. Although he couldn't cure it, he could keep me from dying by gathering élan from the natural world and transferring it to me. We stood in a patch of sunlight beside an open window. Tor stared out at the tree-covered hillside behind the house for a couple of minutes, then stretched out his hands in my direction. I began to tremble in anticipation. I could feel the élan gathering, quivering in the air like the scent of roses and honey. I reached for it and felt it flow over me, into my blood, into my deepest self. I gasped, breathed it in, and nearly sobbed in relief.

"How's that?" Tor said.

"Better." I smiled at him. "You're right, yeah. I'm not frightened anymore."

"Good. It's a miracle that you survived all those years on your own."

"My dad fed me when I was little. I didn't realize it till I was older, but he kept me alive. And we always lived where it was foggy, too, out in the Richmond district in the city, mostly."

"That didn't make it worse?"

"No. It should've, I guess, but both of us felt a lot better when it was cold and wet. It was like the fog, especially the seriously thick ones, gave us élan."

"It should have been the other way around. Cold tires most people out."

"That's what my mother always said, too. But both of us loved swimming and fog and the water. That's why I take so many showers, I guess."

Tor considered me with an odd expression on his face, mostly curious, but a little—not exactly frightened—apprehensive, maybe. He seemed to be about to say more, then gave me a bland smile. "I better get dressed," he said. "I want to go down and cast the runes before I go out."

Tor owned our house up in the hills, the Piedmont area of Oakland. Downstairs was his workshop, as he called it, and we lived upstairs in his beautiful flat, the classiest place I'd ever lived in my life. He came from money, and the hardwood floors, the Persian rugs, the leather furniture and Tiffany lamps showed it. For an art student like me, the luxury meant a lot more than money. Some of the art objects he owned were so beautiful that they soothed my fears better than any tranks could have.

That morning I got a sketch pad and some oil pastels and calmed myself further. From the time I was four years old and got my first box of crayons, I learned to bury all sorts of anxieties by concentrating on drawing. I built up my own little worlds, clumsy at first, then with more skill as I grew older. I drew fiercely, compulsively, whenever my parents fought or money was tight, and of course, when I had my bouts of the mysterious illness that dogged me all through childhood. A rare form of anemia, my family called it, a necessary lie.

These days, however, I needed to be careful when I drew. I'd had a few occurrences of my subconscious mind taking control of my hand to portray things that I never meant to draw. I concentrated on the view out of the west window, a distant prospect of San Francisco touched with morning fog and kept my mind firmly focused on the color and proportion of something real. I'd just finished when Tor came back upstairs. He was carrying an old shoebox. He sat down next to me on the sofa and put the box on the coffee table, then glanced at my drawing.

"That's really cool," he said. "Pretty."

"Yeah, too pretty. I'm out of touch with all the modern trends. I should've been an Impressionist. Art critics just laugh at stuff like this."

"Their loss."

"I'd like to think so. Fat chance they'll ever see it that way. What's in the box?"

"The gold plaque. I brought it up to see if you could use your talent. Y'know, to dispel an illusion covering it. Or see if one existed. We never tried that, not in any formal way."

Tor took off the lid of the shoebox and laid it on the coffee table, then peeled off a thick layer of cotton batting to reveal a pure gold square about six inches on a side and an inch thick. At each corner someone had drilled a small hole to allow the plaque to be sewn onto some sort of backing—my guess was leather horse harness, just because of the weight of the thing. It would have torn free of a tunic or distorted a heavy cloak. On the front, engraved runes ran around the

edge while an equal-armed cross in a circle sat in the middle.
On the back, a spiral of runes pretty much covered the surface. The language was so ancient that Tor could decipher
neither inscription.

"I'm betting that something in Halvar's papers will help
me," Tor said. "That's one reason why I've got to have them."

I tore off my drawing of the distant city, laid it on the coffee table out of the way, then rummaged through my box of
pastels till I found a black stick. I opened the sketch book to
a new page and stared at the gold ornament, not the paper,
while I drew. My hand obligingly made a gestural drawing
of the ornament. I started to fill in the runes at one corner,
but Tor stopped me.

"That looks just like the gold square." He sounded disappointed. "Nothing's changing."

"Then there isn't any illusion on it."

"Yeah. Well, at least we know." He stood up. "I'll put it
back in the safe."

"It's worth a lot of money, all that gold."

"Yeah, but it's not just that. Nils wanted it. It's one of the
things that made him hate me. Started the feud off, in a way."
His eyes had gone slack in a way I'd come to recognize, when
he was seeing some intangible thing. "And someone else still
wants it. Real badly. Maybe Joel. Maybe the rime jötnar."
His eyes returned to a normal focus. "I'm going to cast the
staves before I go."

I went downstairs to watch him do the reading. The entrance to the lower flat led into the library room, a space just
under the living room upstairs. Like the living room, it had
a fireplace and a couple of leather chairs and floor lamps,
but the shelves holding Tor's amazing collection of books,
most of them about magic, took up the rest of the space. To
the right was the master suite, but instead of a bedroom, Tor
had turned it into his workshop. Near the draped floor-to-
ceiling windows, two barstools, the kind with backs, sat on
either side of a tall wooden table like you'd find in a science
lab in a high school.

I perched on one of the barstools. Tor spread a white linen cloth on the table, then brought out a red leather pouch of staves—thin oblongs of wood, about one inch by an inch and a half, each carved with a red-painted rune. He poured them onto the cloth, then looked away while I turned them all face-down and mixed them up. Once I finished, he stood considering the spread for a couple of minutes. I heard a high-pitched squeak, sort of like an oversized hamster, in the library room and turned around to look. I saw nothing.

"Just the nisse," Tor said. "He comes and goes."

The house spirit squeaked again and made a rustling noise among the books.

"Hey!" Tor called out.

The noise stopped.

Tor started with a quick reading with only three runes. He held his hand out flat over the spread, then pounced on one rune. He picked it up and flipped it over: Fehu.

"Gold," he said. "That's the past circumstance." He drew another. "Thurisaz in the present. Someone's directing some kind of force at us or at the gold." He picked up the last stave, the rune indicating what might happen in the future. "Hagalaz. With Thurisaz right there, I'd say there's trouble coming." He stared at the trio for a moment, then drew two more runes and laid them down by Hagalaz to modify it. Naudhiz and then Wunjo inverted—necessity and sorrow. "Yeah, a lot of trouble coming."

Tor had me turn the runes over and mix them up again, then chose one more rune: Thurisaz again.

"I thought maybe the jötnar were after the gold plaque," Tor said. "I might have been right." He glanced at his watch. "I'll do a longer reading later."

While Tor went to the lawyer's office, I had lunch with my two closest friends. Cynthia, with her solid build and brown hair, pulled back in a scrunchie, and blonde slender Brittany with her boyish jeans and tee shirts, looked like opposites. Cynthia was a couple of years older than me and Brit, too—a late-blooming art rebel, she called herself. Didn't matter. We all had a lot in common. The three of us went to our favorite place, a café in downtown Oakland that was right across the street from the park surrounding Lake Merritt. We got our usual table in the front window with its view of trees.

Since we'd just started our last year at a local art college, we needed to come up with ideas for our senior projects, the most important requirement for graduation. Cynthia, who was taking the computer animation curriculum, would make a short film. Brittany's strengths lay in fiber arts. She was planning a series of small versions of fiber modules—combinations of weaving, macramé, and needlework—designed to add warmth and human scale to various public spaces in the San Francisco Bay Area. Me—well, I didn't have any ideas yet.

"I kind of put it off," I said. "Since I'm only going half-time this semester."

"What's that doing to your loans?" Cynthia said.

"I didn't take any. I feel weird about it, but Tor insisted that I let him bankroll me."

"You're complaining?" Brittany wrinkled her nose at me. "Maya, after the way you've been pushing yourself—for years, really—you need the rest. I'm happy for you."

"Me, too," Cynthia said. "There were times when you'd get those dark circles under your eyes and practically down to your neck, and I was worried you were going to die on us right then and there."

"I kind of worried, myself."

"So okay," Brit said. "You're only taking the six units?"

I nodded yes because I'd just bitten into my sandwich.

"So you've only got the project seminar."

"Yeah." I swallowed the bite. "Everyone in Fine Arts is talking about installations. TVs stacked up with weird film loops, or plaster corpses, or junk like that Cremaster guy in New York is doing. I don't want to do anything like that."

"So don't," Cynthia said. "You want to paint, paint."

"I also want to graduate with good grades."

"Yeah," Brittany said, "but Harper's your advisor, right? I bet she'll sign off on the right kind of painting project."

"Maybe, but what's the right kind?"

"Something large." Cynthia laid the remains of her hamburger down on her plate and reached for a paper napkin. "And socially significant but absurdist, too."

"A mural." I felt the beginnings of an idea start moving deep in my mind. "If I can find someone to let me use their wall. I bet I could. Murals are big in San Francisco."

"They sure are," Cynthia said. "But does that make them too mainstream?"

"Yeah, maybe so. Harper's not going approve anything mainstream. Or wait, I could do panels. And they could like fit onto a freeway overpass or somewhere you wouldn't expect to see a mural."

"There you go," Brittany said. "But you couldn't actually put them on the freeway. You can get arrested for that. They're a traffic hazard, Caltrans says."

"Makes sense," Cynthia put in. "You want drivers watching the road, not staring at the art works."

"For sure." I remembered a couple of incidents from past years, when the authorities had pulled down American flags and political slogans. "How about a model to show how they'd look? Or, wait! A Photoshop mock-up. That would be kind of Post-modern."

"That's what I'm going to do for my installations." Brittany paused for a sip of coffee. "Unless one of the malls actually wants to buy one and let me set it up full size." Her voice turned sarcastic. "Ha! Like they ever would!"

The waiter arrived to clear plates and rattle off a list of desserts.

"Chocolate mousse for me," Brittany said.

Cynthia looked mournful. "I'd better not. Thighs."

"Ah come on!" I said. "We've got something to celebrate."

"Oh yeah? What?"

"Tor asked me to marry him, and I said yes."

Brittany cheered, and Cynthia pumped a fist in the air.

"Chocolate mousse all round," I said, "and more coffee."

The waiter grinned and hurried off.

"So okay," Brittany said. "When?"

"I don't know yet. I want to wait until I get my project going, really going, I mean, like maybe almost done. And in the spring I'll have to take a full load of units, too. I don't want anything to get in the way of graduating."

"Smart." Cynthia gave me a firm nod. "Jim and I had the simplest wedding we could come up with, but our relatives made it a huge distraction and upheaval anyway."

"Yeah," I said, "but that was the fight over synagogue versus church, wasn't it?"

"Mostly, and you won't have to worry about that, at least. My family, good grief! You'd think they were all rabbis instead of a bunch of businessmen."

"Is Tor going to get you a ring?" Brittany said.

"Yes, but I don't want some big diamond or anything elaborate. I don't want him spending thousands on it. You guys know what he's like, throwing money around."

They nodded their agreement.

"I just hope this doesn't make me a bigamist," I went on. "Me and Tor and the bear spirit."

Cynthia laughed and nearly choked on her coffee, but Brittany wrinkled her nose at me. "Maya, how can you joke about it?"

"It's that or cry."

My friends shared Tor's secret. Once a month, at the full moon, he became possessed by the spirit of a bear and became, for that few days, and in a really strange way, a bjarki, a shape-changer.

We'd just finished our dessert when I got a text from Tor. He and his friend Billy were driving out to Stinson Beach to "do something" about the box of papers. I took that as meaning that Nils had cursed the collection after he'd packed it. Late in the afternoon, once we'd both gotten home, Tor confirmed my guess.

"I'll give Nils credit," Tor told me. "He's thorough. The curse spells didn't amount to much. I didn't have any trouble dispelling them. But there were a lot of them. On every lousy piece of paper in the box. And the box itself."

"Why go to the beach?"

"I could draw on the sea's power for the dispelling. The ocean has its own kind of élan."

"In that letter, your cousin said something about bringing an ID. Did you find out why?"

"Sure did. The lawyer himself came out of the inner sanctum to tell me. Someone called him asking about Nils' property, but the guy refused to identify himself. He had an odd accent, like maybe English was his second language."

"What did the lawyer do?"

"Told him politely where to get off, but he pressed the point. He was interested, the guy said, in Nils' literary remains. Tried to imply that he was a journalist from some Wisconsin newspaper who wanted to write an article about Nils. Called him a literary figure. The lawyer knew better."

"That's creepy."

"Most things Nils touched are. Look, when I read the staves, Fehu keeps coming up. Wealth, land, gold. I wonder if someone wants the papers to see if they'll lead him to the gold plaque. Can't be Joel, if I'm right. He could have kept the stuff, and I'd have never known the difference."

I glanced around the living room. "Where are the papers?"

"Downstairs. With another lousy portrait of my grandfather. Nils got one, just like everyone else in the family. Now he's dumped it on me. A last insult." He thought for a moment. "Y'know, I'd like to get a good look at Joel. Maybe I can arrange something."

"Tor! You don't even know this guy. You can't use a summon spell on him. It's just so rude."

"Nothing serious, nothing dangerous. If he's got any talent for sorcery, he'll brush it right off, and then I'll know what I need to, anyway. What are you going to do?"

"Work on my laptop. I've decided to start keeping a journal."

"Good idea." He grinned at me. "Especially with your talents."

"Oh, just go away will you?"

With one last grin he headed off downstairs.

So many weird events had happened, too many to keep clear in my mind. I felt in a dim, half-blind way that a pattern lay under them all. There had been a fad some years back for computer generated images made up of dots and squiggles and blobs. At first you could only see messy rows of repeated motifs, but if you let your eyes go out of focus in just the right way, three dimensional forms would suddenly appear. The patterns confused your brain so much that the pictures became stereoptic without a mechanical viewer. My life felt like one of those paintings, and I hadn't yet learned how to see the hidden depths.

I opened a new file on my laptop and started writing down everything I could remember, starting from the day I met Tor. It took hours.

The afternoon turned so hot in the parching East Bay autumn that the air conditioning had trouble keeping up. Rather than cook, we went to our favorite Indian restaurant up in Berkeley and got our usual table in a back corner, near a window that looked out onto a tangle of plants and raspberry canes that had once been a garden. We were still studying the menu when I happened to look in the direction of the door. For a moment I thought Tor stood there at the same time as he was sitting across from me. Had he doubled himself like the vitkar in the old sagas? I caught my breath with a little gasp. Tor looked up and turned in his chair to see what I was staring at.

"There's Joel," he said.

"How do you know that?"

"He looks like me, doesn't he? A logical assumption, Watson. There can't be more than two of us."

"Very funny!"

Tor stood up and waved to the guy, who took one step toward him, stared for a moment, then shrugged and strolled over.

"Tor, no! I don't want to have dinner with—" I stopped

myself. I couldn't say it, 'with the son of the man I killed', not there in public.

I'd spoken too late, anyway. Joel Halvarsson arrived at our table. I'd expected him to dress in expensive clothes like his father's, but he was wearing a pair of jeans and a striped cotton shirt and carrying a beaten-up sweatshirt, an outfit that made him look right at home in Berkeley. Tor got up and held out his hand. Joel smiled—briefly—and shook it—also briefly.

"Kind of a funny way to meet your cousin," Joel said. "But when I came in and saw you, I figured I could at least say hello."

"Sure," Tor said. "Have a seat! This is my fiancée, Maya Cantescu."

Joel nodded my way with a pleasant smile, then took the chair next to Tor and opposite me. Seeing them together made me aware of small differences. Tor was a little taller, and Joel lacked the cute dimple Tor had at one corner of his mouth. Still, Grandfather Halvar's descendants had strong genes. I decided that I needed to pretend to be shy. I don't think I volunteered more than two sentences during the entire meal.

At first neither of the two men talked much. We all ordered, and when the food came, Tor and Joel mostly ate. I picked at a curried vegetable dhosa. Guilt does bad things to your appetite. But after the guys had finished an Indian beer apiece, they did chat, mostly about baseball—the Oakland A's and on Joel's part, the Yankees. Tor ordered a second beer for both of them and a mango lhassi for me. The last thing I needed was to muddle my mind with alcohol. Joel leaned back in his chair and considered Tor over the rim of his glass.

"Could you read the stuff in that box?" Joel said.

"Oh yeah. My college major was Germanic languages. The papers are in Icelandic, all right, most of them. Some are in Old Norse. A few are in German."

"Okay. You could have fooled me." Joel shrugged to underscore the point, then hesitated. "I was wondering if you ever knew my dad."

I went tense. Tor had sworn a vow to the runes to never

lie about himself.

"Not to say knew him," Tor said. "I saw him a couple of times, but he didn't want anything to do with my side of the family."

Which was all true enough. Just barely enough.

"Yeah, that was one of the things he did tell me." Joel frowned into his beer. "He was a pretty odd customer, my old man."

"I got that impression."

"My mother thinks he was mentally ill," Joel went on. "Neurotic, she called it. I'd say she was being kind. Y'know, he told me once he was a werewolf. Can you believe it? Of all the weird delusions to have!"

Out of sheer nerves I giggled, just a little before I choked it back, because Nils had told him the truth. Joel grinned at me. "Don't be embarrassed," he said. "I had the same reaction."

"It sounds like a delusion, all right," Tor said. "When I looked at some of those papers, I got the impression your dad thought he was a sorcerer."

"That, too." Joel hesitated, then spoke quickly, like a confession. "He drank a lot, y'know. One night, the last time I saw him, he was talking about your father. I guess they hated each other."

"My father never mentioned yours," Tor said. "So I've got no idea if he hated Nils or not."

Joel stared into his glass at the last bit of beer, swirled it around a little, then shrugged and drank it off. "Ah crap," he said at last. "Dad's dead, and this can't harm him. But that night, I had a couple of drinks, but he was hitting the scotch pretty hard, and he told me he'd murdered your father by sending him some kind of curse. I sobered up real fast, let me tell you. I couldn't believe he'd talk like that. I mean, bullshit to the max! But the worst part was what it told me about him, that he'd hate someone so much."

Tor turned very still. The expression on his face revealed nothing, an absolute blank, but I knew him. I could feel the fury just under the surface. Joel, fortunately, only saw the blank look.

"Yeah, it's nuts," Joel said. "I know that, okay?"

"Okay." Tor managed to smile. "Too bad. Must be hard to have a father with problems like that."

"My stepfather is a pretty decent guy. He came through for me. I've been luckier than a lot of my friends."

"Good. I saw that interview you gave the news station. If you're the eldest son, you must have brothers."

"Half-brother, just one. And a half-sister. They live up in Connecticut with their mom, Dad's second wife, or she was for a few years. I stay in touch with the family."

"You live back east, then?"

"In New York City. My mom lives near there. She and my stepfather have a house in the Hamptons."

So they had serious money. It seemed to follow Halvar's descendants around. Joel glanced at his watch. "Which reminds me. I've got a red-eye flight to catch." He reached for his back pocket. "Let me pick up the check."

"Hell, no," Tor said. "I'll cover it. Good to meet you."

A few pleasantries, and Joel got up and left. Neither of us said anything until we saw him leave the restaurant. I let out a long sigh of relief.

"That was awful," I said.

"Why?" Tor poured the last of his beer into his glass. "He seemed okay. He's got a little bit of the family talent, not much, but otherwise he's a decent guy."

"Tor!"

"I know, sweetheart. Sorry." He finished the beer in one long swallow. "But it's no wonder I felt I had to meet him. The rune staves said he had something important to tell me." He set the empty glass down and wiped his mouth on his shirt sleeve before he continued. "Now we know about my father's death."

"Liv was right. Nils killed him."

"Yeah." Tor's voice sank to something close to a growl.

"Stop feeling so fucking guilty, will you?"

"I'll try. But sitting here and looking at Joel, and knowing what I did—"

"Yeah. I really am sorry." He leaned across the table and caught my hand. "Let's go home."

Taking a life, after you've been raised to honor Buddhism and to value compassion above all other virtues, is not so easy to dismiss. I could add Thorlak's murder to Nils' list of crimes, sure, but I had no right to set myself up as judge and executioner.

CHAPTER 2

As soon as we got home that evening, I set up my laptop on the breakfast bar and went hunting for news. Even though Tor told me to quit it, he hung around to see what I found. On the web page of a local news station I found an update of the investigation into Nils' death. A forensics expert had been called in to analyze fluids from the bite mark on the corpse's arm and the skin around it. Most of the stuff came from Nils, his blood and lymph. In the expert's opinion the antibodies present showed that Nils had been exposed to some previously unknown version of rabies.

"Huh!" Tor said. "You were right about that virus."

"If it really is the one that causes the lycanthropy, anyway. We don't know that."

"What else would it be?"

In the video the reporter continued talking.

"Saliva recovered from the wound and the surrounding contusion did not display a normal human genotype. Even though the bite mark fit the pattern of a human set of teeth, the recovered DNA differed significantly from that of all catalogued human types. Such a striking abnormality may allow the police to trace the person's ethnic background. If so, the investigative team has a valuable lead."

"Oh god, I hope they never find me," I said. "He has to have messed up!"

"Maybe you're part Neanderthal." Tor was smiling, but his eyes were narrow, a little distant. "Your dad was Romanian, right? Throwbacks still hanging on in the Carpathians?"

"The analyst probably just picked up the genes for my rotten disease. I bet he's never seen anything like it before."

"That must be it, sure." Tor relaxed and gave me a normal smile.

And yet I wondered. Something nagged at my mind, something my father had told me, a long time ago, something I couldn't quite remember. I knew I'd have to work at recovering that memory, no matter how much it frightened me.

My father taught me how to keep secrets. He was terrified that someone would find out about our genetic disorder, our curse as he called it. As a child, I learned to share his fear. I knew I was a thief, constantly stealing life from others in order to keep myself alive. If "they" find out, "they" will kill us, or so I believed without ever asking myself who these "they" were. I also knew that my brother was different, that somehow Roman had escaped the family curse.

When I was eight, my father finally admitted the truth to my mother. She was furious, not about the disease as such, but about his deception. He'd never warned her about the genetic defect when they'd decided to have children. Reluctantly she too started lying, spreading the fiction about my "rare form of anemia."

Secrecy is a dangerous legacy. It's also a hard habit to break.

That evening, while Tor worked downstairs with his rune staves, I sat in the living room with a box of Conté sticks and a sketchbook. I loved sitting on the comfortable leather couch to draw. At times I'd look up to stare into the empty fireplace, which was faced with pale tan slabs of sandstone, cut into irregular shapes but fitted together like pieces of a puzzle. The faint, streaky grain of the stones intrigued me.

First I drew a page of meaningless scribbles, gestural movements to loosen my arm. In the red scribbles I saw my father's face. With the black stick I picked out the contours and let the rust color fill in the shadows and shading. I could see his image so clearly in my mind, his narrow face with the high cheekbones and slender nose, his droopy moustache over thin lips, and his dark eyes, oddly large for the shape of his face.

My own eyes shared that feature. I'd been teased all my life, that my eyes were so large they made me look like a child, especially since I was shorter than average until I got a growth spurt when I was about fourteen. I used to console myself by thinking I looked like my dad and mother combined. I had her delicate Asian build and his eyes—and of course, his disease, his curse, the extra twist in his DNA, as I learned to think of it. A mutation that should have died out but somehow hadn't. A mutation that could kill other people.

What else had Dad told me? Something about the disease, some reason we had it besides the kinked genes—I stared at the drawing I'd done as if it could speak and tell me. Where had we been when he'd mentioned whatever it was? I had a dim memory of trees rustling in the wind and a long lawn stretching away in front of us. A city park, probably. Dimly I could hear his voice, or imagine I was hearing it. Our kind. Those words I remembered. Something about "our kind," people who weren't people like everyone else, people who came from somewhere different.

He must have meant people whose DNA displays a "striking abnormality." The memory and the news report fit together, all right, but what did they mean? I could go no further. Maybe Tor was right about those Neanderthals.

I turned the page in the sketchbook and started a picture of my mother. I'd already written to tell her that I was going to get married and added a little sketch of Tor on the back of the letter. I wondered if she'd ever see it. Her family came from Indonesia, and she'd left us for Bali, where she entered a Buddhist nunnery, turned her back on the West and her children to seek the inner freedom she longed for. The abbess limited contact with the outside world, though I could hope that she'd let Mom hear from her only daughter, especially since the letter carried good news. The last time I'd seen her, I'd been nineteen, three whole years before.

The page in the sketchbook blurred through my tears. I

shut the book and slapped it down on the coffee table. I got up and went to get some tissues from the room I thought of as "my bedroom".

Usually Tor and I slept in the queen-sized bed in the master suite, but during the domination of the bear spirit, the suite became his cage. The bear wanted to run, to claw his way out of the flat and escape to the wild hills and the woods. He might have injured anyone that stood in his way, or he might have gotten lost, found himself miles from home without any clothes or ID once the full moon waned. To keep him safe I locked him in.

So during those nights I slept in the other bedroom—the Burne-Jones bedroom, I liked to call it, with its coffered ceiling and thick red and yellow carpets. A deeply carved pattern of vines and wild roses covered the oak bedstead and matching dresser—very William Morris. A Tiffany lamp stood beside the bed. In the center of the bed's headboard sat a carving of an anthropomorphic moon face. It showed a waxing quarter that day, but it would wax and wane as the Moon itself did. Tor's sister Liv had added the moon face, a lunar calendar of sorts, to the bedstead. You could see it, but if you tried to touch it, your fingers registered only a wild rose and a segment of vine.

I'd finished wiping my tears away when Tor came into the bedroom.

"There you are," he said. "I wanted to consult the barometer."

He meant the writing desk that stood to one side of the room. Under its many coats of black lacquer it resembled a piece made from one of Chippendale's patterns. The top, which lifted up to reveal the desk's innards, formed the background for decoupage. At least, it looked like decoupage, done with illustrations taken from old woodcuts in alchemical texts. Somehow Liv had enchanted it to display images that revealed the psychic state of the flat and its inhabitants at any given moment. We called it the alchemical barometer.

The last time I'd looked at the desktop, it had shown me

a skeleton holding a flask of black liquid. I'd avoided it ever since. That evening, however, the skeleton had changed into a woman with the crescent moon above her head. She held an enormous womb-shaped glass flask, which contained a white bird flying over a pool of blue liquid. All around this central image lay a circle of tiny red lions, standing nose to tail.

Tor slipped an arm around my waist and joined me in contemplating the woman with the flask.

"The red lions are back," he said. "More power's been released."

"What does the whole thing mean? Is the woman a good omen?"

"Good omen? That's too simple. It's alchemical, and that means it's complicated. You need to study the subject, sweetheart. That way you'll be able to interpret these things for yourself."

"Okay. But right now I can't pretend I know anything about it."

"Well, there's never any use in pretending you're something you're not." He gave me a smug grin. "Or pretending you're not something you are."

"Oh, don't start that again!"

"You're going to have to face up to it sooner or later. You've got a lot of magical talent."

I snarled at him. The sound shocked me, a snarl and a hiss like an angry cat. Tor blinked in open-mouthed surprise.

"Sorry," I mumbled. "I don't know where that came from."

"From me badgering you, probably. Okay, I'll lay off. But I've got to say one last thing. One of these days you've got to start thinking about your talents."

I knew he was right. I just wanted him to be wrong. The silence hung between us like a stain on the air.

Tor finally broke it. "Do you have class tomorrow?"

"Yeah, I do. At ten in the morning."

The class I was taking wasn't a class in the sense of going to a room and doing art or listening to a lecture on a given subject. We were having a couple of weeks of orientation to "individual studies," that is, to working alone on our senior project. Our various advisers took turns warning us to get organized and not goof off. Their main message: the year would pass a lot faster than we thought it would. Cynthia took notes on her laptop, but I brought a sketchbook and drew bits and pieces of imaginary landscapes under the pretence of taking notes. I did write down the various deadlines, "check-in times", they were called.

After class Cynthia and I stood out in the hall and chatted for a few minutes.

"Where's Brit?" I said.

"At the hospital," Cynthia said. "She texted me earlier and asked me to tell her what happened in class."

Brittany and my brother lived together. She'd been watching over him and keeping the hospital staff on their toes ever since he'd been shot.

"Have you seen Roman this week?" Cynthia continued.

"Not since Sunday. I'll go this afternoon. Tor's playing basketball with his guy friends."

"Okay, let me know how Roman's doing." She took out her phone and glanced at the time widget. "I've got to run. This color theory class is too good to miss."

"That's good to know. I'll fit it in next semester."

I went home and grabbed some lunch. Before I drove to San Francisco, I changed cars. Whenever I went to campus, I always took my car, the old green Chevy I'd owned when I moved in with Tor. He'd insisted on buying me a fancy German sedan that cost a small fortune. Gretel, as I called her, was a lot safer than my car, so I took her whenever I drove into San Francisco to visit Roman. When my brother had been shot, the ambulance crew had taken him to the nearest ER by the fastest route, an HMO hospital out on Geary Boulevard.

As I hurried down the corridor to Roman's room, I saw Brittany sitting in a chair just outside the closed door.

"Are the doctors in with Roman?" I said.

"Yeah," Brit said. "They chased us out a couple of minutes ago."

Roman's buddy Valdez, an ex-Army Ranger, was sitting on the floor near her. He was wearing jeans, a tee shirt, and an amazing jeans jacket. A picture of the Virgin of Guadalupe, embroidered on linen and then appliquéd, filled the back panel. The artist had stitched it in a multitude of colors, carefully shaded to give the figure depth and solidity. Surrounded by a wreath of satin stitch roses, wrapped in her blue, starry cloak she stood on the crescent moon.

"Wow," I said, "that jacket, it's like an art piece."

"Look at the size of those stitches," Brittany said. "They're tiny. It's beautifully done."

"Sure is," Valdez said. "My sister did it when I was in Afghanistan. She told me that she kept praying I'd be okay. While she was sewing, y'know."

"And it worked."

He smiled at me. "Luck more than divine intervention."

"I was thinking magic more than angels."

Valdez blinked at me and suppressed another smile. He got up and peered down the corridor, back the way I'd come. "Where's the Viking today?"

I figured he meant Tor. "Hanging with his guy friends."

It was some time before the doctors came out of the room. A nurse followed with a plastic bag full of bloody bandages and latex gloves. The young doctor who knew I was Roman's sister stopped to talk.

"The healing's just not progressing normally," Dr. Mellars said. "He should have been ready to be discharged by now."

"It kind of seems like he's been in here forever," I said.

"I'm sure it must. I'm worried about infection. I'm going to start him on a second course of antibiotics."

"Is it one of those resistant strains of bacteria? I read something about that on the Net."

"No, not as far as the lab can tell, and they do a pretty good job of telling." The doctor gave me a reassuring smile. "Sepsis is always a problem in these deep penetration wounds. But we'll get on top of it. I'm more worried about the—" he paused to glance up and down the hall, "about the hospital admin. They want to move him to the VA facility, and I don't want him moved yet. I may have to bring in the big guns. The heavy artillery." He grinned at me. "Your boyfriend."

"I'll tell him to be ready. He likes yelling at authority figures."

"Good. Anyway, I have to go on to the next patient, but you can call my office if you've got questions. I gave you my card, right?"

"Yes, last week."

"Okay. I answer calls around dinner time."

With that he strode off, clipboard in hand. The smell of antiseptics lingered in the air like spoiled perfume.

"The thing about bullets," Valdez said, "is they're not packed under sanitary conditions. I don't like the sound of this."

"Neither do I," Brittany said. "And I've got to talk with the hospital dietician. I don't like what they're feeding him. He's just not getting well."

When I went into the room, the others followed me. Roman had fallen asleep on his side, propped up against a long bolster to keep his weight off his wounded back. His black hair, as thick and straight as mine, was plastered to his olive-tan face with sweat. Brittany hurried over and stroked the wet hair back. He roused and smiled at her.

"I'm exhausted," he whispered. "Isn't fun to have them poking around in there."

"Just go back to sleep, okay?" Brittany leaned over and kissed his forehead. "We all understand."

Roman smiled again and fell asleep so fast that my stomach clenched in fear. Sepsis—not the word you want to hear when someone you care about's been wounded. Nils had used an old-fashioned revolver, the kind you load one bullet at a time. Had he put something on the bullets? Or cursed them, maybe?

An IV pole stood beside the bed with a plastic bag hanging from it. Valdez read the label.

"Morphine," he said. "Shit! I wish they didn't have to do

that, but they do."

"He's addicted again, isn't he?" I said. "What's going to happen when he's well enough to go places on his own?"

"I know." Brittany's voice dropped to a near-whisper. "Right back to his dealers and his druggie friends. It makes me sick, thinking about it."

"I'll help, and our whole group will, too." Valdez said. "That's why group therapy works. We're all tough mean bastards, and we look out for each other. I'll give you my phone number. If anyone can keep Roman in line, it'll be us."

Brittany managed a smile, not much of one, but a smile. "Thank you so much," she said. "So okay, maybe it won't happen."

But we knew damn well that it would happen. Roman had always been the prince of our family, the healthy kid, the successful athlete, the high school hero, until he joined the Marines in time for the Iraq War. When he came home, he brought a drug habit with him.

I left shortly after, because I needed to get back over the Bay Bridge before rush hour. I had a shopping list with me, as well, of things Tor had asked me to pick up at the local supermarket. The bridge traffic was light, the supermarket not very crowded. Everything went so smoothly that I should have known something was about to go wrong.

When I was small, my mother read me fairytales, some from Asia, some from Europe. The northern tales often featured giants. I used to shudder with enjoyable fear whenever a giant came into the story, but I never thought I'd meet a real one. How he'd gotten to Oakland I don't know, but a Frost Giant had arrived in our driveway some weeks previously with a note from his father for Tor. I didn't think he'd come back.

Fail!

In the TV shows and movies it looks so cute when a young teen meets an older woman and she becomes his first real crush, but it's not so cute when the thirteen year old is about seven feet tall and still growing. When I arrived home from the store I found him standing in the driveway with a goopy smile on his dead-white face. His hair was white, too, and the irises so pale a gray that from a short distance his eyeballs appeared solid white. He wore a pair of jeans, way too short in the leg, and a Minnesota Timberwolves tee shirt—an attempt on the part of the Frost Giants to make him pass for human.

When I got out of the car, he hurried over and helped me lift the grocery bags out of the trunk.

"Well, hello," I said. "You came back?"

"I wished to see you. You are well, yes?"

"Very well. And you?"

He shrugged and stared at me with unmistakable longing. "Your man," he said after a minute, "he is a powerful vitki, yes?"

"Very powerful. And very jealous."

"So my father warned me." He sighed. "Vitkar, they are always jealous men." He paused and looked into one of the shopping bags. "You have some vials of the elixir, I see."

It took me a moment to realize that he meant the family-sized bottles of cola. Since I was the one who'd introduced him to the stuff, I took out a bottle and gave it to him. In his hands it looked small enough to qualify as a vial.

"Now drink it slowly this time," I said. "No more of those thunder burps."

He blushed a faint pink. "I will, yes. I will give you a warning in return. There is a dead vitki in your house, too. Not your man, the live vitki. Another one. You know this, yes?"

I turned cold all over. "I didn't, no. Thank you for the warning."

"My grandmother told me so I know it is true. She told me, do not go into that house. The dead vitki will harm you."

"Your grandmother sounds like a wise woman."

"She is, yes."

He smiled and vanished. So did the bottle of cola.

A dead vitki? Nils' ghost, I figured, carrying on his damned feud.

I locked the car into the garage and activated the security system, then carried the groceries upstairs. I had just finished putting them away when Tor returned from his basketball game. He came into the kitchen and rummaged in the refrigerator for a bottle of mineral water. His black Raiders tee shirt stuck to his back with sweat. For a minute he said nothing, just drank the water straight out of the bottle.

"Kind of a hot day for sports," I said.

"Yeah." He paused for a gulp of air and a smile. "How's your brother?"

"Not good. The wound might be infected, and they're really doping him up with morphine."

Tor made a sour face. "Infected, huh? Maybe Nils did something to the bullets. A curse, I mean."

"I kind of wondered about that."

"I bet." He tossed the empty bottle into the recycling bin we kept by the back door. "I'll go in with you tomorrow and look things over."

"Thanks." I hesitated, then decided to just blurt it out. "Uh, something else happened."

Tor turned around fast. "What? You looked freaked."

"I am. That Frost Giant kid came back. He told me there are two vitkar in the house. You and then a dead one."

"Shit."

"It's got to be Nils, doesn't it?"

"Who else, but I don't see how he could get in here, not even as a walking spirit. I've got runes plastered all over the place. Although—" He muttered a few obscenities. "I did invite him in, during that last ritual. I dragged him in, face it. That may be all the entry he needs. At least to the downstairs."

"Can you do something to keep him out?"

"Sure. I can work a spell to make him long to be back in his grave. Although—didn't one of those news reports say he was cremated?"

"Yeah, once the police released the body."

"How long did they hold it?"

"I don't remember exactly, but at least a week."

"A week in cold storage. Maybe a little more. That'd be long enough."

"Long enough for what?"

"Establishing himself as an entity. One of the *afturganga*, the walking dead." Tor frowned down at the floor while he thought something through. "But that's not so easy to do. I'm surprised. I didn't think he was powerful enough."

"You're saying he wasn't really dead?"

"No. His body was dead, sure. Just not the rest of him, not right away, anyway. If he was strong enough to refuse to go onward, he was probably strong enough to turn himself into an *afturganga*."

I could find nothing to say to that. I started to shiver, laid both hands on my face, and realized that my skin felt cold, clammy. Tor put an arm around my shoulders and steered me into the living room, where afternoon sunlight had just started to fall through the western window. He opened it for the fresh air, then gathered élan while I stood trembling in the patch of light. When he raised his hands, the élan poured over me. I gulped it down, soaked it up, whatever it was I did, until at last I felt strong and sated.

"Okay now?" Tor said.

"Yes, thank you. I feel human again." The words struck me as all wrong. "Well, if I am human."

"Most of you is, anyway." He grinned at me. "I'll love you no matter what."

"Thanks. I needed to hear that."

He laughed and pulled me close for a hug. Ever since the shooting, I'd been too stressed to even think about sex, but when he kissed me, I felt the old fire re-ignite. It sounds gross, but I loved the way he smelled when he was sweaty. Pheromones, I guess, but the scent aroused me a lot more than any musk aftershave would have. I rubbed against him and took another kiss. When he stroked my buttocks, I caught my breath in a gasp.

"You feel better," he said.

"Totally. And no, I don't want you to take a shower."

"Okay. The ghost can wait."

We spent the rest of that afternoon in bed. The world

shrank to just the two of us twined together, warm and safe
and sharing pleasures. When he got up to make dinner, I
fell asleep, and for the first time in weeks I slept without bad
dreams. He waited to wake me until close to nine o'clock
that evening.

After we ate dinner, we took his laptop, newer and better
than mine, into the living room and sat on the leather couch
to surf for news. Tor relaxed into the cushions, stretched, and
smiled as he watched me searching on "Nils Halvarsson".
The afternoon had done him good, too. Until, anyway, in
the website of a local newspaper I found a piece of news that
terrified me. Bryndis Leifsdottir had contacted the police
with the information that Nils had been acting strangely. A
family friend–Tor–had told her that he seemed mentally ill.
My voice shook when I read the news to Tor.

"What if the cops follow that up?" I said. "It'll lead them
right to us."

"There's no need for you to talk to the police," Tor said. "I
will. I'm the person Bryndis mentioned, not you." He paused
for a smile. "I can explain to them that she's getting kind of
muddled, too."

"She seemed perfectly sharp to me."

"Uh-uh. Gerda, Nils' mother? Bryndis said she was Swed-
ish, but she couldn't have been. Gerda had to be Norwegian.
That's where the Nazi troops were stationed." His voice turned
into a growl. "That's where they carried out their breeding
program." He shook his head and spoke normally. "Didn't
you realize that? When we talked to her, I mean."

"I didn't know it."

Tor rolled his eyes. "Right. Americans and history."

"It seems weird that she'd get mixed up about that."

"Gerda probably moved to Sweden to get away from the
prejudice against her. She was one of the *Lebensborn* children,
remember? She had plenty of bigotry to run away from."

"Yeah, it must have been horrible, being blamed for something you had nothing to do with. But that's not going to cut
any ice with the police."

"Why not?"

"Because they won't know the difference. Like you said, Americans and history."

Tor looked honestly surprised. He could be so damn naïve at times about the real world!

"Well, anyway," he said. "I'll call Bryndis first and find out what she told them. Sweetheart, leave the police to me! I'll call them after I've talked to her."

"What if you have to lie? You swore that vow—"

"That only applies to me. Not what I know about you."

When he took out his smartphone, I got up and ran into the bedroom. I couldn't bear to listen, I just couldn't. I sat down on the edge of our bed and held out my trembling hands, willed them to stop, took deep breaths. Tor returned after about ten minutes that seemed like ten hours.

"Okay, you were right," he said. "They really didn't care what Bryndis thought about World War Two. Damn it, I'd hoped to throw them off by bringing that up."

"Told you."

He made a sour face at me. "They're sending two men over. The detective on the case and his assistant."

I started to speak, but he held up his hand and stopped me. "Let me feed you. With enough élan, you can conquer the world."

"Not if they arrest me."

"Sweetheart, hush! They'll never believe you bit him to death. You're not a pit bull."

I managed to laugh.

"Besides, if they try, we'll go on the run. All I have to do is hug you and jump, and we can be miles away." He meant it. Tor could move himself and me by magic, what you could call teleportation, I guess. "I'll figure out what to do next once we're at Billy's."

"I just hope we don't have to."

"First the élan. Worry later."

Once he'd fed me, I could face the police without shrieking or fainting like some old-fashioned heroine. The officers turned out to be Lieutenant Hu, the detective, a rumpled-looking, gray-haired guy in a navy blue business suit, and a uniformed officer, a white guy, who said nothing. I guess he was along as a bodyguard. When they arrived, Tor brought them upstairs and introduced me as his fiancée. Hu shot me a troubled and troubling glance. A lot of Asian guys resent Asian women marrying white men. Disliking me at first sight could double Hu's suspicions.

We all sat down, Tor and me on the couch, the police in the armchairs. Out of the corner of my eye I saw a faint shimmer of light on Tor's face. When I glanced his way, I saw that he'd cloaked himself in a minor illusion. His face looked slack, his eyes vacant, as he put on the mask of a nerdy guy.

"We're here because we're investigating Nils Halvarsson's death," Hu said, just as if we didn't know. "I understand that he's your father's illegitimate brother?"

"That's right," Tor said. "Yes."

"Mrs. Leifsdottir told us that you were convinced he was shall we say mentally unbalanced."

"To start with, he thought he was a werewolf. His son told me that. My cousin Joel."

The uniformed cop choked back an unprofessional snort.

"He told me the same thing," Hu said. "What I'd like from you is a report of any actual incidents."

"Okay. My fiancée and I were having lunch with some of her friends from college. Halvarsson came by and stared into the window of the café. When I went out to confront him, he start screaming at me and making threats. He was mostly upset about my grandfather's will."

"Witnesses besides Miss Cantescu?"

"Sure, several, but we were arguing in Icelandic, so—"

Hu looked martyred.

"But," Tor went on, "he was out on the street, waving his arms around and screaming. Everyone saw that. I think he thought he was sending curses my way. He also considered himself a sorcerer."

Hu nodded, considering, then turned to me. "Miss

Cantescu, I understand you're an art student at one of our local colleges."

"Yes." I decided that I could be a big girl and take the initiative. "Has anyone told you about the slashed paintings at my portrait class?"

Hu smiled, just slightly. I took that as a yes.

"Tor's uncle is the only person I can think of who'd do that. Whoever it was, they seemed to be after my painting more than the others, is why."

"I have the report on that incident. We did find evidence, and your surmise seems to be correct." He glanced at the uniformed officer. "We need to contact the instructor at the art school. She deserves to know the findings." Hu paused, smiling, then unleashed his surprise attack. "We've gotten the forensics report back on Halvarsson's gun. We found it near the corpse. It's the same gun that shot your brother."

Tor spoke before I could. "That's what I figured," he said, and his voice was a bit too sharp and strong to fit the nerdy illusion. "I told the officers on the scene that I'd seen Uncle Nils fire. He was shooting at me and missed. Wall Street guys don't spend enough time on the firing range."

Hu's smile turned brittle. "We have your statement, yes." He stood up. "Well, thank you, Mr. Thorlaksson, Miss Cantescu." He nodded our way. "I may need to talk with you again."

"Any time," Tor said. "I can come down to the station if you need me to sign some kind of statement."

"That's not necessary, not now anyway." He emphasized the word 'now.'

With that they turned to leave. Tor showed them out, but I stayed as tight and tense as a stretched canvas until I heard the outside door shut behind them. Tor came up the stairs two at a time. The nerdy illusion had disappeared.

"There," Tor said. "That wasn't as bad as it could have been."

"Except for the bit about the gun. He was hoping to shock me, wasn't he? Into saying something wrong."

"Not wrong, just something he didn't know." He sat down

next to me and put his arm around my shoulders. "It's okay, honest. Go ahead and cry if you need to."

"Thanks, but I don't. I just wish this were all over."

"It will be. People have short attention spans. Something else will take over the news." He grinned. "Like football season."

I hoped so, but my stress level kept burning away on high. I needed to move around and distract myself. I got up and went into the kitchen to finish cleaning up after our dinner—my part of the household food chores, since Tor did all the cooking and most of the shopping. He followed me and leaned against the wall to watch.

"Earlier," he said, "I went downstairs and looked through the library. I found some stuff on the walking dead. Figured I would. They were considered a real problem in the old days. Mutilating livestock, strangling people, killing shepherds and eating their flesh, crap like that. The work of sorcerers, the legends say."

"That's an awful lot of murders! How many evil sorcerers were there?"

"Only a few like me." Tor grinned in my direction. "But no, seriously, the sorcerers animated the dead, the legends run, to make trouble for their enemies. They didn't work the harm themselves."

"So the dead were zombies, huh? I mean, bodies with hands and teeth to do those things."

"In the legends, yes. How true it is, I don't know. Exaggerated, for sure."

"But if Nils was cremated, he doesn't have a body. He must just be a ghost. Can you do anything about that?"

"Oh yeah. I'll work a ritual and summon him into the circle like I did before. This time I'll destroy what's left of him. Every last bit of it."

The cold horror I felt must have shown on my face. Tor walked over and took my hand.

"He's dead, Maya. He needs to go on to the next phase, get ready for his next life. He's doing himself no good by hanging around. He's only living, if you can call it that, as some kind of unnatural energy field. He'll be better off once it's gone. Honest. Just think of it as a second-stage cremation."

"Are you going to do it tonight?"

"No, I need to be careful, use the runes to let me know what we're facing, preparation like that. Tomorrow night, I was thinking."

"You don't think he'll appear tonight?"

"I've set up wards downstairs. They'll keep him out till I'm ready for him."

"Okay. You know what you're doing."

He smiled, but my hands trembled. I concentrated on wiping down the counter. I could still remember the feel of Nils' sweaty arm choking me, and the way he'd clubbed me with his revolver. I started the dishwasher, hung up the dish-towel, and went into the living room. Tor followed, and we sat down together on the couch. He put his arm around my shoulders and pulled me close.

"Feel better?" he said.

"A little. With everything else going on, I didn't need a ghost. Or a giant turning up in the driveway."

"Which reminds me. That rime jötunn. Is he an etin or a thurs?"

"Huh?"

"The thursar are the really stupid, crass, violent giants. The etins have more class, even if they're not real bright. What's this kid like?"

"Very polite. He likes sodas, and when I gave him a bottle of cola, he gave me the warning in return. His grandmother's the one who told him about the dead vitki."

"So she knows magic. They're definitely etins. We can trust him a little if he understands bargains. Just a little. You never really know what they're up to. Some scheme of their own, usually, and I bet the gold's part of it. Be careful if he comes back."

"You don't need to worry about that." What if the kid grabbed me one day and hauled me back with him to

Jötunheim? I never wanted to be one of those maidens in the fairy tales, stuck in a magic castle waiting for some knight to come along and rescue me.

"You haven't told him your name, have you?" Tor said.

"No."

"Good. Don't. Never tell him mine, either, and don't ask him for his. Knowing someone's name gives you power over them in their world."

"I'll remember that."

"I should go downstairs," Tor said. "Cast the rune staves." He slipped his arms around me and kissed the side of my neck. "Or we could go lie down."

"I thought you wanted to cast the runes."

"They'll wait. They're very understanding that way."

This time Tor was the one who fell asleep when we were finished. I lay awake for a while, worrying about Nils. I decided that I'd be better off worrying about my senior project and slipped out of bed.

We had several empty rooms in the house. Tor had offered to let me have any or all of them for my studio and storage. I wanted to avoid doing anything but drawing in the upper flat. Art generates a lot of mess, drips, spills, stacks of supplies, and for some processes, bad smells. Although I wasn't going to paint in oils or do etchings, I might want to incorporate prints, maybe monotypes, maybe not, into the project. Printing inks are seriously messy and sometimes toxic.

So I figured I'd turn the empty rooms downstairs into the studio, although I was worried about interrupting Tor's rune work. That night, I would have gone downstairs to check out the available space there, but I remembered Tor talking about wards. Whenever he set them, they produced a sense of profound irritation for anyone in range. Sometimes they affected me like a high-pitched whine, sometimes like an extremely bright light, sometimes both with a sharp stink thrown in. I decided to wait till the morning rather than try to ignore them.

Or was it really the wards that were keeping me upstairs?

I stood in the dark hallway and listened like a hunted animal to every small noise: the air conditioning and the refrigerator humming and clicking inside the flat, from outside a distant car going up the hill, the tap of a branch against a downstairs window. Normal, safe noises—so why was I terrified? Something was waiting for me downstairs. I knew it suddenly, that something lay in wait, not a physical, live person, not a burglar or intruder, but a Presence.

Who else but the man I'd killed?

I hurried into the Burne-Jones bedroom and turned on the floor lamp. The alchemical barometer had changed its image. A deformed creature sort of like a lobster crawled half-way out of a shallow pool while two ravens flew above. The circle of lions around the image had turned green.

I ran for the safety of our shared bedroom and slipped into bed next to Tor. In his sleep he turned over and reached for me. I snuggled close and listened to the reassuring sound of his heartbeat. Once I drowsed off, I slept till morning, held tight in his arms.

CHAPTER 3

My adviser, Harper, never used her first name, and she disliked being called "Doctor," too, even though she had a PhD in art history to go with her MFA. She was tall and skinny, with rich brown skin and black hair that she kept in long dreads. That morning, for her office hours, she wore a red blouse with a denim skirt instead of her usual overalls. I moved a pile of books off the chair in front her desk, set them on the floor where she pointed, and sat down.

"Okay, Cantescu," she said. "You're doing the painting and drawing curriculum, so you're not going to want to work with video or installations and all the rest of that high concept stuff. Am I right?"

"Yes, totally. I've got landscapes in mind, but I don't want to film myself rolling around in them. Uh, is that okay?"

"Depends on your approach. I'm afraid of your work drifting into illustration." Her lip curled slightly on the word, illustration. "You've got the skills to reproduce anything you see, but that's not going to get you points with the committee. You tend to focus on unnecessary detail."

I winced at the scorn in her voice. At times my painting did fall into the category of illustration, which the art world defined in their slick magazines as anything realistic that wasn't photorealism. I hated photorealism. And dead sharks in tanks, à la Damien Hirst. Harper knew that about me.

"You've got the talent to dig deeper," Harper went on. "And that's what I want to see, something deep. Landscapes that carry personal meaning. Not pictures for middle-class living rooms."

"Okay. I was also thinking about scale. Murals that, like, opened up public spaces and dissolved the walls they were on. Once I found the right walls and spaces, I'd get pictures of those and Photoshop the murals in. So the presentation could be the panels and then a slide show of the locations."

Harper leaned back in her creaky chair and considered me. When she folded her hands on her midriff, I noticed a smear of neutralized thalo green on one sleeve of her blouse. She wouldn't have been Harper if she hadn't had paint somewhere on her clothes.

"I like the idea of art dissolving the wall," Harper said after a minute or so. "What I want to see first are sketches of landscape forms, not necessarily whole views of a place, but studies of the kind of forms you intend to develop. Bring me a sketchbook or portfolio in a couple of weeks. Then we'll talk some more. Don't close the pattern too soon. Panels, Photoshop—sounds like a first pass through the idea to me. Something new could develop under your hands. Leave an opening for it."

"Okay, sure. I didn't know if I should give you some kind of formal proposal—"

"No no no. Get the project underway before you worry about the committee." She grinned at me. "And that's who the proposal is for, the committee. Not for the art. You're working, and that's all I need to know for now."

I left her office on a modified high. Harper approved of part of my idea, at least.

I went straight home afterward. While we ate lunch, I checked my email. In her usual methodical way, Harper had sent me a follow-up to the office visit, reminding me that the year would pass faster than I thought it would. No goofing off when she was your advisor! The last part of the email contained the bad news.

"BTW, I heard from the cops this morning. You probably remember that the vandal who ruined the paintings also left a nasty souvenir in the corner."

Some urine on a pile of paint rags, she meant.

"Well, the DNA matches that of the dead guy they found in that parking lot. I didn't know they could get DNA from urine, but the officer told me that the body generally passes some dead cells along with the liquid. They found enough. Also traces of cocaine. I'll get a mass email out to the class later, but I thought you should know first. They seem to think the guy has some connection to you. I told them I knew nothing about it. If he does, don't tell me, because I don't want to tell them."

I felt too frightened to write a reply. I turned my laptop around so Tor could read the screen. He scowled when he finished.

"Fuck them," was all he said. "The cops, I mean."

I shut down the laptop and concentrated on finishing my lunch.

When we left for San Francisco and the hospital, Tor drove in his usual style, fast but never dangerously. I looked out of the window and studied the urban landscape as it slid past in a jumble of malls and houses and shabby semi-industrial areas. The traffic jammed up, and Tor cut off on Ashby to go over to 580 at the edge of the bay. Once we reached Emeryville I could see the actual bay between the buildings. Distant across the green-gray water lay the low hills of Marin, dark with trees. How would I extract the essential forms from all this? My fingers itched to draw.

Water and trees, particularly trees and their roots, big gnarled roots, twisted, wrinkled, bony fingers clutching the earth and digging in to hold on to life. I could see them, the dark roots of a yew and the pools of water that oozed out between. I walked a little closer and saw how huge the tree was, enormously wide, bigger even than the massive sequoias up in the Sierra, rising so high that I couldn't see the top—

"Wake up," Tor said. "We're here."

"Unh?" I shook myself and yawned. When I looked out of the car window, I realized we'd parked behind the hospital.

"Did I fall asleep?"

"Yeah." He was grinning at me. "You snored."

"Not as bad as you do, I bet."

"I'll concede that point." He unbuckled his seat belt. "Let's go."

When we walked down the corridor to Roman's room, I saw the door standing half-open, a good omen for visiting. I hurried in and found him more or less awake in a web of cables and IV tubes. On the wall above his bed a monitor showed a steady heart beat and a flurry of numbers. His half-smile and slurred hello told me he'd been drugged, even though his dilated pupils made him look startled. Brittany was sitting in a chair by the window and embroidering a geometric pattern on a length of hand-woven green fabric.

"Did you want a break, Brit?" I said. "I can stay here for a while."

"Thanks, but I'm okay. My mom's taking my grandmother to the doctor this afternoon. Y'know, I've decided to drop a couple of classes. I'll concentrate on the project like you're doing. Between taking care of Gram and Roman, there's just not enough time in the day."

"I wondered how you were managing, yeah."

"Taking care of people, it's my karma. I've always known that. It's one reason I stick with fiber arts. It's clean, once you get done with dying your materials. You can put it down and then pick it up later."

I perched on the end of Roman's bed and looked at Tor, who had stayed standing in the doorway. I was about to ask him if he wanted the only other chair in the room when I realized that his eyes looked as sleepy and unfocused as my brother's. In Tor's case, though, it meant he'd gone into trance. Brittany noticed as well. She ran her needle into the cloth and laid her work down in her lap. For a few minutes we sat in utter silence, until Tor moved, smiled at us both, and walked further into the room.

"What did you see?" Brittany said.

"Hard to describe," Tor said. "But something's in here,

all right."

He paused, glanced around, then strode over to the night-stand beside the bed. He opened the top drawer, rummaged around, and pulled out a square yellow envelope. Tor stud-ied the postmark for a moment, then slid a greeting card out. When he held it up, I saw a slick photo of the ocean with the words "Get Well" floating over the image. Tor flipped it open and displayed a bindrune drawn in red. Roman winced and made an odd little grunt of sound.

"What the fuck?" Roman muttered. "That hurt. Or some-thing did."

"I bet it did," Tor said. "According to the time stamp, this was mailed the day after you were shot." He glanced at me. "He used our return address, the bastard."

"Nils?"

"Who else? Roman, do you remember opening this?"

"No. But I don't remember anything from the first couple days. Not a lot after that."

Tor turned to Brittany and quirked an eyebrow.

"I never saw it, either," she said. "A nurse must have given it to him."

"I'm going to go talk to someone at the nursing station," Tor said. "I need to get this out of the room." He strode out before any of us could say more.

As soon as Tor carried the card across the threshold Ro-man let out his breath in a puff of relief. Brittany got up, laid her embroidery down on the chair, and hurried to his side. When she smoothed the sweaty hair back from his face, he smiled at her.

"Feel better?" she said.

"A little, yeah. Like maybe I can sleep now."

"Good," I said. "Nils. The gift that keeps on giving."

Tor returned, but he stood just outside the room in the doorway. "Maya, do you have a pen or something I can write with? A black one."

I rummaged in my backpack and came up with a wide-nib calligraphy pen. I got up and handed it to him, then watched

as he held the greeting card against the wall for a writing surface. I recognized the red runes: Need, Ice, Thorn, drawn in
a tidy design surrounded by a ring of reversed Uruz, that is,
the rune that signifies physical energy and health. Reversed,
it brought the opposite. Tor drew another bindrune over
them in black, made up of Torch, Lake, and finally, Tiwaz,
the spear-rune of his favorite god, Tyr.

"Torch to burn them, Lake to wash them away," Tor told
me. "I'll dispose of it when we get home."

When he carried the card back into the room, Roman felt
no effect. Tor handed me the dead rune card, and I put it in my
backpack, but he held onto the pen and looked Roman over.

"I guess the doctor would flip out if I drew runes on you,"
Tor said.

Roman grinned. "Probably. Or the nurses would."

"I'll stick to paper then." Tor turned to me. "Do you have
a sketchbook with you?"

"Always." I took a small drawing pad out of my backpack.
"I'll tear off a sheet."

Tor drew a bindrune of Yew and Elk, both protective
runes, and added Tiwaz. He put the paper into the night-
stand drawer and gave me my pen back.

"If Nils left any more time bombs lying around," Tor remarked, "that will ward them off."

"Thanks," Brittany said. "Do you think the police are
ever going to catch whoever it was who killed your uncle?"

I felt guilt twist inside me like a hand on my guts. She'd
touched the one secret I could never share with my friends.

"No." Tor shook his head. "Whoever did it was pretty
clever."

"The police were here yesterday," Roman said. "They keep
asking me questions."

"Oh yeah?" Tor said. "Do they think you know who killed
him?"

"That, yeah. The assholes."

"I just hope it wasn't Valdez," Brittany put in.

"If it was, damn right they'll never figure it out." Roman

gave Brittany a tight-lipped smile that struck me as more a warning than humor. "Never ask him. Just don't."

"Who?"

"Valdez. He's a great guy, but he's dangerous." Roman propped himself up on one elbow to look right at her. "We all are."

"So okay." She took a step back. "I won't."

Roman's smile turned gentle. He sighed and lay back onto the pillows. Brittany turned to me and mouthed "you'd better go."

"We'll be back soon," I said to Roman. "We need to get over the bridge before rush hour."

Since his eyes had closed, I doubt if he heard me. I gave Brit a hug, and we left. I waited till we'd gotten outside to the parking lot before I said anything.

"Tor? Why did Nils send that card? How did he know where to send it?"

"He probably saw the hospital on the news. The first TV clip showed a reporter standing in front of it. As to why, I don't know for sure. Revenge, probably. He mailed it the day after the ritual."

"That must have been when he added you to the will."

"Yeah. He was desperate and realized he was losing the war. It was petty of him, sure, but that's the kind of guy he was. That's probably why he's hanging around now. Trying to get back at us."

When I shuddered, Tor caught my hand and gave it a reassuring squeeze.

"Don't worry," he said. "I'll take care of him tonight."

Tor spent most of the afternoon alone downstairs, meditating and preparing the ritual room. About an hour after sunset I went down to join him.

In other half of his workshop, across from the lab table, Tor had put down a black carpet marked with a white circle, about nine feet across, enclosing an equal-armed cross. Spice-scented candles burned at each cardinal point, and, that night, he'd strewn dried flowers around the outer edge of the circle.

The room smelled like old-fashioned potpourri. I sneezed.

"Sorry," Tor said. "Is this going to bother you too much?"

"I don't know." I found a tissue in my jeans pocket and blew my nose. "No, it's settling down. I'll be okay."

Across the room was a walk-in closet that the previous owner of the house had modified. One wall held a solid rank of shallow drawers that looked like they belonged in a museum to store prints and antique jewelry. In the middle stood a lectern, draped at the moment with one of Tor's white tee shirts, decorated with runes, Yew and Elk for protection—my ritual garment. He was wearing a pair of white shorts and the old blue hooded sweatshirt that served him as a sorcerer's cloak. While I undressed and put on the tee shirt, he walked over to the window and pulled back the edge of one of the heavy drapes. He stood looking out for a moment at the view of our back yard and the hillside beyond.

"Moon's just starting to rise," he said. "It'll be full in a couple of days." His voice turned weary. "At least I can deal with Nils before."

Before the bear spirit took him over, he meant, and as always I ached for him. He let the curtain fall and walked into the center of the circle. "Maya, go sit in the west."

I sat down cross-legged where he pointed, clasped my hands in my lap, and waited in silence.

Tor faced north and raised his arms over his head. He took a deep breath, and when he spoke, his voice throbbed and vibrated from deep in his chest, from deep in his soul. He called out the first three runes, Fehu Uruz Thurisaz, then turned to the north-east and chanted the next three, Ánsuz Raidho Kenaz. He turned, chanted, turned again until he'd gone round the entire circle and built a barrier of all twenty-four runes around it. I could see them glowing and flickering like a fire glimpsed through the cracks in a wall.

When he returned to the north, Tor paused, took another deep breath, and began to chant in the language of his ancestors, Old Norse. I understood nothing, but the chanting took me over. The throbbing deep sound of his voice mingled with the herbs and spices until I found myself breathing in the rhythm of his chant. I knew I could never move until he released me, no, until the magic released me, because he was as trapped as I was in the sound of the galdrar, the runespells.

Silence. Tor waited, his arms still held high. In the north, just inside the circle, a shape flickered, hard to see, like a twist of smoke, some tall thing standing on its hind legs, not Nils, no human ghost. Out of the bluish mist an animal stepped forward and held out enormous paws. Shadows defined its head, a flatter skull than modern bears, and a long snout flashing with teeth—a cave bear. I recognized it from the pictures of Paleolithic art I'd studied at school. Tor spoke a few words. The cave bear nodded its huge head, then vanished. Tor lowered his arms, shrugged with an oddly normal gesture, then knelt. With both hands he slapped hard on the floor. The spell broke. I gasped as the released élan flowed over me. For a moment I sat unmoving and breathed in as much as I could gather.

"Nils is gone." Tor stood up. "Dead as he needs to be. It wasn't his ghost that the etinwife saw in here."

I stared, utterly confused. He walked over and knelt next to me in the pool of light from the candle nearby.

"You didn't banish him?" I said.

"I didn't need to. He's dead, gone, moved onward."

"Then who's the dead vitki?"

"Yeah, that's the question, isn't it? We need to know the answer." In the candlelight his eyes gleamed like flames. "But something else came when I called."

"I saw that. The bear spirit."

"You saw her?"

"Yeah. It looked like a cave bear. Is it the same one that possesses you?"

"Yes, 'fraid so. Look, if you saw her that clearly—"

"Did you say her?"

"Yeah. She's female."

I hesitated, stabbed by an utterly weird jealousy. Oh come on, I told myself. It's a spirit, not a woman.

"Maya, sweetheart!" Tor had noticed nothing. "It's time for you to stop denying who you are. If you don't learn how to handle your talent, it's going to control you instead of you controlling it."

My voice clotted with fear deep in my throat. Tor stood up, then held out his hand. When I caught it, he helped me stand.

"Do you have any idea why you're so frightened?" Tor said.

I shook my head, gulped hard, and managed to squeeze out a "no, I really don't."

"Then it's got to come from your last life. The one you can't remember. There are ways, techniques, you can use to—"

"I don't want to!" I started to say more but I hissed, snarled, hissed again as if I were the one possessed by a spirit, a tiger spirit from my mother's deep heritage.

"Sweetheart, you need to get out of the ritual space. Right now! You're in danger."

I nodded my agreement. I could feel the energy pulsing and swirling around us, raw power, terrifying, seductive.

I grabbed my regular clothes and rushed upstairs to change. Tor stayed behind to put out the candles and vacuum up the herbs and flowers. The nisse might have gotten sick if it had tried to eat the mixture.

While I waited for him to come back up, I tried to draw the bear spirit. I could sketch Tor easily, standing with his arms raised. I drew in a portion of the rune circle with no trouble, too. Yet when I tried to focus my mind on the spirit, the image disappeared from my mind. I could envision other bears, ones I'd seen in zoos or TV documentaries, but that particular smoky figure refused to come clear. When I laid down my stick of pastel I did catch a mental glimpse, but as soon as I picked the pastel up again, the glimpse vanished. She didn't want me to draw her, to capture her trace. I knew that as suddenly as if a voice had spoken to tell me. Whatever had happened that night happened between Tor and the bear spirit. I had no part in it.

My jealousy flamed beyond my power to kill it.

Tor came whistling up the stairs a few minutes later. When

he walked into the living room, I said, "You sure sound happy about something."

He stopped and looked at me. "What's wrong?" he said.

"Nothing. I was just wondering what the bear spirit said to you."

"She growled, that's all. It felt like a challenge, but I'm not sure." He shrugged the question away. "Do you want dinner now?"

I wondered if he'd lied about the bear spirit, but I felt too foolish to ask him.

"I can wait to eat," I said. "You look tired. Uh, y'know, I'm sorry I snarled at you like that."

"Don't be. It tells us something we need to know. I just don't know what that is yet." He paused and hooked his thumbs over the waistband of his jeans while he looked me over. "These events with ritual power behind them? They always mean something. They're always important."

I refused to say anything.

"You *are* stubborn," he said. "I got to hand it to you."

"Who else would stay involved with you? You'd steamroll anyone who didn't know her own mind."

"Y'know, a couple of other women have told me that, too. Though they added a few more choice words." He grinned. "When they were breaking up with me, that is." He let the grin fade. "But Maya, your talent isn't anything to be stubborn about. It's dangerous to just let it lie."

"Yeah," I said. "I know that."

"Okay. That's step one."

He waited. I said nothing. He sighed with too much drama.

"Oh shut up!" I snapped.

"Okay." With a grin he turned toward the kitchen. "I want a beer. You want some brandy?"

"Please, just a little bit though."

When he came back with the drinks, he brought a package of corn chips with them, food to help dispel the ritual mood. He sat down next to me on the couch, and for a few minutes, while I crunched through a handful of chips, I could fool myself into thinking we were having a normal evening. Tor broke the illusion.

"It's so damn weird that I didn't pick up any trace of Nils."

"Do you think the Frost Giant kid was wrong? Maybe there isn't any ghost."

"If his grandmother saw it, there's something on the loose here. It might not be a dead vitki in some literal sense."

"That's almost worse."

"There isn't any almost about it. I mastered Nils. I wouldn't have had any trouble sending him on. Who the hell knows what she saw? The etinwife, I mean."

"The bear spirit, maybe?"

"No. She'd recognize that."

"What about the guy who owned this house before you?"

"I didn't pick up any traces of magic when I moved in. I exorcised everything just to make sure. He was some kind of art collector, poor guy. He died of AIDS, and his partner wanted to sell the house fast and move on with his life."

"I bet, yeah. That's really sad."

Tor paused for a long swallow of beer from the bottle. "Huh," he said. "I wonder."

"What?"

"You're not going to like this."

"Since when has that ever stopped you?"

"I wonder if the etinwife saw your talent. It might as well be dead, considering how you ignore it."

"Oh lay off! I'm still thinking about it. What you said, I mean, about the danger."

"If you don't control these things they can control you. Look what happened when Nils attacked you. I know you didn't mean to kill him. But you didn't know when to stop."

I felt too sick at the truth of this to answer.

"I'm sorry," Tor went on. "I know I can be kind of pushy. Well, sometimes."

I felt better enough to laugh, just because it was such an understatement. He grinned and let the subject drop.

Unfortunately, the subject refused to drop me. Why was I afraid of my so-called talents? His remarks about the past life I couldn't remember hit me hard. I'd been having a recurring dream about a window covered with heavy wooden shutters, carved here and there with runes and other ancient symbols. In the dreams I'd approach the window with the idea of opening the shutters, but every time, I'd back away and leave them closed. In the obscure way that dreams have, I knew that they were concealing something about my past.

My mother had often talked about past lives. They were a tenet of the Buddhist faith her family held, part of a small community of believers in their native Indonesia. I'd never really believed her talk of incarnations until I met Tor. He remembered me from the 1850s, he'd told me, and listening to him, I remembered, too. We'd lived in Copenhagen and been adulterous lovers, a furtive, passionate affair until my husband had shot him in a duel. I'd drowned myself in the winter-dark Baltic Sea. I could remember dying far more clearly than I remembered the rest of that life itself. In my memory a few pieces remained—the Romany father who'd sold me to a brutal husband, the husband himself, Björn, and the man Tor had been then—none of them as vivid as the cold water that closed over my head when my heavy winter clothing dragged me under. Remembering made me choke for breath.

Considering how awful the Copenhagen life was, I refused to blame myself for wanting to leave the next installment alone. Let it lie in the shadows of forgetting, I thought, if only it would stay there. Besides, I faced a more immediate problem. That night, before we went to bed, I looked out of the window and saw the moon gleaming in the clear sky. Just one more thin slice of light along its edge, and it would be full.

Tor never ate breakfast except during the build-up to the full moon. That morning he grimly worked his way through a pound of steak so rare I couldn't look at his plate. Not that it disgusted me—I was fighting the urge to ask him if I could lick up the blood after he was done with the meat. This symptom of my disease was something new. I'd never craved blood before I'd bitten Nils.

"What's wrong?" Tor said. "You look like you're going to be sick."

"Just thinking about what happened."

"Nils, you mean."

"Yeah." I concentrated on my pure white yogurt.

"Well, he can't threaten you anymore."

When he finished eating, Tor prepared his lair, as he called the bedroom during the full moon. He put cooked meat and fish into the little refrigerator and laid some old blankets on the floor. The bjarki disliked sleeping on the actual bed.

"Transformation's getting close," he said. "Let me feed you now."

Before the bear took him over, Tor gave me every scrap of élan I could incorporate. He summoned more for himself, too, kept feeding both of us as the afternoon waned. Just before sunset and moonrise I locked him into the lair with a normal lock, a deadbolt, and finally a safety chain.

"I love you, Tor! I'll be right here when you come back."

He made a sound half-way between a word and a roar. I knew the transformation had begun. Although the spirit took over his mind and his behavior every month, Tor's physical body always fought against the spell. It stayed human, though at the price of a lot of pain.

For a few minutes I stood by the door and listened to him shuffling back and forth and growling to himself. He chuffed, then roared and slammed into the door. The bjarki was trying to escape. By the time the ordeal ended, Tor would have bruises all over his body.

I backed off and ran into the living room to cry where he couldn't hear me. Knowing how badly he hurt stabbed me worse than any physical pain. In a couple of minutes I heard the bjarki whimpering and moaning in its lair. Even though Tor's body stayed human, I always thought of the bjarki as a different being, a something, not a someone, and definitely not Tor. Yet inside the bjarki he still existed, and he hurt.

But the bear spirit was female. What was she doing, trying

to turn Tor into a bear so she could have him for herself?

"I'll kill you first," I whispered aloud.

Rage, pure hot flaming rage—but the next moment I felt utterly stupid to be jealous of a spirit bear, female or not. My face burned with embarrassment, even though no one was around to see. I hurried into the bathroom, ran the cold water in the basin, and plunged my face into the soothing chill. When I got myself back under control, I called Brittany.

"I saw the moon," she said. "It must have started."

"Yeah. I just needed to hear your voice. I'll call Cyn later."

"You know we're here for you, so okay, call any time. And I've got some news. Dr. Mellars says Roman's turned a corner. He was really pleased."

"I am so totally glad to hear that."

"I bet! The doctor thinks the antibiotics did it. Huh, we know why."

"Don't try to tell him, though."

"Of course not! But you stay in touch with us, okay? And eat something. Veggies!"

When I clicked off, I followed her advice and forced myself to eat. I had to keep my strength up and conserve all the élan I could until Tor came back to himself. When I finished the few scraps of salad I managed to choke down, I sat on the couch with my sketchbook and pastels and thought about the landscape forms that Harper wanted to see. I started drawing tree trunks and branches, just isolated rough shapes, twisted, barren of leaves. On the next page I drew boulders pushing up through parched earth.

A phone rang—not mine, Tor's—locked in with him. Tor had a wolf howling for a ring tone, his idea of a joke. I heard the bjarki roar and growl at what it assumed was a real wolf, infringing on its territory. Who would be calling, anyway? Tor's guy friends knew about the full moon transformation. The person who'd called the lawyer? How could he have gotten Tor's number, unless he was one of Nils' friends and knew about the hated nephew? After five rings the wolf fell silent. I realized that I'd been holding my breath and let it out with a gasp for air.

The bjarki continued pacing back and forth, growling, searching for the wolf, I assumed, in his lair. I went back to my drawings. If I concentrated hard enough, I could ignore the sound. Finally he fell silent. I crept up to the bedroom door and listened. As far as I could tell from the soft whimpers and breathy snores, he'd fallen asleep right against the door.

Knowing he slept I could try to sleep myself. I went into the Burne-Jones bedroom and lay down, but I kept waking up to listen for a possible prowler. What if someone tried to break into the flat to get Nils' papers? A car going by seemed like a threat. Once I thought I heard something tap at the window. My heart started pounding even though the sound never repeated. I got up and walked around the entire flat, turned on some lights, too, found nothing. Since I was afraid to go downstairs, I knelt by the heater vent in the living room and listened. Nothing moved that I could hear.

Finally I was tired enough to go back to bed. I woke to the gray light of dawn and the sound of the bjarki ramming himself against the bedroom door, a dull thud that echoed through the silent flat. Now and then he roared, as deep as a lion's roar but breathier. I got out of bed and staggered into the kitchen to make coffee. One night down, two to go.

I'd lived through Tor's full moon change twice before. While I could never have gotten used to the experience, by then I did know several important things. He would come back. He wasn't going to die. I wouldn't die from lack of élan before he returned to himself. I could call Cynthia or Brittany every time I felt panic building. By repeating all of these things to myself, I managed to stay calm at least part of the time, at least during the day. I drew ideas for my senior project, and I wrote more chunks of the history of my relationship with Tor.

I also kept wondering about that female bear spirit. What was she doing to my boyfriend in that locked room? I told myself that being jealous was a waste of energy. She was hurting him, not seducing him. I tried again to draw her in the muddled thought that maybe I could pull her out of the room, fix her on paper, and make her leave him alone. I never got a convincing image. She stayed out of my reach. When I looked bears up on the Internet, I found out that the female bear is called a 'sow'. I'll admit I found that insulting term satisfying.

No one ever called Tor's phone again. But still, on the second night I had trouble sleeping. Noises that had seemed normal, reassuring even, just a few days before now made me wake up and lie in bed with my heart pounding. Approaching cars in particular seemed to announce danger coming, even though they always drove on by. I'd calm myself and manage, eventually, to go back to sleep.

Tor had given me so much élan before he went into the lair that I felt fine until moonrise on the third night. At that point my hands began to ache. I rubbed them, but inexorably my knuckles turned red and swelled. My wrists followed suit. By midnight, my knees and hips hurt so bad that I could barely walk. I left the light on in the Burne-Jones bedroom because I'd become afraid of the dark as well as of the evil eye of the moon, glaring down over the city outside. I took off all my clothes except for an oversized tee shirt, because my bra and the waistband of my shorts hurt where they touched my skin. Even though the thermometer told me the room was warm, I felt cold.

Symptoms like these always made it clear that without a source of élan, I'd die. For years I'd stolen it in bits and drips from healthy people. I never wanted to have to live that way again. Maybe, if I found my talents, I could learn to harvest élan for myself. I wouldn't be feel so dependent on Tor. Right then I had to conserve every scrap of élan I had.

I huddled under a blanket. I'd just dozed off when a buzzing, beeping alarm went off. I sat bolt upright. The harsh noise came from outside, from somewhere behind the house. I got out of bed and pulled on my shorts, then ran to the kitchen window. Up on the hill behind our house, lights flashed on and off in rhythm with the screech of the alarm.

The landline phone in the kitchen rang. The security system! I grabbed the receiver.

"Mrs. Thorlaksson?" a male voice said.

"Yes." Of course Tor would put me down as his wife. "The alarms—"

"A prowler alert, yes. We're sending police. Where's Mr. Thorlaksson?"

I had a sleep-fogged inspiration. "Away on a business trip."

"The police should be there within five minutes."

"I can hear the siren now."

"Excellent! We'll follow up with the police, but call back if you need anything else."

I hung up, then punched in the code to silence the alarm. I ran to the Burne-Jones bedroom and put on shoes, jeans, and a cardigan sweater so I could look a little bit respectable. The siren wailed closer and closer, then stopped in front of the house. As I went down, I turned on the stairwell lights and the lights in the library room of the lower flat.

Two officers waited at the door. I opened it just as far as the safety chain would allow until I could see that they really were uniformed cops with badges and police-issue utility belts, guns and all. At that point I opened it wide.

"Is the house secure?" one of the police officers said.

"Yes, it was the outside alarm that went."

"We'll take a look around back." He paused, listening. "Do you have dogs?"

Distantly we could hear the bjarki, growling and making a sound that could have a bark from a very large dog.

"Only one, and I've locked him in the bedroom."

"Good. He sounds angry enough to take a bite out of one of us."

As well as their guns, the policemen each had a big heavy flashlight that looked like it could double as a weapon. They set off around the side of the house. I shut the front door and shot the deadbolt, then sat down on the stairs to wait. Upstairs the bjarki fell silent. I wondered if in the prison of his spirit possession Tor knew that help had arrived. It was uncomfortable, sitting on the narrow stairs, but I was afraid to go into the library room, where a restless spirit might be waiting for me, a threat that neither the cops nor the alarm company could touch.

The police officers returned to the front door in about fifteen minutes. All clear, they told me, but they suggested I leave the security lights glowing on the hillside.

"By now the prowler knows that you've got a good alarm system," one officer said. "So he'll probably stay away. But let's not take chances."

After they left, I went back upstairs and re-armed the entire security system. I figured I'd never get back to sleep, but once I lay down, I was so tired that I drifted off. I woke just before sunrise. When I looked out of the window, I saw the pale and gibbous moon lingering on the western horizon. I wanted to scream at it to hurry up and set. Instead I took a shower, which gave me just enough energy to put on a pair of loose shorts—nothing else—and go into the living room. I took the keys from the mantel and watched the sun rise from the eastern window. As the golden light brightened, I heard Tor call me from the bedroom.

I limped as fast as I could down the hall and called back, "I'm right here!"

"Good! You can open the door."

My aching fingers nearly dropped the keys, but I forced them to behave. Inside lay the help I desperately needed. I managed to get the locks undone at last. I shoved the keys into the pocket of my shorts and hurried into a room filled with sunlight and élan. I felt as if I'd plunged into a pool of scented warm water. Tor was casting off all the élan he'd stockpiled to allow him to deal with his body's attempts to transform. I sobbed once in relief, then concentrated on breathing, soaking up every shred of the precious life force that came my way.

Tor stood naked by the window and grinned at me. I stepped out of the shorts and rushed to his arms. He pulled me close, kissed me open-mouthed, then walked me backwards to our bed. Energy swirled around us as his body threw off élan. The smell of roses and honey overpowered me as I breathed it in. I was barely aware of his hands, turning me around, his hands on my breasts as he bent me over the edge of the bed and took me from behind.

I cried aloud with pleasure and felt him climax. With a gasp he let me go. We fell on the bed together and rolled into each other's arms.

CHAPTER 4

We stayed in bed all morning. Lust was only part of it. We both needed to feel safe and close while we talked over the moon nights just past. Tor had realized what the alarm noise meant, he told me, and he knew that the police had come.

"I suppose they made a report about it," I said. "I bet that Lieutenant Hu will get a copy, too."

"Probably. I wonder if they think I'm a drug dealer?"

"Why do you think they would?"

"A lot of shootings come down over drugs. Consider: a witness sees you hand Roman a wad of cash, Nils appears, fires at me. Deal gone wrong? To a cop, drugs would make more sense than arguing over a will." He grinned at me. "They've got no idea how rotten rich people can be."

"Well, maybe." I was in no mood for jokes. "But what about the other night? Do you remember your phone ringing?"

"Yeah. Let me check something out."

Tor got out of bed and fetched the phone from his dresser. He lay back down and brought up the messages.

"No message from the middle of the night. It might have just been a wrong number."

"Do you really think so? I'm worried about that guy who wanted Nils' papers."

"The lawyer never would have given him my phone number. Not even my name. The prowler worries me a lot more."

"Unless it's the same person."

"It could be, yeah, but I suspect some ordinary kind of break-in artist. Everyone knows that you need money to live up here. That means you've got stuff worth stealing."

"But a pro would know what a security system means. We've got signs posted in the front window and up on the hill."

Tor started to speak, then clicked off the phone and put it down on the nightstand. "That's true," he said. "But I can't see what else it would be. I need to go through the papers more carefully. So far I haven't seen anything anyone but me would want."

"What about information on the gold plaque?"

"Now there's a thought, yeah! I'll cast the staves and see what they can tell us." Tor stretched his arms over his head and winced. "Do we have any of that sports rub?"

"I bought some at the store last time I went. I knew you'd need it."

We took a shower together before I rubbed him down with Ben-gay. His shoulders and upper arms were bruised from the bjarki's attempts to escape, but the damage looked much lighter than it had after the previous full moon.

"I had a little more control of the bear this time," Tor said. "I'm pretty sure it's because I know now that I don't physically change. I still see a bear when I look in the mirror, but now I know it's an illusion." He paused to kiss me. "Thanks to you."

Take that, you stupid sow! was my first thought. Aloud, I'm afraid I kind of simpered. "Well, it wasn't all me."

"Yes, it was! Don't be so damn humble! You're the one who saw through the illusion. You're the one who came up with a way for me to see it. Maya, claim it! It's your success. Take the credit!"

"Okay, okay. You're right."

And why, I wondered, hadn't I wanted to claim it? Female conditioning had to be part of it, but not all. Maybe because avoiding the credit seemed safer than admitting my talents.

Once we dressed, Tor made us both coffee and pulled up a stool at the breakfast bar to keep me company while I ate. Now that he'd come back safely, I felt normal hunger again.

I loaded up a plate with bran muffins and fruit and cheese and pitched in.

"Don't you want lunch?" I said.

"No. The bjarki finished half a salmon last night. Which reminds me, I need to clean up the bones. The refrigerator's a mess now."

I made a yuk! face.

"Bears have lousy table manners." Tor grinned at me, then let the smile face into thoughtfulness. "But this time I learned a lot. I could think while I was possessed. At least during the day, not so much at night."

"I bet, with the full moon shining down."

"The big question is the moon's role. Why would the moon phase affect the shapechanger? That doesn't make sense. It's got to affect the spirits instead. The ones trying to possess us, the human victims, I mean." He paused for a sip of coffee. "It must open a gate or signal some kind of power tide that gives the spirit an edge."

"But what about the virus?"

"That's what makes the shapechanger vulnerable. It weakens you enough so you can't fight back. The spirits can creep in and take over. They see their chance to get a body, Maya. They don't understand that they can't live here permanently."

"But you're male, and she's female."

"True." Tor frowned in thought. "She must be up to something else."

"Huh! I bet I know."

"What? You're not jealous of her, are you?"

I felt my face heat up with a blush. He laughed, the jerk! I swear he looked pleased that females might be fighting over him. I concentrated on eating for a few minutes, then decided to get back to the original subject.

"About the virus," I said. "If it gives the spirit power over you, then why don't you change permanently?"

Tor let his arrogant grin fade. "Once the moon wanes, they lose power, and a healthy shapechanger can throw them off. That's what I mean about the moon's role. It's crucial to the process. Somehow."

"What if someone's sick or weak? Really sick, like with a chronic disease, not just a cold or something."

"I'm willing to bet that they'd be trapped with the spirit in charge."

"You don't think they'd stay a wolf or a bear, do you? Physically, I mean."

"Probably not that, or only at the full moon." He considered the coffee in his mug and frowned. "I don't know, but I'd guess that the human body shape would come back for most of the month, revert to its own genetic nature, but the spirit would still live inside it somewhere."

"God, that's creepy!"

"Yeah, it sure is. I've got to get control of this thing, Maya. I can't live like this for the next forty years, fighting her off every fucking month until I'm too old to fight anymore." He spoke quietly, but his eyes narrowed and turned cold, as if he were looking down a tunnel of time and seeing the horror waiting for him. "I've got to translate the inscription on that gold plaque, just to start with. I'm pretty sure it's got information about the curse." He hesitated, then shrugged as if he were dismissing an objection to something. "Y'know, I wonder why you haven't picked up the virus from me."

"You've never bitten me."

"And I never will." He smiled and held up one hand like a boy scout. "I promise." The smile disappeared. "But you bit Nils and—well—"

"Don't make me remember!" For a moment I felt completely nauseated. I took a deep breath and calmed my protesting stomach down.

"I'm sorry!" Tor caught my hand in both of his. "But we need to figure it out."

"I must be immune. It must be part of those different genes."

"It's the only thing I can think of." He raised my hand to his lips and kissed my fingers, then let it go. "And I'm damn glad of it, too."

Tor spent the rest of the day downstairs, brooding over the runes inscribed on the golden square. When he came back up to cook us an early dinner, he told me that he'd done a couple of rune stave readings and meditations as well.

"I'm kind of worried about Joel," he said. "I hope he's not in danger. He showed up in one reading, but the second one wasn't good or bad. Something's hanging in the balance. That's the only conclusion I can reach."

As it turned out, we heard from Joel Halvarsson the next day. In mid-morning, I was sitting on the couch drawing tree forms when Tor came upstairs, waving a handful of mail. "Here's something I should have expected," he said. "A letter from my cousin. The runes were ambiguous, but some kind of contact looked pretty possible." He dumped the bills and junk mail onto the breakfast bar, then opened Joel's letter. "Huh, Joel's an IT guy at some big company." He showed me the letterhead stationery. "The head IT guy, no less."

"Working with computers is a lot like sorcery, all those codes and images and stuff. I guess he does have the family talent."

Tor laughed, then read the letter aloud.

"Hey, cousin, something I thought you should know. I just got a phone call at my day job from a man who wants to buy that box of Dad's papers I sent you. He said he knew Dad and wanted something to remember him by. He had this weird accent, like maybe he'd just learned English. Reminded me of Grandpa Halvar's accent. He kept dropping strange hints and questions about magic. I guess he thought I should know some kind of mysterious crapola. Which I don't. The whole deal was fishy. I can't put my finger on what was wrong with it, but I decided against telling him about you. He kept pressing me for info, and I finally cut him off. Said I couldn't keeping wasting the boss's time. I've got no idea how he even knew where I work. I don't have your email, but mine's in the letterhead. Let me know if you want to sell that stuff, and I'll give him your name. I've got this weird feeling that this guy will be back."

"So do I." Tor laid the letter down on the breakfast bar. "That's Joel's talent talking, what he's got of it. Warning him, and a good thing, I bet. I don't like the sound of this. Not at all."

"If this guy reads the will, he can find you."

"Yeah. If."

"Wills are matters of public record. If he knows where Joel filed it, all he has to do is go to the county courthouse and read it. I bet he can even find it online. And Nils put our address in the codicil."

"Oh." Tor considered this for a long moment. "Great. That's all we need, one of Nils' crazy friends looking for his papers."

"How do you know he's crazy?"

"Just a wild guess." He gave me one of his sly grins. "Anyone who'd want to be Nils' friend has got to be crazy."

He laughed. I couldn't.

"I'll email Joel right away," Tor continued. "Tell him no, I'm not selling."

"You don't think that maybe the guy's a Neo-Nazi? You said that some of the papers were in German."

Tor stared at me as if I'd barked instead of spoke.

"I don't know why I said that," I said. "It must sound dumb."

"Not dumb, no, but luckily I don't think it's relevant. The German pages are just some notes Nils copied out of a book on the Armanen rune system. Things he wanted to remember. Nothing political about it. Although—" He paused, thinking. "When it comes to the runes, you always have to be careful about edging toward the fucking Nazis." His voice dropped toward a growl. "They believed some real shit things, distorted everything, twisted it. Polluted the runes." He stopped to catch his breath. "Sorry. I get worked up, I know."

I tried to answer, but my throat had gone dry, and my heart was pounding.

"Whoa!" Tor said. "You look terrified."

"I am." I managed to croak out a few words. "I don't

know why."

"It might mean something. Think about it, okay?" Tor was re-reading the letter. "Joel says the guy's accent reminded him of Halvar. Can't be German, then. Something Nordic. Unless—"

"Unless what?"

"I keep thinking of the jötnar. But how in hell could one of them learn to use a telephone?" He shook his head. "Makes no sense."

Later that day the police, in the persons of Lieutenant Hu and his back-up cop, arrived at our door and asked for a few minutes of our time. Tor invited them upstairs like the innocent householder he was pretending to be, nerdy illusion and all. Although the uniformed officer sat down, Hu stood and glanced around the living room. I noticed that he seemed particularly interested in the jade mountain sculpture.

"I saw the report on your prowler the other night," Hu said to Tor. "It looks like you've got some things worth stealing, all right."

"Yeah, I do," Tor said. "I own some European antiquities, as well, but those are small enough for me to keep them in the safe downstairs. One of them is solid gold."

"You're very wise to keep those locked away."

"Thanks. I'm glad you stopped by. I remembered something you might want to know."

"Good." Hu reached into his jacket and took a small notebook and ballpoint pen from his shirt pocket. "Do you mind if—"

"Not at all. Did you know that Nils Halvarsson's father was murdered?"

Hu's eyebrows quirked, and he coughed. The information was a shock to me, too. I suppressed a gasp, but the uniformed cop was looking my way with some interest. He wasn't quite as indifferent to the case as he pretended to be. Hu sat down to make writing notes easier.

"He was my grandfather, of course," Tor said. "His name was Halvar Svansson, that's s-v-a-n-s-s-o-n. The naming system—"

"We know about that." Hu looked up from his notebook. "Someone at the office looked it up."

"Ah, okay. Anyway, this happened in New York City in 2000, the summer. I don't remember the exact date. I was just a teenager at the time. Not quite fifteen."

Hu nodded and wrote on.

"Halvar was eighty that year. He was living in a suite in a real expensive hotel—I can find the name for you, if you can't get it from the New York police. He'd moved to the city to be close to his son Nils, who was I think between wives at the moment."

"I take it he had plenty of money. Your grandfather, that is."

"He sure did, and the family was full of rumors as to how he'd gotten it, too. Some of his investments were kind of dubious, especially those he made in the 1940s after the war. Swiss industrialists who'd been a little too close to the Nazis, is one thing I heard." Tor grinned at the lieutenant. "The family joke was, Iceland got too hot to hold him."

The uniformed cop snorted. Hu ignored the humor.

"Anyway," Tor continued, "one summer night he went for a walk and never came back. The hotel staff put out the alarm, and the police found him. His throat was cut, and his body dumped in an alley. Right in the middle of the city, but no one had seen a thing. If you believe them, anyway."

"That's New York for you," Hu said. "Did they ever catch the perpetrator?"

"No. My father was pretty upset by that."

"I bet. Your immediate family—where were they, and I presume you, at that time?"

"Living in Mill Valley. Do you want that address?"

"Not necessary. Your parents, is it possible for me to interview them?"

"My father's dead. He died of elder-onset leukemia two years ago. My mother moved back to Iceland to live with my sister and her family there. But I'm sure she'd be glad to answer questions if you want to reach her."

"Iceland again." Hu sighed like a Roman Christian hearing the lions roar. "In the Bay Area we have police officers who speak over a hundred languages between them, but not one of them speaks Icelandic." He thought for a moment. "You mentioned that Nils Halvarsson was living in New York City at the time of the murder."

"Yes, I'm sure he was."

"Did he take part in any of his father's dubious business dealings?"

"I honestly don't know. No one would have told me anything about it, since I was just a kid."

"Yes, most likely not. Well, there are other sources, now that I know Halvarsson's father's death was a police matter. Thank you, Mr. Thorlaksson. You've been very helpful." Hu nodded my way. "Miss Cantescu, sorry to disturb you again."

On this wave of alleged good feeling, Tor showed them out. When he rejoined me in the living room, he looked totally pleased with himself.

"That'll give the dogs a new scent to follow," he said.

"I hope so. I didn't like the way the guy in uniform was looking at me. Like he was judging my reaction to everything."

"What? Maya, you're getting paranoid. You're beautiful. He's male. Of course he was looking at you. I noticed. He's a cop, or I would have challenged him over it."

Somehow this obvious explanation hadn't occurred to me. Tor must be right, I thought. I am getting paranoid.

"Come to think of it," Tor went on, "I wouldn't be surprised to learn that Nils was involved in whatever Halvar's dirty business was."

"I wonder if Nils killed him."

"He'd finally had enough of the old man's shit? Could be. If Nils cast one of his aversion spells, it would explain the lack of witnesses. Or if Halvar was killed inside somewhere and then dumped, that would explain it, too."

"Have you found anything about his suspicious business deals in those journals?"

"Not yet. I've only just started reading them. I've been classifying them by date and type first. Doing a quick skim through of each, to see what's in it."

"It's you mentioning Nazis that made me wonder."

"Nazis again, huh? Tell you what. Let's go downstairs, and I'll read your rune staves."

Down in Tor's workshop, a brown cardboard banker's box was sitting on the high table with a couple of tidy stacks of yellowing, dusty papers and leather-bound notebooks next to it. Tor pointed to the stacks.

"Halvar's journals are there, and then in the box there's some notes about rituals in a different handwriting. Nils' work, I bet. He was trying everything he could to drive the wolf away."

"And none of it worked."

"No, it sure didn't." He paused and glanced away, abruptly grim. "Well, he's free of it now."

The red leather pouch of rune staves lay on the table where we'd left them, next to the neatly folded white cloth. For the reading Tor moved the family papers, one careful handful at a time, to the end of the long table. While Tor scrambled the staves on the cloth, I walked around to the far side of the table and sat on the high stool waiting for me. I avoided looking at the staves until Tor told me I could. He laid a clean piece of paper, dotted here and there with numbers, down in front of me.

"You'll be picking out nine staves," he said, "but do it one at a time and put them face up on the number. Y'know, the first one on One, the next on Two, and like that."

For a moment I studied the odd-looking template. Five of the numbers lay in a straight vertical line but out of order: eight, six, one, seven, and nine. Four and three lay to the left of this line, and two and five to the right of it. I picked out a stave and laid it on One.

"Mannaz, human things, in Midgard," Tor said. "Appropriate."

Two was Othala, ancestral holdings, in Niflheim, the

mistlands. The memory rose in my mind of telling Tor how thick fog and misty rain made my father and me feel more alive, as if we drew élan from the cold. I glanced up and saw Tor smiling, an odd little twist of his mouth.

"That means something, doesn't it?" I said.

"Maybe. Go on."

"I'm not sure I want to."

He made a little snorting sound.

"Oh okay," I said and drew the third stave.

"Kennaz in Muspelheim, torch in the land of fire," Tor said. "This could turn out to be a strange reading."

It grew stranger as every stave I drew fell into an appropriate world: Thorn to Jötunheim, the Birchtree for Vanirheim, the home of the old fertility gods. The Sun fell in the land of the Light Elves and the Dice Cup of Fate in the home of the dwarves. Ánsuz, meaning a god, fell in Ásgaard, and finally, Ice, the cold at the end of everything, landed in the deathlands of Hel. Tor stared at the finished layout for a long time while the silence in the big room grew around us and the sunlight sprawled across the floor. When Tor finally spoke, I nearly yelped in surprise.

"Okay," he said, "this is not an ordinary reading. Forget the usual fortune telling shit."

"Well, what—"

"It's a message. From yourself to you. Niflheim, the world of mists. Your patrimony. Those discrepancies in your DNA that baffled the expert."

"I don't understand."

"Really?" He was smiling at me, but his eyes stayed cold. "Look at where the runes fall. Every one of them lies where it should be, just as if this reading's a map. It's saying that we should take the positions, the world names, literally, not as some kind of metaphor. All of them except one. Othala in the land of mists. Your ancestry, your patrimony. Can't you see it?"

My hands started shaking. I clasped them together to make them stop. "Okay, yes, I do," I said. "You think this reading's telling me my father came from Niflheim. How?

I mean, he was a human being. He and my mom had kids the usual way. He died of heart failure like a human being."

"He had a human body, sure. But his soul—"

"Soul? What's that supposed to mean?"

"Maya, I don't know. It's a shit word, sure, over-used. Makes you think of angels and crap like that. But we've all got to have something that I guess we could call a soul. It's got nothing to do with the gods or the idea of one god, either. It's got to be some natural thing, because it's what travels from life to life. It's why you and I remember loving each other in Copenhagen. The human brains we've got now couldn't remember, but some part of us does."

I started to speak. He held up one hand flat to stop me.

"I don't understand this," he continued. "I don't have any answers for how this happened. Okay? I'm not laying down the law about it." He grinned at me, and his eyes lost their cold glare. "For a change."

I had to smile in return. My hands stopped shaking.

"Okay," I said. "You're saying that my father's soul, whatever that is, belonged to some other part of the universe."

"Yeah, just that, and he passed it on to you. His genetics gave you something that changed the body you have, when you were growing in the womb. Think of the piece of code as a magnet, kind of, that drew your soul to it. Whatever the affinity is, it's got to be seated in some recessive part of the DNA. Your brother got the dominant human coding. You weren't so lucky. Neither was your dad. Somehow or other what we're calling his soul got trapped in the wrong world. I wonder if he even knew it?"

"I think he did." Memories began to fall into place. "I bet that's why he studied magic so—so obsessively. He was searching for something, and he was desperate to find it. I knew that. I thought it was about our disease, and yeah, in a way it was. But I bet there was something more to it than that."

"So do I." Tor's voice turned soft, gentle. "Can you remember anything he said about it?"

"When he was in the hospital and really sick, y'know?"

This memory brought tears to my eyes, but I forced the words out. "When he was dying, he told me, don't mourn, I'm just going back. Back where? I said. I don't know, he said, but home. It was hard for him to talk, but then he said, it's a long long way away. He might have told me more, but my stepmother said he was hallucinating and chased me out of the room."

"The bitch!"

"Well, she was jealous of us, me and Roman, I mean, and the way he still loved us after the divorce."

"Real generous of her! Can you remember anything else?" I shook my head no. "I'm exhausted. Not now. Please?"

"Sure. Sweetheart, I'm sorry."

Tor strode around the end of the table and held out his arms. I got down from the stool and let him hold me. I could feel the élan flowing around me and breathed deep. Strength, his strength as well as the strength of the life force itself, soothed me.

"Feel better?" he said.

"Yes. Thank you."

"We can talk more later." He let me go. "No rush."

Tor began picking up the staves and putting them back into the leather pouch. I wandered over to the sliding glass door that looked out onto our pathetic back yard—ratty grass, one Japanese maple that needed pruning. To one side lay a hunk of old concrete, left over from someone's attempt to put in a patio. I could remember a lot about my father, all our good times and the bad as well, lying in bed as a child and listening to him and my mother fighting in furious whispers. They never wanted Roman and me to hear what they said to each other in those fights, so I only perceived the sound of rage and frustration. I lacked the words carrying its meaning. Maybe it would have been better if I'd understood them. I don't know.

But none of those memories told me anything more about my heritage, my patrimony, as Tor called it, the strange place my dad came from, the place that marked us deep in our genes. The Mistland, Niflheim, a chunk of old mythology, not a real place, how could it be real? Symbolic, that's all, a symbol, a marker of some meaning beyond conscious functioning, an archetype, maybe, powerful but not really real. It didn't belong in the same world as DNA and science and ordinary human beings.

But did I?

"Maya?" Tor said. "You okay?"

"Not really." I turned around and face him.

"It's a lot to think about."

"Yeah. Sure is."

"I can give you a book on how to meditate on themes like these. Well, if you want."

At least he wasn't pushing on me. I started to agree, but I remembered Harper, telling me to dig deep for my senior project. I felt a rush of energy like a fountain bursting upwards into the air.

"Thanks but no thanks," I said. "I'll paint it. That's what I've always done. Whenever I had a problem or something awful I had to face, I used to draw for hours. That's what I'll do with this, turn it into art and see what it looks like."

"Great! That's always best, do it your own way." He paused for a sheepish grin. "But you won't mind, will you, if I do a little research?"

I laughed. "No," I said. "I won't mind."

When he held out his hand, I walked over and clasped it. He smiled again and kissed me on the forehead, nothing sexy, but warm and sweet all the same. We started toward the staircase to go upstairs, but something caught my attention, a welcome distraction. Leaning against the lectern in the walk-in closet area was a large rectangular object, about three feet by four, muffled in a green baize zippered bag.

"What's that?" I stopped and pointed.

"The portrait from Nils. We should take a look at it, I guess. See if it's scratched or anything like that."

Tor carried the bag to the table in the main room. He took the portrait out and propped it up on one of the barstools. Against a dark background, a middle-aged man sat in a red velvet chair and stared unsmiling straight out at the viewer. He had silvery gray hair and eyebrows, but otherwise he resembled Tor, or I should say, Tor resembled him—same strong jaw and broad hands, same brown eyes, but Halvar's were narrowed slightly as if he disliked the world he saw in front of him.

"It's just like the other two," I said. "It was totally strange of him, to have all these identical portraits made. Especially since he didn't let the artist sign them."

"He was a strange man. That's another reason I wanted his papers. I've always wondered what made Halvar tick. But if you're curious about the artist, I found his name in one of the notebooks."

"I'd like to know, yeah."

"I'll find it again. Let me just get rid of this."

Tor slid the portrait back into its bag, zipped it up, and put it into the long drawer that held the other two portraits. "Halvar's coffin," he said. "That's what I call it."

"Where was he actually buried?"

"In Iceland. They shipped him home after the police autopsy. I'm not sure of where, exactly. I don't give a damn, either."

Tor rummaged through one of the notebooks on the high table, found the entry, and wrote out an English version for me on a scrap of paper. "Final payment to Florian Windrup for four portraits. June 19, 1992."

"Four?"

"Liv has the other one, back in Iceland."

"Florian Windrup? That's quite a name! I wonder if he made it up to sound artistic."

"Could be, though Florian's a common enough German name. Kind of old-fashioned, maybe. Grandfather found him in New York City." Tor pointed to an entry in the journal. "Here's the second note that mentions Windrup's name, about a week later. 'Matter settled' is all it says."

"That's enough information to narrow my search."

"Good. Go on up if you want. I just remembered a book

that might have some information we can use. It's in the library somewhere."

While he hunted for the book, I returned to the living room and my laptop. All the data together, Florian Windrup artist NYC, turned up exactly one person, a young portraitist, and some totally grim information about him. I'd just finished that search when Tor came upstairs, carrying a book. When he laid it on the coffee table, I noticed that the title was in a Scandinavian language—I wasn't sure which one. He walked over to the breakfast bar, where his laptop was sitting, and booted it up while I did another quick search on Windrup. I found nothing more.

"Hey, Joel answered my email." Tor stared at his screen for a long minute, then looked up. "When he got home from work tonight, his apartment had been torn apart. Burgled—except they left his TV, the laptop, and some cash he had in his dresser drawer."

"Some burglary!"

"Yeah. He thinks they were after the papers, because, like he says, what else? Y'know, I think I'll just go put them in the safe. Right now."

"Wait a minute, okay? I found that artist your grandfather hired. He was murdered in Brooklyn on June 26, 1992. It looked like a mugging. They never caught the killer."

"Oh shit." Tor whispered the words. "One week after the final payment, huh?"

"I have this creepy feeling it's not a coincidence."

"So do I." His mouth twisted in disgust. "Matter settled. Yeah, I just bet it was."

"Your grandfather, would he really have someone killed?"

"I wouldn't put it past the old bastard."

"But why? He gave the portraits away. It wasn't like he wanted them kept secret."

"That's a real good question. Florian must have done something or known something that dear old Grandad didn't want spread around. Unless it's just coincidence. Windrup might have flashed some money around, since he'd just gotten paid. Attracted the wrong kind of attention."

"You really think so?"

"No, because I knew Halvar. If he had a reason to want this guy dead, he would have arranged it. Huh, I wonder if it's got some connection to his own murder?"

"It sounds like he knew some really creepy people."

Tor grinned at me. "Including Nils, yeah."

"I don't suppose Nils loved his father. Considering how much he resented all the rest of the family."

"I don't suppose anyone loved Halvar by then. He'd turned into a real nasty son of a bitch. Even when he was young, he was a lot like me. Ruthless. A barbarian at heart."

"You keep saying that about yourself. I don't see it."

"Who's upset about Nils' death, you or me?" Tor smiled, just faintly. "Don't let the way I love you make you blind."

I felt ice slide a warning down my back.

"Let me go put those papers in the safe." Tor's voice was perfectly calm, perfectly ordinary. "I'll be right back."

As I listened to the sound of his footsteps, clattering down the stairs, I was wondering which one of us was less than human, me or Tor.

I turned off the laptop and set it down next to my sketchbook. A box of pastels lay on the coffee table where I'd left it. I was just leaning forward to pick them up when a sound shattered the air—a crack like lightning, or a gunshot, clean and sharp, and so loud that I screamed before I could stop myself. I heard Tor pounding up the stairs and yelling my name.

"I'm all right!" My voice swooped up way too high.

Tor burst into the living room and ran over to me. He caught my shaking hand and helped me stand up, then slipped his arm around me.

"What the hell was that?" He glanced around and swore under his breath. He let me go and hurried over to the sandstone fireplace. I followed more slowly. I gasped and felt like swearing myself.

One of the largest slabs of decorative stone, roughly three feet high and a couple of feet across, had split down the middle,

a long deep crack still plumed with a trace of dust in the air.
"Poltergeist," Tor said. "The dead vitki just said hello."

CHAPTER 5

Tor spent the rest of that day carving protective runes into every lintel of every door in the upper flat, every frame of every window, and for good measure the mantel of the fireplace. He finished the living room first and told me to stay there, then did the rest of the flat. I sat huddled on the couch with my sketchbook and watched him work, when I could see him, and just listened to his voice intoning spell after spell when he was out of my range of vision. First he'd intone a galdr, then use his rune knife to carve a protective formula. Chips of paint and wood pattered down like snow and fell on his shoulders and arms. He'd irritably shake them away.

Once he'd carved all the lines of runes, he brought an old mayonnaise jar of paint and a fine brush up from downstairs. While he painted each carved rune with red ochre, he sang another spell.

Just after sunset I heard him washing his hands in the bathroom. When he came striding into the living room, I noticed that he was holding his left hand out a little ways from his body. He had a couple of Band-aids in his right.

"You put blood in that stain?" I said.

"Yeah, just a little." He sat down next to me on the couch and proffered the bandaids. "Could you put these on it for me?"

"It" turned out to be the cut, about half an inch long, on the back of his left arm at the wrist. He'd reopened the old scar from the ritual battle with Nils. I took off the paper coverings and covered up the wound with the gauze pads.

"I thought of using blood straight up," Tor continued, "but it would have taken too much."

"That's for sure. I'm glad you saw that."

"I'm going to need my strength." He smiled and patted my hand. "I've got to eat something. I'll make us some dinner, and then I'm going to put wards downstairs. I wish I could use them up here, but it would drive both of us nuts, feeling them."

"Will the runes work the same kind of spell?"

"Yeah. Maybe not as well, though. We'll have to see." He stood up. "But if not, there's other stuff I can do. Don't worry." He headed for the kitchen.

Don't worry. I felt like throwing something at his retreating back. Instead I picked up my sketchbook and rummaged through the old wooden box full of pastels and Conté and charcoal sticks. The sight of them, my tools as an artist, calmed me. I took out a black Conté stick—the color seemed appropriate—and began scribbling circles just to soothe my nerves. In the mess of lines and smudges forms began to appear. I turned the page and let the images come to me.

In the foreground, snow lay heaped up against a wall of some sort. Beyond, I saw low buildings, a wharf, water, wide wide water, an ocean, a tiny harbor, on an island. I remembered the island, but I couldn't place where it lay. In the north, obviously, I thought as I added fine lines to define the heaps of snow. I messed up the snow drifts on the wharf, or so I thought at first. They looked dirty, as if I'd overworked them, until I realized that the drifts were dusted with soot. Someone burned coal in the cabin nearby. At the end of the wharf a woman was standing, dressed in long skirts and a heavy cloak.

I heard a shout, but only in my own mind, not audibly, a man's voice, screaming two words, over and over, but she leapt off anyway, the woman on the pier, and drowned. I drowned. I'd heard Björn's voice speaking what must have been Danish, "Nej, stop!" But I hated him, and I let the ocean claim me.

Another voice summoned me: Kristjan's. But he's dead too, I thought.

"Maya?" Tor was standing in the kitchen door. "Dinner's ready."

I stared at him, my mouth slack, the Conté stick clutched in dirty fingers.

"Are you okay?" he said. "I called you twice."

"No." I tossed the stick back into the box. "I was remembering."

He strode over and took the sketchbook from my lap.

"Do you recognize that island?" I said.

"No. Ugly kind of place."

"Yeah. It was."

He waited for me to say more, but the memory hurt too much to describe aloud. The cabin belonged to some friend of Björn's, a wealthy man who used it as a vacation spot in the summers. Björn took me there after Kristjan's death. No one would hear me scream when he raped me, is why. Or I should say, as they did in those days, when he "claimed his marital rights", his privilege no matter what his wife thought about it.

Tor laid the sketchbook down on the table and considered me. For a moment I thought he was going to speak, but he just shrugged and led the way to the kitchen and dinner. Over the doorway the new runes glistened red, as wet as wounds. He'd put a line of runes over the breakfast bar, too.

After we ate, I cleaned up the kitchen, and Tor got out the vacuum and swept up all the paint chips and splinters. We pretended we were a normal modern couple, sharing the housework. I started the dishwasher and returned to my sketchbook while Tor went downstairs and set magical wards. Not so normal after all. This time, when I started working, my fingers followed orders and drew what I wanted, memories of snow lying on tree branches or streaking the trunks, details for my senior project.

Since I was born and raised in California, I'd only experienced snow a couple of times in my life. Once, when there was a freak winter storm that dropped snow on Mount

Diablo, my father pulled me and Roman out of school and drove us over to play in it before it melted. He was as excited as we were, laughing as he tossed snowballs and helped us build a snowman. By the end of the afternoon, Roman felt exhausted from the cold and wet, but both Dad and I had so much energy that we could barely get to sleep that night.

When I was a freshman in high school, my parents decided to split up. For the holiday break some family friends took Roman and me on a ski trip at Tahoe. They wanted to give my mother time alone to deal with the divorce. Even though our parents' break-up grieved both of us kids, the trip did help. Roman learned a new sport, skiing, while just playing in the snow soothed me and gave me a mega-dose of élan. I never seemed to get cold. My friends kept nagging me about wearing a parka because I kept running outside in a pair of jeans and a sweater. I even kept forgetting to wear a hat.

Now, years later, the experience finally made sense. Niflheim on Earth.

Tor came back upstairs and sat down next to me on the couch. I laid the sketchbook aside and slid over to snuggle against him. He put his arm around me, and my human side felt safe again, warm against his strength.

"I was wondering," I said, "if we could maybe go up to the snow during Christmas break. Tahoe or Boreal, maybe."

"Sure! Great idea! We'll have to plan it so we go between full moons, is all. Do you know how to ski?"

"No. I mostly want to take photos—references for my senior project. I bet you ski, though."

"Yeah. I love it. We'll have to get you some proper gear. None of my stuff would fit you."

"Oh, I don't get as cold as most people." I didn't want him spending wads of cash on buying me expensive ski clothes.

He pulled a little away so he could turn and look at me. "Well, yeah," he said. "I don't suppose you do. But we can get you a few things, anyway, just in case there's a major storm." He suddenly grinned. "Maybe you can attract snowstorms if we find the right galdr. We could rent you out to ski resorts.

Make sure they have plenty of powder."

I laughed and turned my face up for a kiss. Tor bent his head, kissed me, then abruptly pulled away. He let me go and stood up fast.

"What?"

He held up a hand for silence. He turned, very slowly, until he faced the wall that held the door leading to downstairs. He was staring as intensely as a cat spotting prey at a spot next to the door—the heating vent, I realized, that went straight down into the lower flat. Slowly, a bare inch at a time, he raised his other hand, paused, then swept both hands through the air in a tight ritual gesture. I heard a muffled sound, a dull thump as if something blunt had slammed against the wall. Tor grinned in satisfaction.

"Thor's hammer," he said. "I need to show you how to sign that. Defense as a good offense."

"Something was there."

"Oh yeah. I never thought of the heating vents, but they need runes, too. My mistake. I'll do it now. Go sit in your bedroom, okay? Till I'm done. You'll be safe there, because it doesn't have a vent. We know now that the runes keep the damn 'geist out. The vents are weak points, and I'll fix that."

I gathered up my drawing stuff and fled. I sat down cross-legged on the bed in the Burne-Jones bedroom and considered the drawing of the island. It lacked something. I remembered that a scraggly tree, bare-branched for winter, stood next to the cabin. As soon as I drew that in, the drawing felt complete. I could almost feel the cold, crisp air, smell the dry mineral smoke from the coal—no, I could feel the cold. I held my hand over the picture and felt the tingling chill in my palm and along my fingers. The smoke alarm on the wall over the bedroom door pinged. Its tiny red light came on as it sensed the coal smoke. Somehow the picture of that place I'd hated had come alive.

I tore the drawing out of the book and ripped it to little pieces. The alarm fell quiet. Its light darkened to off. I got up and walked over the writing desk. On its shiny black surface, the alchemical barometer showed an image of a red lion, its mouth open, its head tipped back for a roar. I knew I should tell Tor about the exhalation of cold and the smoke from the drawing. I was planning on telling him as soon as he finished his spell. But as I watched, the lion image changed color, turning a muddy brown, then a greenish neutral, and finally a bright green as the lion's mouth closed.

Something had drawn off its power—my power. Tell Tor, I reminded myself. But as soon as I stepped away from the desk, I forgot what I wanted to tell him. Since I'd torn the drawing up, it no longer seemed to matter.

In the morning we heard from Joel again. Tor sat down next to me at the breakfast bar and showed me the email while I was eating. The police had searched Joel's apartment and given him their report. The burglar had entered through a rear window protected by an outside wrought-iron safety grill. The burglar had bent the bars until they broke, then reached through and opened the window.

"Seriously scary dude," Joel wrote in his email. "They found fingerprints all over the bars. I guess this guy didn't even bother to wear gloves while he was twisting solid metal. Nothing to it, ho ho ho. Shit! The prints were huge, the cop told me. On beyond one of those iron man types on that ESPN show. The cops think they're fake, left there somehow to throw them off. I don't see how anyone could do that, and neither can they, but I guess they gotta say something."

Tor quirked at eyebrow at me and waited for my reaction. I pushed the laptop back toward him.

"Frost Giant?" I said.

"Who else? Or what else, I should say. What's ESPN?"

"A cable sports channel. Not that you'd know."

"TV sucks." Tor put the laptop into sleep mode before he continued. "Typical jötnar thinking. Smash whatever's in your way. Deal with the consequences later, if there are any."

"They wouldn't know about security systems, either, would they? What if that prowler who was up behind our house was a jötunn? Those signs from the security agency wouldn't mean anything to him."

"You're right. He probably thought they were magic symbols. Huh, when the lights and siren went on up there, he must have freaked. The vitki's spirits were attacking him, is how he'd see it." Tor reached for the laptop. "I'm going to email Joel. Tell him to be careful. And tell him that if anyone phones about those papers again, he should make sure they know he doesn't have them. If they insist on knowing who does, he should just lie and say the lawyer didn't give him the name."

It turned out that Joel had done that already. He answered Tor's email only a few minutes after Tor sent it. "I'm home today," he told us. "I'm taking a couple days off work. I've got to clean up the fucking mess the guy made of my crib. Landlord's coming to fix the back window, too. With steel bars, this time."

"Leaving a mess sounds like a rime jötunn, all right," Tor said to me. "Not that I can tell Joel that." He got up from the bar stool. "I've got to finish reading through Halvar's journals. Say, are you going to campus today?"

"No, but I'm going to the mall. I need some female supplies."

"Okay, but be careful. The poltergeist is probably bound to this house, but you never know with these things."

"Is it the same as the dead vitki?"

"No, but I bet it's something he created."

When Tor went downstairs, I put the rest of my yogurt back into the refrigerator. I'd lost my appetite.

Before I hit the mall, I stopped at the post office. A few weeks back I'd gotten a post office box because Tor had taken over my mail. I don't mean he would have read personal letters—I never got any anyway—but he insisted on paying all my bills. I'd been so far in debt from school and the crummy part-time job I'd been working that my credit rating had hit bottom, so he'd paid off all my credit cards and given me one on his account instead. Before you say "sounds great!", you need to realize this means he could see everything I bought when the statement came in. If I ever watched a TV show on my laptop, he'd bitch about it.

So to re-establish credit I'd applied for a charge card at the fancy department store in the mall. I could buy small things and pay them off each month. I was counting on the way those expensive places hand out credit, and sure enough, my new card had arrived. I tucked it into my wallet and threw the envelope away in a public trash can. Then I went to the mall, bought what I needed at the drug store with Tor's card, and bought myself a red cotton tank top with my new card.

When I got back home, I put the car into the garage and locked the door after me. As I headed back to the house, I saw the Frost Giant kid magically appear at the end of the driveway. A wisp of fog blew across the lawn, formed an oval, and disappeared, leaving the boy behind. It all happened so fast that someone passing by might not have noticed, or if they had noticed, they would have assumed that something must have gotten in their eyes or come up with some other excuse to explain it away.

The young giant smiled, waved, and hurried down the driveway to meet me. I kept my keys in my hand and waited for him right by the side door of the house, in case I had to make a fast exit.

"I have come with a message," he announced. "Will you take it to the vitki?"

"I will if you answer a question for me. But first, let me tell you that I don't have any elixir to give you today."

"I see this." He heaved a sigh. "Too bad. Very well. I will answer your question. Here is the message." He looked away and let his eyes go slightly out of focus. From the stilted way he spoke, I got the impression that he was repeating the exact words that had been given to him. "Why have you not answered our note? We have given you the note as you wished. Will you do what we want? Answer soon."

I considered telling him that Tor couldn't understand the note's language, but to do so meant admitting a weakness. In the old sagas powerful men never admit weaknesses, even when they should.

"I'll give him your message," I said. "Here is my question. Where did you learn English?"

"My grandmother taught us. She is from the island where they speak it. Here in your world, that is. My grandfather stole her heart many years ago, and she came home with him to live among us."

"So you've got human blood."

"Only a little!" He gave me a jutted-chin scowl.

"Do the other kids tease you?"

"Yes." He looked down with a sigh. "We have fights."

"I don't see anything wrong with that. You had to defend your honor, right?"

He looked up with one of his goopy smiles. "Yes," he said. "You understand."

"I've got human blood too," I said.

"True. But you are not all human, yes? I smell this. You smell like ice and beautiful rain, not apes." He frowned. "But you are very small."

"I'm not a jötunn, no. Is your grandmother tall?"

"Short for us, very tall for humans. Even for a Jorvik woman, she was very tall. But, she tells me, since she has lived with us, she has grown much taller still."

I heard the scraping sound of someone raising the screen on an upstairs window. I looked up just as Tor stuck his head out.

"Maya!" he called out. "Is the jötunn still here?"

The Frost Giant yelped and pointed. "The vitki! I go now."

"No!" Tor shouted. "I heard you ask a question. You stay for my answer." He leaned further out of the window and pointed at the jötunn. "Stay!"

The boy stayed. He was trembling so hard that when he tried to speak, he only stammered.

"Here is my answer," Tor continued. "No. Understand? Just no."

The boy tried to speak, stammered again, then managed to force out, "I tell them this." He took one step back and disappeared.

Tor laughed and left the window. My own hands shook as I unlocked the side door, which led to the staircase. I hurried up and found Tor opening a bottle of dark beer in the kitchen.

"You must have deciphered the note," I said.

"No." He took a swig from the bottle. "It just never pays to agree to do what a giant asks you to do."

"Say what? You don't even know what they want, do you?"

"Yeah, so? I mean it, Maya. It doesn't pay to give in when the rime jötnar demand something of you." He had another swallow of beer. "So I won't."

I made a squealing sort of noise in sheer frustration.

"Besides," Tor went on. "I've got a good idea of what the note said. Give us back our gold plaque."

"That would fit with the stuff Joel's told us."

"Yeah. It's the only thing I can think of that they'd want. We always wondered who could wear the thing, it's so heavy."

"I thought it was maybe for horse gear, but it would suit a giant, too."

"Sure would. Look, while you were at school this morning, I read more of Halvar's journals. I focused on the ones from the last couple of years of his life. He never came right out and used the words rime jötnar, but he kept writing things like 'they want it back', or 'they made another demand'. He did talk about Nils, who was still living in New York then. Nils was pissed off because he wanted the same thing that the mysterious 'they' wanted. Halvar refused to give it to either of them. He sent it to my dad instead."

"And either Nils or the 'they' killed Halvar. For the ornament?"

"Maybe, maybe not. There were a lot of people who had reasons to hate the old bastard. He didn't get rich by playing fair." Tor considered the beer bottle with a small frown, as if it could tell him the answer. "But I'd put my money on the Frost Giants being the killers if we were going to bet on it. They're like that."

"And you just royally pissed them off."

Tor grinned and shrugged. I took a deep breath to keep from screaming at him.

"Why won't you give it back, if it's theirs?" I said.

"Because first, we don't know if it *is* theirs. Yeah, it probably was at some point, but we're not a hundred per cent sure. They could have stolen it from someone, anyway. Second, it might help me control the bjarki."

"Might?"

"Why else would Nils have wanted it so bad? I bet it's because he knew it had something to do with were-creatures. I can't throw that away. And finally, it's mine now, and I don't give in to threats."

Tor finished the beer, wiped his mouth on his shirt sleeve, and set the empty bottle down on the counter. With a crack and crackle like gunfire it shattered. Glass sprayed. I yelped and jumped out of the way. Tor stepped back, wincing. A couple of pieces had stabbed the back of his right hand. Skinny runnels of blood wound their way between his fingers.

"I left the kitchen window open," he said. "Shit, this is what I get for being stupid."

I ran across the room, pulled down the screen, and slammed the window shut. Tor very carefully stepped clear of the broken glass on the floor and crossed to the cabinet where we kept clean dishes. He took down a saucer and let the blood on his hand drip into it, glossy red blood, oozing élan.

"Too valuable to waste," he told me. "I've got to carve some more runes."

"Whatever." I forced myself to look away before I salivated. "I'd better sweep up all this glass before one of us gets cut."

"The bleeding's stopping." Tor was frowning at the back of his hand. "If you get me some Band-aids, I'll rinse this off and then get to work."

Going into the bathroom for the Band-aids, away from the sight of blood, was a relief. When I came back into the kitchen, he was drying his cut hand off on a couple of paper towels.

"Does it hurt?" I said.

"Not much, no." Tor held out his hand. "I've been thinking. Y'know, I don't want to go on living with a fucking poltergeist. I don't want to keep carving up the flat to ward it off, either. I've got an idea about this dead vitki. Who he is, and if I'm right, I've been overlooking the obvious."

Since it wasn't obvious to me, I concentrated on patching up Tor's hand. Once I got the cuts bandaged, we cleaned up the broken glass from the floor and the counter. By the time we finished, Tor had a grimly satisfied smile. He'd been thinking, all right.

"Come downstairs with me," he said. "If you're game. I want to get a portrait out of Halvar's coffin."

It finally dawned on me. "He was a vitki when he was alive."

"Sure was." Tor gave me a smile of approval. "And I wonder if he still is."

Tor went downstairs first to banish the wards he'd set. By the time I came down, he'd taken a portrait out of the drawer and set it up on the lectern. Together we stood in front of it and looked it over. I studied the technique, impeccable though so old-fashioned, painted in oils and then varnished. The eyes caught my attention, held my attention. I couldn't look away as the image shimmered and changed into a face I remembered all too well. The same eyes, the same scowl, but his hair was dark, and he wore mutton-chop whiskers.

"Björn." I whispered the name aloud.

For the briefest of moments the portrait smiled, the icy smile of the hunter who spots his prey. Tor barked out one word in Icelandic. The smile disappeared. I wrenched my gaze away.

"Maya," Tor said, "go upstairs! Fast! Before he tries that again."

I ran for the stairs and started up. I glanced back once to see Tor shoving the portrait back into its green cloth bag. For a moment I thought I heard laughter—not Tor's laughter, but Björn's. He'd made that same cold howling sound when he'd told me my lover was dead. I ran the rest of the way upstairs and stood panting in the living room by the fireplace, where the runes would keep me safe.

Tor came up directly after me. "So," he said, "I'm more glad than ever that the old bastard's dead. Halvar, I mean, but Björn, too."

"Did you see the face change?"

"Oh yeah. And I saw what he was trying to do. Take you over. Capture your will and make you obey him."

"How could he—"

"I don't know, but I bet Liv does. She made that writing desk, didn't she?" He grinned, a gesture that left his eyes cold. "Now I know where she got that particular talent. Image magic, I guess we can call it. She must have inherited it."

"What are you going to do? With the portraits, I mean."

"I don't know. I wish I could talk with her about it, but I got an email from her yesterday. That means she won't be going back into town for another lousy week." He paused, then gave me a normal smile. "Unless—I just got an idea. Come into your bedroom with me."

For a minute I wondered if he wanted to try a sexual rite again, but when we walked into the Burne-Jones bedroom he sat down in the green armchair facing the writing desk. He motioned me over to stand next to him. The alchemical barometer displayed an elaborate picture of an oak tree. On one side of the tree an armed knight pinned a huge snake to the trunk with his sword. On the other, a second knight stabbed a king.

"I might need to borrow some of your energy," Tor said. "I'll try not to."

"Okay. Should I touch you?"

"Only if I ask. Then put your hand on my shoulder."

Tor leaned forward and put his own hands flat on the writing desk. The picture abruptly changed to a smooth black void surrounded by a circle of red lions. Tor's mouth twitched in a brief smile. For some minutes Tor stared into the void without moving, barely breathing, it seemed, while I stood ready beside him. Slowly images began to form in the black void, fragments of the snake, fragments of the king and the tree, until one piece at a time the original image had reappeared. Tor lifted his hands off the desk and sat back with a long, exhausted sigh.

"Well, shit," he said. "I don't know if anything you could call a message got there. I'll send her email for back-up. But it gave me an idea. I wonder what would happen if I laid hands on the portraits and concentrated? Like I just did with the desk, I mean."

"No!" I practically screamed at him. "It'd be too dangerous."

Tor turned in the chair and quirked an eyebrow at me. I got the distinct impression that he was fighting to keep from smiling.

"I don't know how I know," I said. "But I do."

He did grin, then. "Okay," he said. "I bet you know a lot more about image magic than you think you do. I wanted to see if I could make you admit it."

I felt like slapping him, just because he looked so smug. Tor crossed his arms over his chest and waited with an infuriating little smile.

"Oh lay off!" I snapped at him. "I'm tired of you always pushing on me. Why won't you just hang it up?"

"Because I want you to be my equal."

I found myself caught with an open mouth and nothing to say.

"Well, come on!" Tor said. "I've got the money to make your life easier. You need me to feed you élan. You're part of my household, and I'll take care of you as long as you want me to. It's all fine with me. But what happens when *you* get tired of feeling like a patient in a clinic? Or a pet?"

I went on staring without a word at my disposal.

"You'll leave me, that's what." Tor's voice softened, became quiet. "And I'll fall apart. and when I put myself back together, I'll just be the cold kind of half-dead bastard who feels nothing but contempt for the whole fucked-up human race. And I don't want to turn into a monster." He forced out a twisted smile. "I'm too close to that already."

I took a deep breath and got my brain back online. "Okay," I said. "I get it. You're right. I don't want to be any-body's pet cat."

"Good."

"But you're not a monster."

"Not yet, no."

"Tor! I don't fall in love with monsters."

His smile changed into something warm. I'd call it grate-ful, but with Tor, that might be going too far. I wanted to say something normal—well, as normal as anything could be between us. "How long do you think it'll be before you hear from your sister?"

"Depends on when she goes into town." Tor got up and stretched before he continued. "I don't know why she wants to live way the hell out there. The farm's on the east side of the island. Not a lot of people around."

"The isolation's probably why, with your family talents to hide. I mean, most Icelanders are normal people, aren't they?"

"Very." He grinned again. "Which is one reason my father moved to California. Here, we fit right in."

"Fit right in? You got to be kidding."

"Yeah? Think about it. You, Brittany, the occult book-stores, the tarot card readers, the occult lodges down in L.A. and San Fran, your dad, the—"

"Okay, okay, I see what you mean."

We walked into the living room together. I sat down on the couch, but Tor paused at the fireplace. He laid a finger on the long crack in the sandstone slab.

"We're going to have to get rid of him," Tor said, "one way or another. I need to figure out how to do the right ban-ishing ceremony."

"Can't you just send him on, like you were going to do with Nils?"

Tor turned around. His eyes had gone wide, and his mouth looked oddly slack. "I don't know if I can," he said. "Maybe he's half-dead now, but when he was alive, he was one strong son-of-a-bitch. And if I tried and failed—" He let his voice fade into silence.

"What? What would happen?"

"I don't know for sure, but I might end up as the soul living in those pictures. And he'd be the man in this body."

I nearly vomited. The sensation grabbed my stomach, rose with an acid burn in my throat, and made me gasp for breath with the pain. Tor took a step toward me, but I got up and ran down the hall to the bathroom. I hadn't eaten enough that day to let go and hurl, but I drank glass after glass of water until the last of the acid got driven back into my stomach where it belonged. In the mirror I could see my face, beaded with sweat. I turned away from the sink and found Tor standing in the doorway.

"You okay now?" he said.

"Yeah. It was just the idea of him being you, or you being gone, and him touching me again." I shuddered.

"He had that effect on people even when he was still alive." Tor managed to smile, a weary twitch of his mouth.

I realized that I was seeing something I'd never seen before: Tor afraid. I began to tremble.

"Let's get out of the house," Tor said. "Go for a drive in the sunshine."

"Good idea. I'd like that."

We ended up having dinner out, too, then stopped by Cynthia and Jim's apartment for a little while. We came back to house about ten at night, and neither of us wanted to go anywhere near Tor's workshop and the portraits. Tor took a bottle of beer out of the fridge, looked at it for a few seconds, then put it back unopened.

"I've got a better idea," he said and grinned at me.

"Huh! I bet I can guess what it is."

He confirmed my guess by striding over and catching me by the shoulders for a kiss. As we walked to the bedroom, I was unbuttoning my blouse, hurrying to take it off and unzip my jeans. He pulled his shirt over his head, caught me again, and picked up me up to dump me onto the bed. That night our passion for each other felt like a drug, as if I'd gulped down a big glass of brandy on an empty stomach, and now the alcohol was spreading through my entire body until I could no longer think, only feel what Tor was doing to me. The pleasure so close to pain drove all the fear out of my body. Afterwards we fell asleep, but I woke about an hour later. The drug had worn off. Despite the wards downstairs and the runes all over the upstairs, I was worried enough about Björn's presence, his spirit living in the paintings, that I found it hard to get back to sleep. I couldn't think of him as Halvar, Tor's grandfather. To me he'd always be Björn, the man who'd murdered my lover, who'd driven me to suicide. I remembered him as the captain of a whaling ship, and I knew enough about whaling that all those deaths sickened me, too, intelligent animals, speared, bound to the side of the ship, cut up while they were still alive, in agony as the salt sea lapped into their wounds. Brutal, horrible, all the things he'd done, monstrous actions from a monster.

Yet in his way Björn had loved Magda, the girl I'd been back then.

I suddenly saw it. At the time, as I crept around our house after Kristjan's death, and when we'd gone to our little island for a "holiday", I thought that Björn had only been defending his honor, that he'd hated Kristjan for taking something Björn thought of as his property. But that night in California, while I thought I was still awake, I heard Björn's voice speaking English, "I loved you because you were so vital. You made me feel alive. You made me understand magic. You made me crave magic."

I sat up in bed and screamed. Tor woke with a grunt and sat up next to me.

"What?" he said.

"Someone's in the room!" I was sure of it, suddenly, that Björn stood in the shadowed corner.

Tor reached over and turned on the bedside lamp. No one was there. The runes cut into the molding, rusty with paint and Tor's blood, gleamed in the golden light.

"Couldn't have been," he said, yawning. "Were you dreaming?"

"Yeah, I must have been. I heard him talking."

"Shit! If he can reach your dreams, we've got a problem." Tor got out of bed and stretched. "What did he say to you?"

Already the dream memory was breaking up into a murmur of disconnected words. "He said I made him feel—I don't know—he understood magic or something. Like I gave it to him, the understanding."

Tor picked up his jeans from the floor and put them on before he spoke. "I can remember that Magda had a magical aura around her. Seeing her, it felt like coming into a warm room out of the snow. Even when I was Kristjan I felt it, and I was a dull guy, a lawyer, pillar of the Lutheran church, all that crap until I met her. Loving her, I changed, like down to my soul." He hesitated for a long moment. "Did he change?"

"Björn was brutal. He killed for his living. I don't remember him being anything else, that last couple of months. He—" The memory stabbed me. "He raped me. I mean, it wasn't legally rape then, because we were married, but every night he threw me on the bed, and he was furious, and I ended up bruised all over."

Tor went deadly still. His face showed no emotion, except for a muscle under his left eye that twitched repeatedly.

"That's why I drowned myself," I said.

He nodded and took a deep breath. The twitching stopped. "I wonder how long he lived after you died?" he said. "I bet he didn't have another life between him and Halvar. Or I should say, that his spirit didn't incarnate in between the two. They were too much alike."

I shrugged to show I had no idea.

"I wonder," Tor continued, "if you changed both of us. Kristjan didn't give a damn about magic. Lars—that's me the next time around—did. Maybe that's why I remembered you so clearly when I was reborn. That's probably why I was thinking of you when I was dying in the snow, after the Nazis shot me. Your magic could have marked both of us. Magic?

No, it had to be your nature. Who you were. Who you still are, that half-human spirit."

"But Magda didn't need to steal élan. She wasn't a vampire. That deviant DNA, it has to be something from my dad in this life. She can't have belonged to Niflheim."

Tor gave a little grunt of surprise. He sat down on the edge of the bed.

"I just realized that," I said. "Okay, yeah, I do need to remember more of what happened." I couldn't quite bring myself to say 'in past lives.' "Before now, I mean."

He nodded and looked away, thinking. Finally he said, "Well, back to the old drawing board! I thought I had it all figured out, but I don't. I was wrong."

"I never thought I'd hear you say that."

He laughed. "Okay, I deserved that. I need to think about all this, Maya. Sort it out for both of us. But right now let's do something to keep him out of your mind. I want to draw some symbols on your forehead." He thought for a moment. "I think I'll draw them on your chest, too. Why take chances?"

"Bindrunes?"

"Not exactly. They're from a tradition called stave spells."

I'd left my backpack in the living room. I got a calligraphy felt-tip and returned to the bedroom. Tor sat me down on the edge of the bed in the pool of light from the lamp and got to work. The two patterns of runes took him a long time to draw, and he chanted spells, too, while he did. When he finished, I got up and looked at myself in the mirror in his bathroom. I was expecting a tight, beautiful design like on the pendant he'd made for me earlier that summer, but this figure looked strange and ungainly. A circle had five lines emerging from it, three on top, two on the bottom. Different little squiggles crested each one. Well, I guess they were magical symbols, but they looked like squiggles. In the center lay five dots and the Hagalaz rune, basically an H.

"That stuff in the center represents Halvar," Tor told me. "The other lines will suck in any force he sends to you and direct it right back to him. He won't like it."

Strange-looking or not, the magical patterns worked. When we went back to bed, I felt totally safe. I drifted right off and slept straight through till morning.

I was having breakfast, and Tor was drinking his second cup of coffee, when the cellphone in his shirt pocket howled. I yelped. He took the phone out, glanced at the caller ID, and grinned as he answered it. When he spoke in Icelandic, I figured that Liv had gotten the message. Tor glanced my way.

"She knew something was wrong," he said, "and drove over the hill so she could pick up her wireless access."

"Say hi for me." Inane, yes, but I wanted to acknowledge the woman who was going to be my sister-in-law.

I listened to his side of the conversation, not that I understood any of it. I could see him growing grimmer and grimmer, hovering on the edge of anger. At one point Liv yelled at him loudly enough for me to hear her voice, all strange and tinny over the distant connection. Tor winced and answered, suddenly meek. They spoke normally after that.

Finally he clicked off. He sighed once and slipped the phone back into his pocket.

"She's right, of course," Tor said to me. "I've got to destroy the paintings. Like, right now."

"What else did you want to do?"

"See if I could learn something from the old bastard. Evoke him and make him speak to me. But Liv's right, it's too dangerous." He shrugged. "Who knows, he'd probably only lie to me, anyway."

I felt the hairs rise on the back of my neck. "He's really alive in the paintings, then?"

"Kind of alive. Kind of dead. Not really either, but waiting his chance to come alive. Nils had no way of knowing I already owned two of them. I bet he gave me his to let Halvar carry on the feud for him. A little revenge."

"So if you destroy them, Björn, I mean Halvar, he'll be gone?"

"We hope so. Neither of us really knows what to do. Liv burned her copy last year, she told me. She had a dream telling her to. So the ones I have are his last hope."

I felt the urge to vomit again. I choked it back and ran into the bathroom for water. Tor followed me. He studied my face.

"The staves are still there," I said. "I didn't want to wash them off this morning."

"Yeah, they don't look smeared or anything. I'd tell you just stay away till I'm done, but it's too dangerous. He could come after you."

"I wondered about that. Besides, I have to know what happens." I have to know if you're still you at the end of this, is what I was thinking.

"Okay," Tor said. "There's some firewood in the back of the garage. I'll go get it."

The downstairs hearth stood in the library room, not Tor's workroom with the consecrated circle. Tor built a tidy stack of wood in the hearth and laid in some scrunched-up junk mail for tinder. Before he lit it, he sat back on his heels on the hearth rug and considered his handiwork.

"Think that's enough wood?" he said.

"The portraits are canvas covered in oil paint and varnish. They should burn like crazy."

"Okay." Tor got up and glanced around. "I've got a fire extinguisher. Let me get that."

Tor rummaged around in a cupboard in the kitchen of the lower flat and brought out the fire extinguisher. He set it down near the fireplace.

"Okay." He took a box of long matches from the mantel. "Let me just light this, and then we'll bring the old bastard out."

The junk mail caught, some wood splinters with it, and then the bark along the thick chunks of dry wood. When Tor went to fetch one of the portraits, I realized with a clench of my stomach that we were about to burn a witch—not exactly alive, but close enough. I stepped back from the fire and refused to look at the canvas when Tor took it out of the green bag.

"That's right." He said, misunderstanding. "Don't let him look you in the eye."

Without a second's hesitation Tor walked over and set the picture, face to the wall, directly into the crackling flames. The fire went out, stone cold out, with nothing more than twist of black smoke and a waft of the smell of charred wood. "You bastard!" Tor knelt down, struck a second match, and tried to light the remaining junk mail. The match blew out. Tor pulled the portrait out of the fireplace and set it face-down on the concrete slab in front of the hearth.

"All right, you." Tor was talking to the painting. He said something in Icelandic, then got to his feet. "Maya, shut the drapes over the big window, will you?" He picked up the portrait in one hand. "Join me at the circle." He strode through the bookcases and disappeared into his workroom.

I did what he asked. When I walked into the other room, I saw that he'd lain the portrait face-down in the center of the ritual circle, right at the point where the two arms of the equal-armed cross met. He still wore his ordinary jeans and Raiders t-shirt, but he was holding his rune knife in his right hand.

"Sit in the north," he said. "I'm not going to evoke the runes, because he can feed on them just like I can."

I took my place between the outer edge of the circle and the wall. Tor knelt beside the portrait and raised the knife. Before he could lower it, he gasped and choked with a grunting sound like a boxer hit in the stomach. His arm trembled and bent as he arm-wrestled his invisible opponent. For a long few minutes they fought. I could see Tor's arm begin to move the knife downward, then spring back up again as his opponent pushed it back. Björn–Halvar–I couldn't see, but I knew by the coldness in the air that a presence struggled to win this match. This second duel–the first time, back in that other life, Björn had won.

Tor set his mouth in a scowl and swayed backwards, just a few inches. The tension in his arm eased. He barked out one word and plunged the knife down in the center of the stretched canvas. A voice, barely human, shrieked aloud. Tor yanked the knife hard toward him. Despite the layers of paint and varnish the canvas ripped all the way to the frame. Tor raised the knife again and slashed the painting from corner to corner.

"He's gone," Tor said, "but I bet he's back in that damn drawer."

Tor got up and stalked into the huge closet where he kept the safe and the drawers in question. I was afraid to move. I saw just a trace of motion above the ripped portrait, a gray curl like a wisp of smoke.

"Tor!" I said. "What—"

The wisp disappeared. Tor came back, carrying another portrait, and he was staggering and panting as if it weighed a thousand pounds. One slow step at a time, but at last he reached the circle and threw the painting face-down next to the mangled remains of the first one. Tor barked out three words in a language I didn't recognize. He stood for a few seconds, breathing hard, then stepped into the circle and knelt down. When he raised the knife, I saw the wisp of gray forming above the first canvas. Tor snarled a word. The wisp thickened, rose up, and dove into the second painting even though Tor called out the galdr again.

"Magda!" Bjorn's voice begged in my mind. "Help me!"

"No!" I screamed aloud. "I hate you!"

Tor brought the knife down and plunged it into the second portrait. He ripped it, he stabbed it, he slashed it, over and over until at last nothing but a tangled mess of painted ribbons sat in the middle of the empty frame. He got to his feet, staggered a little, then strode out of the circle and returned to the drawer.

The last portrait was just a portrait. Tor carried it in with no trouble, cut it a couple of times with no trouble, and let it lie. He sat back on his heels and panted for breath while he looked at the shreds and the scraps still clinging to the stretcher bars of the second portrait. He smiled, a grim tight berserk grin, and laughed a little, a barely audible chortle. Red blood dripped from the blade of the rune knife. It neither repelled or attracted me. It was just blood.

"You cut yourself," I said.

"No." Tor's voice was perfectly mild. "This isn't my blood. It's a manifestation." He turned the crazed grin my way and chortled again. His eyes were cold, unblinking, almost blind, as if he hardly knew where he was.

"Tor," I said, "do you know who I am?"

"Of course. Your name is Maya Cantescu, and I'll love you forever. I'm not possessed."

"What's my mother's first name?"

"Kusuma. It means flower."

"And what's my middle name?"

"Lila." He looked puzzled, then smiled, a weary twitch of his mouth. "I'm still me."

"Yeah. I know that now. I just had to make sure."

He nodded to show he understood. He glanced at the mess of canvas scraps and the red knife. "I've killed a kinsman. The worst dishonor of all." His shoulders slumped, and a trickle of tears ran down his face.

I wanted to run screaming out of that room. I wanted to hold him and comfort him. Caught between the two I just sat there and trembled. That day I realized why I fought so hard against my own talents.

Magic is terrifying when it's real.

CHAPTER 6

I don't understand what happened," I said. "What was that gray stuff that came out of the portrait?"

"Ectoplasm." Tor paused for a smile. "An old word, but it'll do. Think of it as whipped élan. Etheric mayonnaise."

"Too weird!"

"The whole thing is weird. Also wyrd."

I ignored the pun. We'd come upstairs to the living room after cleaning up the ritual space downstairs. After the battle to banish Halvar, I'd felt nothing but numb relief, but now my mind was working again.

"Usually I respond when there's élan close by," I said. "But if anything, it creeped me out."

"You hated him, right? Of course it repelled you."

"And then the blood on the knife—I didn't feel any élan."

"It didn't have any, that's why. It was a manifestation. Dead man's blood. It sucks up life force, which is probably why Halvar brought it through. Tried to weaken me with it."

That's when I remembered the picture of the island and the red lion.

"Something I meant to tell you," I said. "On the barometer, I saw a red lion. That means power flowing, right?"

"Right."

"But as I watched it, it slowly turned green, like someone was draining it."

"Was that before or after I drew the runes on you?"

"Before."

"Then it was Halvar. He couldn't act directly, not even with his poltergeist, so he got a claw into you. Shit, I'm glad he's dead now! Too much longer, and he might have gotten control over you."

I turned icy cold and felt the room jerk suddenly to one side. I sat down on the couch fast before I collapsed.

"I'm right here." Tor sat down next to me and caught my hands in his. "What's wrong?"

"I was just so scared for a minute." I took a deep breath. "Thinking about what might have happened if you'd lost. The thought of being in his power again." I shook my head and trembled.

"Well, you won't be. And neither will I." Tor gently let go of my hands. "He was into controlling people. He wanted to use my mother as a medium. Maybe for sex as well. That's the main reason my dad left the family lands. Halvar had plans, and my mother wanted nothing to do with them." He smiled. "Halvar couldn't admit it, though. It was all left unsaid, nothing but hints and significant looks. You know, like an Ingmar Bergman movie. So the old bastard had to let us go." He stopped smiling and shrugged. "My dad told me about this just before he died."

"God, how awful." It wasn't much of a thing to say, but I felt too exhausted for eloquence. "I'm just so glad you won."

"No, we won. When you told him you hated him, he—well, it was like he looked away. Got distracted, just for a couple of seconds, but it was enough to let me get the upper hand."

"He can't have loved me that much."

"Oh yeah, he did. I bet he wanted to hang around because of you." Tor's voice tightened in anger. "I guess we could call it love, anyway. He wanted possession. He was obsessed, maybe, is more like it."

I slumped down on the soft cushions and rested my head on the back of the sofa. "He's gone, isn't he? I mean, really gone on to wherever souls go. So he can't come back."

"I think so. Liv figured he'd have to go, if I could pry him out of his hole."

"But you don't know it? I mean, really know it?"

"No, not for one hundred per cent certain. Look, this is another reason why you've got to stop running from who you are. You need to be able to defend yourself."

I sat up to face him and gathered my breath. "Okay," I said. "Yeah, you're right."

Tor smiled, but thank the gods, he didn't launch into one of his smug lectures. He patted my hand, then got up and went into the kitchen. He came back with a bottle of dark beer for him and a snifter with a splash of brandy for me. He handed me the glass and sat down again.

"I hope Liv calls soon," he said. "She told me she would. I bet she's already sensed that—" he put an ironic twist on the words, "—that the matter's settled."

Was it? I felt a cold knot of wondering near my heart. Yet Tor would know how things stood, wouldn't he? So I nodded my agreement and had a sip of brandy. I stared into the glass, just without thinking, while I swirled the golden-brown liquid around. In the moving fluid an image began to form: runes, but ones I couldn't recognize. I looked away fast. Tor was watching me.

"You saw something," he said.

"Shapes like runes, but they weren't the runes I know. I feel like my mind's got holes in it, and things can creep in."

"Holes or open doors?"

"Both, probably. I think it's spillover from what just happened with the portraits, the power, I mean."

"Maybe that's it, yeah. We've got to be more careful from now on. Your talents are coming online, all right, but in a kind of dangerous way. Unorganized, I guess I mean."

"I wish I could talk with your sister."

"That's a good idea. You can email her."

"I don't know any Icelandic."

"She speaks English. She was raised here in California same as I was. I just like to speak the old country language with her so I don't forget it."

Tor's phone rang. He fished it out of his pocket, glanced

at the caller ID, and laughed. "Right on schedule," he said and clicked the phone on. "Hi, Liv? Did you know we were talking about you?"

I could just hear her laugh and answer yes, her ears were burning. They lapsed into Icelandic once they started discussing the spirit battle. Both of them laughed a lot, but out of relief, not joking around. My mother and I had laughed the same way when we'd just barely escaped a car crash. A drunk driver ran a red light, she'd swerved just in time, and we'd sat in the parked car and giggled hysterically for maybe five minutes. Liv and Tor laughed with the same desperate edge.

Eventually they calmed down. From Tor's serious voice, from the way he spoke in clipped sentences, sure she'd understand, and his occasional nods of agreement, just as if she could see him, I could imagine them as siblings, heads together as they discussed some important event or decision. It was a good twenty minutes before Tor handed me the phone.

"She wants to talk to you," he said.

I liked Liv's voice, a pleasant alto, and sure enough, her English sounded like she'd left California the day before. She wasted no time on pleasantries.

"The brother tells me you have image magic," Liv said. "If you want to be an artist, you've got to get control of it right now. Otherwise it'll take you over and drive you to drink or drugs. Maybe even total psychosis like Richard Dad. The only way you can escape is to never draw or paint again."

"That would drive me crazy even faster," I said.

"Okay, then. Email me. The phone service in my little part of the island is ridiculously bad when it comes to connecting to the Internet. I only go into town once a week, but I'll do what I can to help. I don't really understand my own magics. They're what are called wild talents. I thought I was the only one in the family, but Halvar must have had some knowledge of them, the nasty old creep! I've lived with them for years, and that's taught me a few things."

"Anything you can tell me will help. I've been so frightened."

"I don't blame you. When a wild talent hits you, it's like a slap in the soul. Look, I've got to hang up and get back to the house. But email me. I always take my laptop into town when I go, and I'll answer."

"I will, for sure."

"Good. Oh, and congratulations! I don't know why anyone would want to marry my brother, but as long as you're happy."

"I feel the same way about mine."

We snickered in unison.

"Mom and I will come to the wedding," Liv said. "Set it for early summer, okay? Otherwise we could be snowed in."

"I will. And thank you so much for your help. I'll email you as soon as I can think straight."

"Do that. Bye!"

I handed the phone back to Tor. He clicked it off and put it back in his pocket, then picked up his beer again.

"Feel better?" he said.

"Weirdly enough, I do. Sometimes it's hard to remember that all this magic is real. Maybe that's just as well. I can just put it to one side that way and go on with school and life and stuff."

"The trouble is, you can't keep putting it to one side."

"I knew you were going to say that."

Tor gave me a normal smile and finished the last of his beer. I also knew that he was right. That evening I sent Liv a long email describing what had happened with my art after I'd moved in with Tor.

For some days, while I waited for her answer, I managed to keep my talent in the margins and pretend I had a normal life. The battle had left both of us exhausted, Tor more than me, of course. We did a lot of normal things with our normal friends—went to a movie with Cynthia and Jim, visited my brother and Brittany in the hospital, went to the local park so Tor could play basketball with his guy friends, Billy, Aaron, and JJ. Tor cooked a couple of really fancy dinners to let the planning and work ground him, he told me, in what he called physical plane matters. I probably gained a pound each, but they were worth it.

I worried continually about the police, but we heard nothing from them. The jötnar, however, were another matter. One morning when I was leaving for campus, I found symbols painted on the garage door. I got out my smartphone and called Tor.

"Come down and look at this," I said.

"Where are you?"

"In the driveway."

"Why didn't you just yell?"

"I was raised in apartments. It was so hard finding rentals that would take kids. My parents totally drilled us in not disturbing the neighbors. Y'know, like by yelling."

He sighed and clicked off. While I waited for him, I examined the sloppy, distorted runes more carefully. Red ochre, and a real earth pigment, at that, coarsely ground and mixed with some kind of animal skin glue—the gritty paint had dripped and hardened unevenly on the metal panel of the door.

"What the hell?" Tor came up beside me. "Oh great! A misspelled curse!"

"Is it dangerous?"

"Not really, but I'll remove it, anyway. Whoever wrote it tried to curse our wagons so the wheels fall off and the harnesses break."

"They don't understand cars, do they?"

"No. Has to be jötnar work. I guess we're at the graffiti stage of the feud."

"You don't seem real worried about this."

"I'm not, as long as they're trying to work magic. When the battle axes come out, then I'll worry."

Somehow I didn't find this reassuring.

By the time I got home, Tor had neutralized the curse and scraped the runes off the garage door. The paint left an ugly stain on the panel, though, that bothered me every time I saw it.

During those days, I also kept drawing, but I only did sketches of the life around me and studies of landscape details for my school project. I avoided the mysterious talent that revealed things other people couldn't see or things I didn't know I knew. The talent caught up with me when Liv answered my email.

Liv had so much to tell me that she ended up attaching a PDF file to a short note. I read the material through three times. I felt as if she'd thrown me a lifeline when I didn't even know I was drowning. I saved it, of course. My subconscious mind took her final piece of advice particularly seriously, "Make sure you start working with your dreams. Don't ignore them."

That night I dreamed about the wooden shutters, carved with runes, that covered the windows of a mysterious room. These shutters had appeared in my dreams before. Sometimes the window seemed to be in the bedroom I shared with Tor; at others, in my childhood room. This time they appeared in a totally different space, barely more than six feet on a side, with dark walls and a low beamed ceiling. I got out of a bed built directly into the wall and walked over to the shutters. When I flung them open, I saw a snowy landscape, ringed by mountains, and felt a blast of cold air. I slammed them shut and woke up shivering in our warm bedroom in California.

Tor had ended up sleeping on his back, and he was snoring so loudly that he never heard me get out of bed. I went into the living room, picked up a sketchbook, and made a loose, deliberately sloppy drawing of what I'd dreamed. I didn't want the picture coming alive on me. In the corner I drew the runes I'd seen carved into the shutters, two on the left shutter, two more on the right. Doing the sketch brought with it an immense feeling of relief, as if I'd been holding my breath for a long time and had finally released it to pull in clean, fresh air.

I went back to bed and poked Tor until he turned over onto his side. In the relative silence, I fell asleep with no more dreams. When I woke up in a room bright with sunlight, Tor was gone, and I could smell fresh coffee. I got dressed and hurried out to find him sitting at the breakfast bar and glaring at something on his laptop's screen.

"What's wrong?" I said.

"Nothing. I was just checking the lunar calendar I've got on this machine. The moon goes dark tonight. Two weeks to the next bjarki battle."

I sighed in sympathy and kissed him good morning. I fetched myself coffee from the glass carafe and yogurt from the fridge, then sat down next to him at the breakfast bar. While I ate, I debated showing him the dream-picture I'd drawn. Secrecy is a habit that dies hard. Finally I got strict with myself and retrieved the sketchbook.

"Something I dreamed last night." I found the right page and laid it open on the counter. "This room looks medieval to me."

"It sure does, yeah." Tor moved his laptop out of the way and slid the book over in front of him. "Though I don't know, there are plenty of rooms in Europe that still look like that. Especially in Eastern Europe. These runes—where were they?"

"On the window shutters, two on each shutter. I just drew them bigger up on the corner like that."

"Okay, first, the left pair. There's Othala again, your patrimony." Tor laid a finger on the rune. "Paired with Need. And then we have the pair on the right, Wunjo reversed, Elhaz reversed." He drank some of his coffee while he studied the page. "I wouldn't call these real good omens."

"When I've dreamed about them before, they always seemed really scary. It's why I didn't want to open the shutters. I did, though, in this dream and looked at the view outside. Whenever this room existed, it was in the mountains, lots of snow and sharp peaks." A thought sidled into my mind. "Like Austria or Switzerland."

"Then it could have been any time since about 1200 up to—well, up to now, for that matter. They build them that way to save heat. The bed should have curtains or even doors to keep the drafts out."

"It might have had them. This was just a dream."

"Huh! There isn't any 'just' with dreams like this. I'm

hoping you slept in that bed more recently than 1200, though. We've never untangled your last life. It's bound to be important." He tapped the sketch with his index finger. "Especially if these runes apply to it and not something way back in your past."

My stomach clenched around a painful truth. Again, I had to force myself to talk instead of keeping what I'd just realized secret. "It was the life before this one. I just don't know how I know."

"Okay, that uncertainty? It's common when you start remembering past lives. Let's see what we can figure out. First, the runes Othala and Naudhiz, the ones on the left shutter. You brought those with you into your last life, the mystery life. Got that?"

"Yeah."

"Okay, so the way Magda's life ended, suicide, meant you inherited a grim Necessity, a wyrd to work through." He frowned down at the page. "These two reversed on the right hand shutter, they indicate you were stagnating, alienated from life, and stripped of protection, vulnerable." He shook his head. "I wish we had more runes. It's hard to move on from these four without others."

"It's weird, but when I dreamed about these shutters before, there were more runes. Now it's just this four."

"Well, if you dream about them again, write them down, will you? It's important."

"Would they still apply now in this life?"

"Maybe." He closed the sketchbook. "We need more information. We could start with Halvar."

"Do we have to?"

"Yes. Iceland was neutral—sort of—in the Second World War. Real confused situation." Tor paused for a sip of coffee. "Halvar was already connected to the government, just as a flunky, but connected. He sat the war out. Afterward he went traveling in Europe. I don't have all the journals for those years, but later he talks about searching for someone. He never gives a name, but she was female. He never found her." He quirked an eyebrow in my direction. "Were you dead by then?"

Caught off-guard I could only stammer.

"I bet you know, Maya. Think!"

I wanted to throw my coffee into his face. The feeling translated itself into an ache in my wrist and hand, as if someone had grabbed it and twisted. Someone had taken not a mug but a glass away from me before I could throw it at him. A glass of water. Someone long ago. Not Björn, not Kristjan.

I spoke in a language that my current mind couldn't understand. I saw a fragment of a shadowy image—a good-looking man with dark hair coming through a door and snarling an order. The man who held my wrist let me go. I spoke again.

The breakfast bar and the kitchen reappeared. Tor had set his coffee mug down and turned on his chair to look straight at me.

"What did I say?" I said. "What was that?"

"You spoke in German, a southern dialect. Not Swiss German, maybe Bavarian. Or an Austrian dialect."

"Tor, you idiot! I don't care about that. What did I say?"

"Sorry." He smiled, but not his usual arrogant grin, more a nervous twitch of his mouth. "First you said, 'Let me go! If he were here, you wouldn't dare!' Then you seemed to be listening to someone speak. Finally you said, 'Otto, you're back! Oh thank God.'" Tor smiled again, the same twitch. "Otto wasn't or isn't me, that's for sure. Do you know who you meant?"

"No." I had a gulp of hot coffee. The burn going down jarred me out of the strange trance state. "I saw someone, this Otto, come into the room where this other guy was harassing me. When he saw Otto, he let me go."

"No memory of when or where?"

"No. They both wore military uniforms. Black ones." I shut my eyes and got a brief, hazy impression. "With silver trim."

"Shit! I was afraid of that."

"Of what?"

"The SS."

I set the coffee down before I spilled it. I'm no history buff, but I knew what that meant. Nazis. The worst kind of Nazis.

"What did he look like?" Tor said.

"Tall. Dark hair, real dark, slicked back. And a gaunt face. The uniform looked a little too big for him." I hesitated, waited, felt a memory starting to rise. "He had something to do with runecraft."

"He was young or old?"

"Youngish. Maybe thirty-something?"

"Not Wiligut, then, and thank Tyr for that! Huh. What about the Grail legends?"

The memory rose in a burst of the language I could no longer remember.

Yes," I said. "That was important, the Grail."

"Otto Rahn. Does that name mean anything to you?"

Knowledge hit me like a slap to the soul, as Liv had put it. I nodded. "That's the name of the guy I saw."

"He was part of Himmler's special SS unit, the one that worked with occult theories. The Ahnenerbe, they called it. Rahn had written a book about the Grail, and Himmler wanted him on the team."

"Like that movie?"

"No, nothing like that stupid movie, if you mean the Indiana Jones one." Tor's usual arrogance came back in force. "Billy and JJ dragged me to it when it came out. Bunch of shit! No, Rahn was a medievalist, a scholar who made the mistake of playing with the big boys, Himmler and his crew. Though I don't suppose he had any choice when they recruited him."

"I don't think you could say no to the SS."

"Not if you valued your life. Rahn was part of that outfit until—I think it was '39—he died. Officially he was killed in a mountaineering accident. It's more likely he committed suicide because he was gay, and Himmler found out. Rahn knew mountains. He wouldn't have made a fatal mistake, not where they found him, practically on a bunny slope. It was in the Tyrol somewhere."

"I guess that fits, if what I saw is real." In my mind I saw the view from the window again, a rounded hill with a long snowy slope, gently rising between dark banks of forest to either side. Behind it rose the high mountains.

"If, yeah. I'm betting it is because it came to you spontaneously." Tor frowned. "And because of the language you heard. And every time the Nazis have come up, you've freaked."

I realized that I was trying to keep secrets from myself, not him. Don't lie! I told myself. You know it's real. "I remember getting upset," I said. "I guess it is a lead."

"This is worth pursuing. I want to go downstairs and get a history book my father had. Can you draw me a portrait of Otto Rahn? While I'm not in the room."

I started to snarl and say no, of course I couldn't draw someone I'd never seen, but his image appeared in my inner vision—no, *he* appeared, whole and alive, in a lot of different memories, as if I were looking at a video montage.

"Okay." I picked up the sketchbook. "I'll try."

And so I took my sketchbook into the living room, sat down on the couch, and drew what some people would call a 'spirit portrait' of a man who'd been dead for seventy years. I worked in Conté, mostly black and grey, just a touch of burnt sienna here and there. Memories rose with every stroke I laid in. I refused to draw him in uniform—he'd hated wearing it, there at the end—and put him instead in a soft shirt, open at the throat, because he hated stiff collars and ties, too. As I drew I remembered other things, that I'd loved him but hopelessly because I knew he preferred men. He told me though that he loved me in his own way. I could be his lady, like in the days of the troubadours that meant so much to him, and he'd be my knight. I clung to that fantasy for years. I'd thought he was just being nice to a woman he considered little more than a child, but in the end, he showed me how true it was.

When I finished the drawing, I signed it.

I tossed the Conté stick back in the box and woke up. It felt like waking, anyway, when the trance broke and the images drained away from my mind. I realized that Tor, with a book in his hand, had been standing and watching me for some minutes. He sat down next to me and opened the book to the page he'd marked with a slip of paper. When he put it down on the table, I saw a photograph of Otto Rahn. Tor took the sketchbook from my exhausted hands and laid it down beside the book. The history book's text was in German, but I didn't need the caption. The same man looked out from both pictures.

"Evidence," Tor said. "Can you remember more about him?"

I didn't want to tell Tor how much I'd loved another man, even if it was in another life and a long time before. "How much he hated being in uniform," I said. "I must have known him pretty well. He was supposed to be a civilian adjunct or something, but they made him join the SS, and then he had to wear the uniform."

"That's what this particular book says." Tor was frowning at the open volume. "But we can't trust everything in it. It's one of those lurid histories, the kind that believe the whole Nazi movement was crazy for the occult. It wasn't."

I knew that, too, from somewhere or some time. "You told me that they perverted the runes," I said. "They put the swastika on everything, didn't they? Sowilo doubled."

"That was propaganda, playing on a lot of older sentiments. The folk tradition, the *völkisch* sentimental crap. They exploited that and the dangerous themes, too. Pure Aryan blood and past Germanic glory and shit like that." He leaned forward and glanced at the portrait. "Huh—Mia? You signed the picture Mia."

"I did?" I leaned forward and checked the name at the bottom of the page. "Whoa, that's a surprise!"

"That must have been your name then. It's a nickname for Maria."

"Maria sounds right. When I was looking out the window in the dream, I saw mountains, Alps, but they weren't the famous Swiss ones. No Matterhorn, nothing like that."

"Maybe Austria, then. Your childhood home?"

I shook my head no. "A ski hostel of some kind. I honestly

don't know more'n that."

"Past life memories can be bitches, yeah. You get broken pictures, pieces of conversation, a couple of bars of music, sometimes. Hard names and dates, no, they don't cough those up easily." Tor was flipping through the pages of the history book while he talked. "There's something more in here, if I can find it, about Rahn and—yeah! Here!" He looked up. "The SS sent Rahn to Iceland in 1936. An archeological expedition, they called it, and his part of it might have been just that. I wonder—some high-ranking men came with him, probably to negotiate with the government while he went around researching pure Aryan culture crap."

Tor returned to reading. In a minute he made an odd snorting sound and looked up.

"What?" I said.

"Rahn bought some Dark Age Icelandic gold objects for the German government while he was there, runic artifacts, this book calls them. I wonder if some of my family's treasures were part of the buy? The ones that Halvar's father dug up on the farm. He'd sold some of the pieces to Germans for a really high price."

"Halvar was how old in '36?"

"Sixteen, maybe seventeen, old enough to have written something about it in his journal." Tor considered for a moment. "I think I've got some journals from the '30s. I'm not sure. It would be interesting if he'd met Rahn."

Interesting. Does a fly find it interesting when it feels the spider's strands wrapping around it, holding it tight and hopeless in the web? One of the strands around me: a memory of drawing a precise, careful record in pen and ink of two gold rings, each with a square bezel that had lost its stone. Around each band ran a line of runes. I was working at a wooden drafting table in some kind of office. I could hear voices murmuring behind me in a language that sounded like German and the clack of a mechanical typewriter like the ones in the old movies.

"Maya!" Tor shut the book with a snap. "What is it?"

I came back, woke up, whatever you want to call it, at the sound of his voice.

"I was hired by the SS as a civilian worker," I said, "and I drew the stuff Rahn brought back. Photographs weren't clear enough to really show every detail of an artifact in a scientific way. I guess they're still not. I'm willing to bet that some of that stuff came from your grandfather—or your great-grandfather, I mean. Everything's all tied up together. I feel like I'm caught in a net."

"I can see why, but nets are meant to be unraveled. You've got me to pull it apart, don't forget."

"As long as you don't pull me apart, too."

Tor tossed the book onto the table. He caught my hands in his and moved close to kiss me.

"Don't worry," he said. "I know these things take time."

I took another kiss and clung to him, my solid, real, present-day lover, the man I was going to marry. The past is dead, I told myself. What happened then doesn't matter. Even Otto—Audo was my pet name for him, the way he'd called me Mia—even Audo doesn't matter anymore. This time I knew I was telling myself the truth.

What did matter was what I'd learned. I began to understand what Tor meant about the value of knowing your past lives. Would I ever have fallen so hard for a gay man, an intellectual lost in his dreams of extreme religious heresies, if he hadn't been the opposite of the brutal hunter, Björn? I doubted it. My dim memories of being Mia told me she'd been no fool, even though she'd acted like one.

The importance of those memories lay elsewhere. Where? I needed to find out. Something painful lay behind those memories, like poison locked up in a coffer. The man I'd loved in that life would give me the key, if only I could find the lock.

CHAPTER 7

That Sunday the Raiders played a home game. Tor and his buddies had tickets to the Black Hole section of the stadium, down close to the field behind one of the end zones. Although Tor offered to take me, I turned him down. Now that I no longer needed to bump into strangers to steal élan, I could avoid the noise, the awful restrooms, and the crowds.

"It can get dangerous for a girl," I said to Tor. "Especially with guys like you there."

He laughed at me. The game made me see a whole new side of Tor. While he waited for Billy to come pick him up, he dressed in black jeans, black Raiders tee shirt, and silvery-gray Raiders baseball cap. He even painted his face silver with black stripes across his cheekbones.

"I won't kiss you goodbye," he said. "It'd spoil my make-up."

I had to laugh at that, and he grinned through the face paint. When Billy drove up, he stopped his Land Rover at the curb and honked the horn. Tor grabbed his Raiders' hoodie and ran down the stairs like a teen-ager. I waved from the window.

I had a standing invitation at Jim and Cynthia's to come watch the games on their enormous TV, since Tor refused to have a television in his house. Now that I'd decided to get serious about researching my past, I called them to beg off. I spread my drawing tools and sketchbooks out on the coffee table and started with my memory of the office and the drawing table.

The image of the drawing I'd been working on, the two rings with the runic bands, built up so clearly that I could reproduce it. Using a Pelikan fountain pen for the drawing helped retrieve the memory, because that brand had been available in Germany in the 1930s, though I did own a modern version. Dim images of other objects floated to the surface of my mind: a round, flat decoration called a bractate, a heavily damaged drinking horn, and a rectangular fragment of metal, each one inscribed with runes. I drew them all, and at times I could add a few German letters underneath from what had probably been the original captions. Not being able to retrieve the complete words reminded me that my memory might have garbled the details after so many years, no matter how perfect the images seemed to me. While I worked I could hear the clacking of the typewriter and the murmur of voices, speaking a language I could no longer understand.

I closed that particular book, capped the pen, and got up to pace around the living room. When I opened the fridge, looking for soda, I found a sandwich wrapped in plastic on a plate with a note "for Maya" in Tor's handwriting. I took it to the breakfast bar with my cola and ate it gratefully. When I finished, I realized that the memories had gone dead on me. I remembered the first time my talents had manifested, and Tor had insisted I drink a sugary soda to "close things down."

I got out my laptop and opened the radio app. I started to listen to the Raiders losing the game, but 2010 began to look like an awful season. I turned that off and surfed the Internet for images of Otto Rahn. I turned up a whole page of them—but it showed pictures of at least three different men, all classified under the same name. One even had white hair, which meant he'd lived way beyond thirty-five, the age when Audo died. Another man, who must have been in his late forties, looked like an evil elf. Only a few of the old photos thumbnailed there matched my memories.

I panicked. My mind raced around and around a loop of possibilities. Maybe I was wrong. Maybe he didn't look like

the person I remembered. Maybe I was remembering someone else. Maybe my whole story came from some movie I'd
forgotten seeing. I took a couple of deep breaths and calmed
myself down. No one had ever said that exploring your past
lives was going to be easy. When Tor came home, he'd help me.

No, I told myself, you don't have to wait for Tor. You can
try to prove or disprove it yourself like a big girl.

By then I'd digested enough of my lunch to get back to
work. I decided to start at the first memory, the one where
the SS officer had grabbed my wrist. Why had I wanted to
throw cold water in his face? The usual explanation for that
impulse presented itself: a clumsy pass. Since I never caught
more than a glimpse of him in the memory images, I figured
that he had no real importance, just some crude dude trying
to make time, like they called it in the old movies, with a girl.
I made a sketchy layout drawing with charcoal, his position,
mine, a drafting table nearby, and the door. Some of his sneer-
ing little speech came clear enough for me to write it down.
That is, I wrote down a version of it in horribly bad German
spelling. I won't dignify it by calling it phonetic.

The memory images deserted me there. Just as Tor had
warned me, they'd arrived in fragments of unrelated pictures
and sounds. I did remember that Otto Rahn had written a
couple of books. When I checked the Internet, I found they'd
been translated into English. In the lower flat Tor had an
enormous library. A little knot of fear formed in my stomach.
What if Björn still existed in some strange form? I reminded
myself that this time around, Kristjan had won the duel. I
got up my courage and went downstairs.

The library room housed a forest of expensive oak bookshelves arranged in tidy rows. The books looked like Tor had
arranged them, too, in some kind of order, but since I couldn't
read most of the titles I couldn't figure out what that order
was. Since I'd seen Audo's books on the Internet, I at least
knew what the English-language trade paperbacks looked like.
I did eventually find them, placed beside the same books in
German. I pulled them out, blew off the dust, and carried

them back upstairs.

At first I felt triumphant. I held the keys to locked memories in those books. But I found myself oddly unwilling to open them and read. Even the short translator's introductions repelled me. I took the books into the Burne-Jones bedroom and set them down on the floor next to the green armchair. Later, I told myself. Tomorrow, maybe. The alchemical barometer displayed an image of a black man with the sun for a head crossing swords with a white woman who wore the moon for hers. Conflict—I was conflicted, all right.

I returned to the living room and sat down with my laptop. I felt not exactly drained, just too tired to draw any more loaded pictures. Instead I wrote more on the history of my relationship with Tor. I made sure to lock the files with a password in case the police could somehow access my machine.

The guys returned over two hours after the game ended, not that I worried. The stadium was all the way on the south side of Oakland, and the traffic leaving the parking lot was always horrendous. Billy and JJ came upstairs with Tor, who announced that we were all going out for dinner at a local ribs place. The other two men were dressed just like Tor. Billy, a red-haired white guy, a little on the plump side, wore the same face paint as Tor, but JJ had only a couple of silver stripes on his face.

"I'm black already," JJ told me with a grin. "It's easier for me."

"About the only thing that is," Billy broke in. "If that fucking security guard hassles you one more time—" He slammed a fist into the palm of his opposite hand.

"No, leave him to me," Tor said, and he mugged an evil grin, totally convincing with the face-paint. "He'll be an insecurity guard when I'm done with him."

JJ held up both hands flat for silence. "Thanks, bros," he said, "but no need to make things worse. Yeah, the guy's a shit. But—no need to make things worse. I don't want to get us all bounced from the games."

"You're probably right," Billy said. "It just fucking gripes me. You pay through the nose for a ticket, and then some greasy white dude . . ." He let his voice trail away.

JJ shrugged. When an uncomfortable silence lingered, I decided I needed to play hostess or maybe den mother.

"I'll make some coffee," I said. "We're not going out till you guys drink some of it. You all stink of beer. I'm just glad you made it back okay."

"Ah, the traffic was crawling," Billy said. "Maybe five miles an hour on the freeway. Easy driving."

"We won't be going on the freeway this time," Tor said. "So Maya better drive, even with the coffee."

They all laughed, and the awkward moment finally died.

"Where's Aaron today?" I asked.

"He can't take the crowds," JJ said. "Or the noise. He probably watched the game on Tor's Bane."

My turn for the laugh—he meant television, of course. Tor very loudly said nothing.

The ribs were great, and the company even better. Raiders fans, still wearing their face paint, crammed the restaurant. Billy ostentatiously drank only diet cola with his meal. We all laughed a lot during the dinner. For an hour or so I could forget about the police and Nazis both.

By the time we returned to our house, Billy was sober enough to drive himself and JJ home. When we went upstairs, Tor hurried into the bathroom to wash the paint off his face. I turned the lights on in the living room and sat down on the couch. My sketchbook still lay on the coffee table where I'd left it. Slightly damp around the edges, Tor joined me. He pointed at the book.

"Anything interesting?" he said.

I figured he meant 'relating to image magic and past lives.' "Maybe," I said. "I heard someone talk, but I know I didn't write it down right."

When I showed him the sketch of the jerk in the office, Tor laughed at my attempts at spelling German. "I think this means," he said, "Why don't you stop going around with that *schwüchtel*—" He paused to think. "That faggot, I guess you'd translate it. It's a derogatory name for a gay guy. So, stop going around with that faggot and see what a..." again the hesitation, "what a real man is like. You're right, your spelling is lousy."

"Well, I don't know any German really."

"True. Huh, he must have meant Rahn. Who may have overheard him, since he was just opening the door. In your memory, anyway. I wonder what he had to say about that?"

This memory rose as a sound, a lot of sounds. "He decked him," I said. "Hit him really hard in the stomach, and the dude went down, and chairs went over. I think I screamed. And someone came running, a lot of people." I could vaguely remember the meaning of my angry yelp. "I yelled something like don't spill my bottle of ink."

"Spoken like a true artist."

"The guy got up, and Rahn hit him again. This time he stayed down." I frowned, trying to remember. "And everyone made fun of the other guy when he came to. I have this vague idea that someone told him to stop listening to stupid gossip."

"That's one way to kill a rumor about your manhood, all right. Do you remember when this was?"

"It's weird, but as soon as I try to think of a date, I feel like I don't know anything, like I'm just making all this up or something."

"That's the way the process works. You're bringing up emotional memories, and then something makes you doubt yourself. Wham! The bottom drops out, and you can't trust anything."

"That's exactly how I feel. And I tried to do some research on the Internet—"

"Don't! That's dangerous."

"Well, this sure was. I found pictures. Some looked like my memories, but others were all wrong. There were at least three different guys in the thumbnails, and a couple were way too old. Everything I'd dredged up, it all seemed fake."

"Yeah, that's standard, when you first start remembering, and a good sign. Skepticism is a valuable corrective. A lot of people think they remember past lives. But they believe they were an old movie star or Cleopatra or an aristocrat, because they jump on the first stray thought or image that comes to mind."

"So you think I'm right after all?"

"Sure, probably." Tor shrugged, but his smile reassured me. "Don't try to remember too much at once. When I was a teenager, I got my first clear memories. Of being Lars, those were. And I got fascinated with the circs, the Nazi invasion, the Nazis themselves, and I read everything I could get my hands on. I ended up so confused I didn't know what I was remembering and what I was just inventing, trying to fill in the gaps of the memories. My dad had to help me straighten it all out again."

"Is that why you know so much about Rahn?"

"Yeah. But let him go for now. I don't want to confuse you worse."

"I don't want you to, either. This is all so weird."

"You'll get used to it. What else did you draw?"

I gestured at the sketchbook. "If you turn back, like maybe three pages back, you'll see some artifacts. I remembered drawing them."

Tor obliged, then frowned at the first drawing, the broken drinking horn. "Shit, I've just seen a picture of this, an old photo." He looked up. "In the papers from my grandfather."

"I'm not surprised. Did he say anything about it?"

"No, it's just a faded old black and white photo. Nothing on the back." Tor turned another page, nodded, turned to the last one, nodded again. "I've got photos of all of these." He shut the sketchbook and tossed it onto the coffee table. "Well, now we know."

"Yeah. I guess Rahn must have known your great-grandfather. Your family, they seem to be totally involved in this story."

"Which must be one of the karmic things that brought us together in this life. So don't knock it." He thought something through before he spoke again. "What I wonder is how your father got involved. Your father in this life, I mean. The guy who was half a wight."

"Half a what?"

"A wight's just the name for any non-human intelligent being. Come to think of it, these sound more like wraiths, because of the way your father could drain élan from living beings. He must have had genes from the snow wraiths, the ones who live in Niflheim. And he passed them on to you."

Snow wraiths. Frost Giants. The room turned colder, I felt, just from repeating those names in my mind.

"Jötunheim, the place where the giants live," I said. "Is it all ice and snow?"

"No, only in the north where it fades into Niflheim." Tor frowned in concentration. "Not sure where I read that, one of the Eddas, probably." He shrugged the problem away. "But the giants have farms and steadings in the valleys and along the rivers."

"So they have like real lives? They need houses and food?"

"Yeah, the giants do, but in Niflheim, the wraiths must harvest chi, élan, directly from the air. Like you can learn to do."

That statement destroyed my last few doubts. If developing my talents could let me feed myself, I could face any fear. Well, I hoped I could. At least I could try. Tor was smiling as if he knew he'd just changed everything.

"You really think I could?" I said.

"Why not? I had to learn how. I did it when Dad was so ill. I helped him live a little longer by feeding him chi."

"But you'd been studying the runes for years by then."

"Yeah. I didn't say it would be easy for you to learn, did I?"

"Okay. Where do I start?"

Tor laughed and threw his arms around me. He looked so triumphant that I finally believed what he'd said about becoming his equal.

Until that evening I hadn't put any thought into our actual wedding. Too many other things, like my senior project and the weird magics, had occupied my mind. Tor, however, had been thinking about it. The next morning at breakfast, he repeated what Liv had already told me, that early summer would be a good time.

"We need to get you a lawyer before we draw up the official marriage contract," Tor told me.

"I need a lawyer? That's scary."

"If you don't have your own representation, and something happens to me, the court might have trouble adjudicating your inheritance. Not that I think Liv would dispute it, but there are cousins lurking around."

"I don't get why we need a contract."

"I'm setting it up to protect you, not cut you out of the family goods."

"I didn't think you were going to shaft me. I just never thought money would be an issue when I got married. Not even when I was playing with Barbies and fantasizing about marrying a prince."

Tor grinned at me, then turned solemn. "You're the first girlfriend I've ever had who didn't think about the money. I think they put up with me as long as they did because of it."

"That really sucks!"

He smiled again. "There are so many reasons why I'm marrying you."

We kissed a few times, but how cozy can you get when you're sitting on tall stools at a breakfast bar?

"Before we get married," I said. "I've got to graduate. Which means I've got to get serious about my senior project."

"Do you want studio space downstairs?"

"I can get some at school to start with. The panels I have in mind are going to be huge."

Fancy art schools have big buildings where senior students can have real studio space. At my school, we had an ancient gymnasium that had been "repurposed," as the Admin people called it. The basketball hoops were gone. Scruffy, paint-stained linoleum protected the wood floor, and the cheapest possible office partitions divided the space up into 12 by 12 foot cubes, one per student. Each cube did include a section of the real walls, at least, where we could hang things up properly. The partitions wobbled too much if you taped any-thing heavier than a photo or drawing on them. For a water source and clean-up space we had the old locker room, which still smelled of sweat on damp days.

I got a decent cube near the door where I breathed fewer fumes from the turps, printing inks, and chemical mediums than the other students did. The prof in charge that day is-sued me an easel. I put up a placard with my name on it to ensure that no one else took the space, but I left my supplies in my locker. I needed to get home, because Tor and I were driving in to see Roman in the hospital.

And a good thing we did, too. We'd only been in Roman's hospital room for about five minutes when Lieutenant Hu and his uniformed back-up joined us. Hu greeted Tor with perfect politeness, which Tor returned, but oddly enough, neither Hu or the other officer so much as looked my way. Brittany glanced at them, then strode out of the room without saying a word. Neither cop remarked on her leaving. I helped Ro-man sit up against a stack of pillows. He was staring narrow-eyed at the two cops.

"We just want to ask you a few more questions," Hu said to Roman. "Nothing serious."

Tor dropped his illusory pose of nice guy and stepped forward. "We'd better have a lawyer present. I have my fam-ily lawyers on retainer." He took out his smartphone. "Just take me a minute to call."

Hu gave him a look like a general on the North China frontier might have given an uppity barbarian. His voice, though, stayed mild. "It's hardly necessary."

"Oh, I'm sure it's not." Tor smiled in the bland way that meant he was furious. "From your point of view."

Hu opened his mouth to reply just as Doctor Mellars charged in with Brittany right behind him.

"I told you," Mellars snapped at Hu, "that my patient can't be disturbed this way. If you'd simply set up a time for an interview, I can have the nurses manage his medication." He turned to me and Roman. "He should be lying down on his side."

Roman winked at me. I helped him lie down again and arranged the bolster along his back. Mellars was just getting warmed up.

"Look," the doctor said, "do you see that IV unit? Do you know what it's delivering? Morphine, that's what. The bullet damaged major ganglia. Without sedation he'd be in serious pain. Questioning a witness under the influence of morphine—would anything you learned stand up in court?"

"Mr. Cantescu is the victim," Hu said, and I could imagine the frontier general staring down a whole horde of barbarians. "He's not a suspect."

"Then why do you keep disturbing him?" Mellars said. "You have eyewitness testimony to the crime. The shooter is dead, isn't he?"

"Very true." Hu turned to the uniformed cop. "Okay, let's go."

They stalked out without so much as a goodbye. Tor put his phone away, then went to the door. He stared down the hall for a couple of minutes, until he could tell us they'd gotten into the elevator. Mellars turned to Brittany.

"Why do they keep coming back?" the doctor said. "Do you know?"

"No." Brittany walked over to Roman's bedside. "I just wish they'd stop doing it."

We all did know, of course. They wondered if Roman's buddies in the ex-military PTSD group had killed Nils, and they were hoping he'd slip and give them a lead. As much as I hated lying to such a good ally as Dr. Mellars, I figured he'd be better off ignorant. Something he knew nothing of wouldn't trouble his conscience. Only Tor and I knew how wrong the cops' suspicious were. On the drive home, I kept brooding about it. Once we got off the freeway and reached the quiet streets near our house, I began rehearsing my fears aloud.

"How can I even confess? They'd want to know how I killed Nils. Would they ever believe the truth?"

"They'd only think you were lying to shelter me," Tor said. "Maya, look. If what you did was really evil, then it will come back to you in some way. If the universe sees it the way I do, self-defense, that is, then it won't. What the local laws demand is nothing compared to what the karmic balance exacts."

"Well, maybe, but—"

Tor glanced my way, then returned to watching the road. "But what? Isn't there a Buddhist law, if you kill someone to prevent him from working evil, then your action has its place in the scheme of things? I'm not saying it's cool. Just that it had to be what it is."

"Like Krishna told Arjuna. Hindu."

"Well, whatever. Don't worry so damn much."

I could think of nothing to say in answer. Tor's attitude troubled me as much, if not more, as what I'd done. Yet that day my own attitude began to change. I had the right to escape. And if I hadn't killed him, what would Valdez and his buddy have done if they'd found him? Nils would have ended up dead, either way. Although the guilt still made my stomach twist and my hands shake at moments, maybe, eventually, I could accept the necessity of what I'd done.

A few days later, I received a letter from my mother, only a blue fold-up airletter, but a letter. I kissed it before I opened it. The abbess had relented, Mom told me, and let her communicate with the outside world, even though it had taken a while to wear her down. I smiled when I read that, because I knew how Mom got her way. Dad used to call her the "flower badger." She was always very polite and sweet, but she never gave up when she really wanted someone to do something. She was well, she told me, and happy that I was getting married. In the picture I'd sent, Tor looked very handsome, and she knew he'd take good care of me.

"But darling, my dearest girl," she finished up, "please think twice before you have children. I know you know why I have to say this. Don't be offended."

Yeah, I sure did, maybe better than she. No, I wasn't in the least offended.

I answered the letter, even though I doubted that the abbess would let Mom see it, not two whole letters in one year! I saved hers in the carved wooden box where I kept my few pieces of jewelry.

Tor's mother and sister were going to come to the wedding. I began to worry that they'd dislike my being Asian. My father's family emigrated to the States from Romania, and some of their ancestors were Turkish. My mother's came from Indonesia. Between them they gave me straight black hair and skin that's an olive tan, I guess you could call it. Growing up, even in cosmopolitan San Francisco, I knew that the color of my skin mattered. Now I was going to meet Tor's silver-haired mother and his sister, the blonde, blue-eyed woman I'd seen in his snapshots. I started to discuss the subject with Tor, but he tried to shrug it off.

"Liv grew up in the Bay Area," he said, "and my mom lived here for years. It's not going to matter to them. They had lots of Asian friends. They still do write each other. And visit."

"Friends are different. You're marrying me."

"Yeah, I am. And even if they didn't like it, so what? You don't think I'm going to change my mind, do you?"

"No, of course not. But I'm just afraid of causing, y'know, friction in the family, because I'm different."

"Different?" Tor laughed under his breath. "Look, my mother has visions and talks to fox spirits. Liv can do all kinds of weird magics. Her kids are little sports of nature. Why in hell would they look down on you?"

I began to feel better. "You've got a point. Sometimes I forget what kind of family I'm marrying into."

"Sometimes I forget how strange my family is. You don't want to back out, do you?"

"What? No!" I laid my hand on my cheek. "But there's no use pretending I'm not scared of what they'll think of me. Your mom, anyway. Liv and I have a lot in common already."

"I don't—" He stopped in mid-sentence and thought for a moment. "I don't understand, but I'll take your word for it. I don't think I can do more than try to understand. Look at me, Mr. White Male. And with money. What would I know about how it makes you feel?"

I reached up and kissed him.

"Thanks," I said. "And I'll try not to worry."

"Which reminds me, I need to buy you an engagement ring."

"Nothing too fancy, okay?"

"You mean too expensive."

"Well, that, too. But look at my hands." I held out the left. "They're small, and I've got slender fingers. Some big flashy diamond thing would look all wrong."

"You've got a point. Okay, a small diamond. Tell you what, draw up some sketches of what you'd like, wedding rings, too. I know someone to make them."

"That's such a cool idea! Thank you!"

Tor grinned, and we shared a couple of kisses.

"But don't sketch something cheap, okay?" he went on. "You really don't like it when I spend money on you. Why? Sweetheart, I like doing it."

"It makes me feel like I'm in debt to you. Y'know, obligated to do something in return."

"No, it's part of *my* obligations, being generous."

"Obligations to what?"

"My membership in the master race."

He was trying to keep a straight face, but the cute dimple at the corner of his mouth quivered and gave him away. When I laughed, he gave in and laughed with me.

The joke made me wonder, though. What had I looked like in that German life? The next time I looked into a mirror to comb my hair, I saw a shadowy impression of Someone Else, Mia, I supposed, standing just behind my left shoulder. Blonde hair, cut short and waved in a 1930s fashionable perm, big blue eyes—she could have been Brittany's sister, and about as Aryan as you can get.

I finally got up the courage to take another look at the pictures of Audo online. Several I recognized immediately, there among all the other men who weren't him, one where he was wearing an overcoat over a civilian suit and a hat at a dashing angle. It must have been winter in Berlin when it was taken. There was another of him in winter, in uniform with a jacket over it. It made me think of Tor's past life as Lars, the Resistance fighter, who wore a heavy Nazi jacket he'd looted from a dying German officer.

What a horrible, awful, gruesome time! I put the laptop away and went into the bathroom. In the mirror I saw Mia's shadowy image, standing behind me. And what had she thought of it all, the Fatherland, the glorious thousand year Reich? At the question Mia took me over. I smiled, a crazed berserk almost animal grin. I felt tall, strong, full of life and faith in the future.

"Deutschland," I said aloud, "über alles."

The spell broke, and I nearly vomited. Finally I saw why I'd tried to avoid remembering my last life. I'd believed in the Reich. I'd been the perfect little Aryan princess.

"Go away!" I whispered. "Get away from me, you bitch!"

The image vanished. I covered my face with both hands and wept.

"Maya!" Tor came hurrying into the bathroom. "What's wrong?"

My mind froze. I don't know what else to call it. The room grew distant, and I seemed to be seeing it through torchlight, torches flickering in the wind while thousands of voices cheered, a mindless roar of joy, over and over. Tor grabbed me by the shoulders. My vision cleared.

"Awful memories," I whispered.

"Let's go sit down."

Tor guided me into the living room and onto the couch. He sat down next to me and pulled me close into his arms.

"What?" he said. "What do you remember?"

"I was a party member." I started to tremble. I could not bring myself to say the word Nazi. My revulsion rose physically in my throat. "I swallowed the whole line. I—"

"That's enough. I don't mean to push you too far. This is horrible stuff to remember."

"It's a good thing Lars never found me." I could barely speak. "He would have hated me, what I was then."

"He would have saved you from it."

I shook my head no. "I never would have gone with him, not as long as I still believed."

"Did you stop believing?"

"Yes. It was after he—Otto—came back from Dachau. He'd been sent there as a guard for a few months, as a punishment. He came back changed. He told me what he'd seen and heard. He told me the truth. I didn't want to believe it, but he made me believe it." I took a deep breath and choked back more tears. "I keep thinking, they would have taken Cynthia, if this were then. I mean, does that make sense? They would have killed my best friend. Jim, too, for race mixing. Isn't that what they called it?"

"Oh yeah. Miscegenation. Marry a Jew—verboten."

"But at the time, I believed them! Tor, I've got to know—I mean—can you forgive me?"

"For what? Wait, you mean for what you were then?"

"Yes." My voice shrank to a whisper. "That."

"I can't forgive you because I don't blame you."

I started to speak, but he laid a gentle finger on my lips

"Never blame yourself for what happened before you were born." He took the finger away. "It's that simple. It's like your disease. You're not being punished for something. It's a whole new problem."

"You sure?"

"Yeah, I am. That was then, this is now, and who knows what drove you to it? Millions of women fell for the Nazi line, the uniforms, the torchlight parades, the runes and the flags. Look at all the women who got pregnant for the sake of the pure Aryan race. It's not like you were the only one." He took my hand in both of his. "But I can see why you didn't want to remember this shit."

It was one of those moments when you realize why you love someone. He held me until I could stop weeping.

It took me until the evening to realize I'd broken through

a karmic barrier. I'd faced what I'd feared. I'd seen my old self in the mirror. I hated her, but at least I'd confronted her. Finally I could move forward.

While Tor worked downstairs, I went into the Burne-Jones bedroom, sat down in the green armchair, and picked up Otto's book on the Cathar heresy and the Albigensian Crusade in southern France. This was the book about the Grail that had brought him to the attention of the Ahnenerbe SS. Before I settled in to read it properly, I dipped into it here and there, looked at the table of contents to see what was in it, skimmed a few passages. A word caught my attention and led me to a painful treasure.

Endura. It's the name of the Cathar fast, forty whole days, mandatory for those who wanted to take the final set of holy vows. People died during it, but in their way of looking at things, such a death was glorious. The Cathars saw nothing wrong with committing suicide when you'd had enough of the life of this world, the life they hated above all else. You weren't allowed to kill yourself out of boredom, or to get out of debt, but if your life was utterly intolerable, suicide became a holy act that would send you straight to their version of Heaven, the immortal realm of the spirit, the true home and destination of all human souls.

The lid of the poison casket sprang open. I let the book lie in my lap unread. I was remembering. Most of the images came and went with less order and logic than those in a nightmare. At times I heard voices. There were gaps, big ones. But I remembered the core. He'd killed himself, and Mia wanted to die with him.

The senior staff had sent Audo as a guard officer to Dachau because they'd finally heard the rumors about his sexuality. The camp showed him what could happen to men who disgraced the SS. He decided that he and Mia might escape from Germany to his friends in Southern France if they could somehow throw off suspicion. Everyone around them thought you could just stop being gay if you tried, kind of like quitting smoking. Stupid, yeah, but when you consider the rest of the insane stuff the Ahnenerbe SS men believed, it's no surprise. So Audo asked Mia to marry him.

And she said yes. That I remembered, how oddly happy she was despite the danger all around them, despite how hollow such a marriage would be, a ruse, a part to play, she the adored lady to his chaste knight. He had to get the permission of the Reichsführer, of course. He told her afterwards that Himmler seemed genuinely happy for them, that he'd smiled and congratulated his scholar-officer and wished Mia the best. Looking back on it from my life in California, I found this the most incredible thing of all, that such a cruel man would be so happy for the friend he'd tried to break.

The dagger struck the next day. When he'd been forced to join the SS, Audo had never filled out the Racial Purity form. He had to do so before he could marry. That night he told Mia his terrible secret. He had a recent Jewish ancestor. He couldn't lie on the form. The officials would scrutinize every line and demand it be notarized. No one could lie and get away with it. He expected Mia to reject him because of that grandmother or whoever it was, but Mia said no, she'd seen what he'd seen. She told him that she could no longer live in the nation Germany had become, but really, she felt she couldn't live without him.

I no longer hated Mia when I remembered the way she'd stayed faithful to him.

He wanted to die in his beloved mountains. He told her to stay behind, to play a different part, to make a big show of rejecting him as a disgusting Jew after he was safely dead. Safely dead. He used those words a lot, that night. But she went with him. I couldn't remember the details. They must have kept up the pretence of a happy couple going on holiday to the ski hostel in the Wilderkaiser, the hostel with the medieval bed cabinet and the long view up the snowy slope, bordered by trees.

At this point, the memories became so vivid that I knew I was reliving them in my mind. I became Mia again for that little space of time. Audo had it all planned out. Death by exposure, hypothermia, relatively painless, especially since he'd brought a bottle of British whiskey along. Drinking in the snow makes you feel warmer, but it actually helps kill you faster. The morning came when, or so I thought, we'd go up the slope together. But he crept out while I was asleep and locked me in. He left a note that said something like I was too young and lovely to die. He apologized for risking me. He told me that he truly loved me.

I was furious. I remember pounding on the door and yelling until the elderly man who ran the hostel heard me and opened the door. I rushed out of the room and ran for the slope. I could remember how my lungs ached in the cold air and how the snow crunched under my feet. I don't remember what I was wearing, but I bet they were just ordinary clothes, not even a coat. I saw a dark shape lying part-way up the gentle slope. I was panting and gasping by the time I reached him. He was already dead, his face a ghastly pale blue color. The empty bottle lay on his chest. Like the fool Mia could be, I stripped off my outer clothing and lay down beside him in the snow. I threw my arms around him one last time and tried to weep, but my breath would not come.

While I lay cuddled next to his corpse, the snow wraiths arrived. Those I remembered so clearly, the tall misty shapes, human but attenuated, glittering with frost. They had ice-blue eyes that looked down on me in sympathy as they gathered round. When they spoke among themselves their breaths made trails of frost, as if they drew their words with crystals on the still air. One female with long white hair and pale blue lips knelt beside me and laid a hand on my face. Her nails were made of ice, sharp as daggers. I told her I wanted to die. She smiled, nodded, and sank the nails into my throat. She said one word, "Soon."

But the old man at the hostel had gone down to the village and rounded up the locals, who came after me, after Audo, too, because the old man had found the note and figured out what was happening. At their approach the wraiths fled. The villagers found me alive, but the she-wraith kept her promise.

I caught pneumonia, just like the Cathars who chose death by cold. When I died, I drowned again, this time in a hospital ward, as the disease filled my lungs with fluid, a drop or two at a time.

I retrieved a clear memory image of a nursing sister in a gray habit, praying the rosary for me as the ward disappeared into darkness. Despite her prayers, the snow wraiths were waiting for me on the other side. As I stepped into the white mists of their world, a male wraith with huge pale eyes came forward to greet me. I recognized the soul who would become my father in my next life. He held out delicate white hands and smiled, revealing teeth like slivers of ice.

"At last," he said. "Again."

I held out my hands to him—A voice jerked me back to the present moment, into the Burne-Jones bedroom in California.

"Maya?" Tor was standing in the doorway of the bedroom. "You've been in here for hours. Are you okay?"

"Oh yes." I got up and gestured with the book. "Just reading."

Later I'd tell him the truth of what I'd remembered. But first I had to draw my memories, wrestle them onto paper and fix them in the real world. First I had to understand them, especially the wraiths, and in my own way and on my own terms, not Tor's. Besides, he had troubles of his own.

On the bedstead, the sorcerer's moon had reached its first quarter. Another week, and Tor would be facing the bjarki change once again.

CHAPTER 8

As bitter as my memory of my last death was, it gave me the theme for my senior project. I started by trying to draw the snow wraiths, first in white pastel on white paper by building up forms that caught the light in a different way than the matte surface. Didn't work. I tried white Conté on black paper. Those looked like Halloween decorations.

I decided to concentrate on the first landscape painting, a four by six foot view up the slope of the Wilderkaiser hill. I spent the next week drawing at home and painting in my shared studio space at school. I started by drawing the view in detail with charcoal on the canvas. I'd just finished when I was reminded of one of the drawbacks of art school: trendy art students. A guy I knew from a bunch of classes stopped by to say hello. Jason, a decent looking white guy with longish dark hair and light eyes, had asked me out twice, but nothing ever clicked between us. We'd parted friends, well, as much as anyone could be friends with Jason.

He stood in front of my canvas with his hands in his jeans pockets and his head tilted a little to one side. "Jeez, Maya, you're doing landscape?"

"Yeah. So?"

"With that composition it's going to look like a backdrop for a Disney movie. Too simple. Illustration."

I looked heavenward and snarled.

"Yeah, yeah, I know." He grinned at me. "You're sick of hearing that."

"You bet I am."

"Then why do you keep doing it? All this unnecessary detail!" He waved his hand at the canvas. "Realism is so over."

I counted to ten, then said, "And what's your senior project?"

"A way of re-perceiving a common object through transformations."

"Which means?"

"Toilet paper tubes. You know how they rip apart on the spiral seam? I was fiddling around with one of them one day when I—"

"Too much information!"

He snickered. "I'm distorting them into different shapes and taking photos, and then the exhibit will be the tubes backed by a wall mural of the photos. A hundred of 'em! And oh yeah, some have pieces of toilet paper clinging to them."

"Not used, I hope?"

"Nah, come on! Just the little pieces that sometimes stick when you tear off the last sheet. I'm calling it the random factor."

"I suppose you've got to call it something."

His turn for the eyeroll. Fortunately, he wandered off to sneer at the next person's work.

Unfortunately, he was right about the composition. I knew the landscape demanded the image of Audo lying dead in the snow, but I hesitated to add it. The problem: I saw no way to use this painting as part of my original plan for murals. When I took some sketches and a smartphone snap of the canvas to Harper, she reassured me.

"I figured that the mural project might morph into something else," she said. "Let it. It's still October, so you've got time. What's interesting me now are these sketches with the superimposed Nazi insignia. Where does that come from? In your mind, that is."

"Well, it's kind of relevant again, isn't it? I mean, when I surfed the Net looking for pictures of the Alps, I found all kinds of totally scary Neo-Nazi sites. And it's not just Jewish people they're going after. Most of them rant about the 'mud races.' They mean people like us. Some of them don't even mention Jews. Just the N-word. And yellow peril stuff, too."

"Oh yes." Harper shuddered. "I know about that."

"I keep thinking that I need to include—" Talking about past life memories in front of Harper was a bad idea. "Well, some kind of statement. A lot of these white power rants talk about landscape, the northern natural landscape, they call it, and they think it belongs to the white race, to the Aryans. They blame people of color for breeding too fast and harming Nature. They talk about saving the planet by purifying it."

"And folks like you and me are the sludge overdue for a clean-up."

"Yeah. Which is why I want to put a dead man in that painting."

"It'll balance the composition, too, keep it from falling into halves, if you place it just right." Harper picked up an Osmiroid and wrote a few words on my page of her project journal. "You might see where this line of thought takes you. Maybe rather than doing any more big panels, you might want to think about a series of smaller images. Photo-collage is a possibility for works on paper. If you find something perfect that's not on Creative Commons, I can probably get the college to buy you the rights."

I thanked her—a lot of times—and left with a head full of new ideas. One of them: smearing mud across one of the paintings, incorporating dirt somehow, to show the world what I was, to mock the mud race meme by claiming it. Or crumpling and staining a drawing to indicate that some people would see it as garbage, just because a woman like me drew it. We were supposed to include a small image of ourselves in the project. I could do a photo of myself with 'verboten' across it in red stenciled letters. The landscape would still fit right in, especially if I reached back in art history and drew on Expressionist techniques to avoid the put-down, "illustration." The snow fields would represent the Aryan fantasy land, all pure and glistening and white.

With a dead man, a dark shape against the snow, lying in the foreground with an empty whisky bottle on his chest. I debated adding a yellow star somewhere on his clothes. It seemed kind of blatant. And illustrator-ish. Instead I decided to put him in the SS uniform. Still illustration, I supposed, but so true that I no longer cared about art critics.

I came home to find Tor sitting upstairs and translating a long email from Liv. The Oakland police had arranged for an officer of the Icelandic police force to interview Tor's mother about Halvar Svansson's death. Tor gave me the papers so I could read the English version, then leaned back on the couch to watch me .

"I've got to hand it to my mother," he said with a grin. "She didn't hold anything back."

The substance of her testimony came down to, "Halvar was an awful old man, and everyone was glad he was dead." The New York City police must have had enough suspects to fill Yankee Stadium, to hear her tell it. Although the men in the family had kept the details from her, she did know something about Halvar's unsavory business dealings. She held papers that proved he'd collaborated with the defeated Nazis who'd fled to South America with stolen German gold. She was convinced he'd helped set up the policies that eventually led to Iceland's big bank crash in 2008. She knew that Nils had profited from that crash somehow. She also suspected both Nils and Halvar of bankrolling profiteers, particularly those who trafficked in women, on the Russian market after the fall of the Soviet Union.

"If they take all this seriously," Tor said, "the police here are going to have a whole new gang of suspects for Nils' death. Which is all to the good."

"I hope so. You're right about your family, y'know." I set the translated letters down on the coffee table. "You're lucky that I'll stoop to marrying you."

He laughed and kissed me.

"How did the session with your advisor go?" he said.

"Really well. You know, I've changed my mind. I think I

will want to work downstairs, at least on part of the project, because I'll be doing smaller pieces for most of it. If it won't disturb your work."

"No, if you don't mind me chanting now and then."

"I'm used to that. I'll need to get a work table and shelves for the empty rooms downstairs. And I'll need to clean them out, too. I bet there's a lot of dust."

"Yeah, I'm sure of that. I can help if you don't mind waiting. There's nothing I can do about it right now. The moon's almost full."

"Tomorrow night?"

"Yeah." He got up and stood looking out the window. "When I think about the way Halvar got his money, I sometimes feel like his family deserves a curse. Not my mother or Liv or even her feral spawn. Maybe it's right that I take the curse and keep it off them. Accept the bjarki. Face whatever wyrd lies ahead. I'm the head of this family now that Dad's gone. It's part of the job description, y'know, taking on the family curse."

"What? No! It's not your fault. But if it bothers you so much, maybe you should give all the damn money away. I don't care. We'll get by."

For a moment I thought Tor was going to weep. He swallowed hard and forced out a grin. "Yeah, we could manage," he said. "But if we do dump the family money, I'll get the job in the burger joint, not you."

"You really do love me, don't you?" I grinned at him. "But from what your mom told the cops, anyway, Nils is the one who deserved the curse. He profited from all that dubious business stuff. The wyrd came down on him, and then he made you share it. It wasn't your fault."

Tor stared at the floor and considered what I'd said. Finally he looked up.

"Okay," he said, "we'll keep the ill-gotten gains. For now, anyway. Which means it's time to see what I can do about getting rid of the bear spirit. I'm going downstairs, but I'll be right back."

When Tor returned, he was carrying the rune plaque in its shoebox. He set the box down on the coffee table as casually as if it didn't hold a small fortune's worth of ancient gold.

"What's that for?" I said.

"I'm going to try putting the plaque in the bedroom for the full moon nights. I'm guessing that the runes spell out a galdr that's got something to do with were-creatures. It's time to find out." He fished in his jeans pocket, took out a curl of slender leather thongs and laid them on top of the shoebox. "These are for the plaque. I'll hang it up somewhere in the room before the spirit comes for me. Somewhere I can see it and touch it if that seems right."

Before we went to bed that night, he hung the gold plaque from the drawer pulls of the dresser. He also set up the nanny cam we'd bought to observe what happened to him during the transformation.

"Do you want me to record you again?" I said.

"Yeah. I need to know if the talisman makes any difference. If she gets hold of me, I won't remember enough to tell."

Her again. You ugly sow! I thought. You won't take my man if I can help it.

The transformation started the next morning. Tor had time to feed us both with all the élan we could absorb before he felt the lunar influences gathering around him. He strode over to the bedroom door, then turned to look back at me. Something about his facial expression and his posture struck me as different from the other times I'd witnessed the bjarki moon. He looked like a warrior, ready for battle.

"Lock me in," he said. "And start recording."

Although I did what he asked, I refused to watch him transform, not even on a laptop screen. I went downstairs to clean up the two empty rooms that would be my new studio space.

The bigger of the two stood just under the Burne-Jones bedroom and the smaller, under the pseudo-secret room at the end of the hall. Both had plain museum gray walls. The smaller had built-in bookshelves, but the previous owner must have used the larger as a gallery for his art collection. The remnants of museum-quality picture hangers marked the walls, and on the ceiling he'd installed spot lighting. It also had a much bigger window than the one upstairs, and the hardware to hang drapes, though the cloth was long gone. At the moment both rooms contained dust and not much else. I got out the downstairs vac, put in a new bag, and got to work.

By the time I finished, noon had come and gone. I returned the vac to its closet in the kitchen area and headed for the stairs. I was thinking of not much more than taking a shower when I heard a sad little whine, a noise like a lost cat might make, behind me. I spun around and saw the nisse. He appeared as little more than a shape made out of shadow, about two feet high, sort of human, sort of simian, standing at the end of a bookcase.

"What's wrong, little guy?" I said.

He whined and jigged up and down in an agitated dance.

"It is Tor? The bjarki?"

He was gone, just like that. For a moment I doubted that I'd seen him, but the whine and the shadow-shape stayed clear in my memory. I hurried upstairs and drew him to fix the image, before I took the shower.

At intervals during the afternoon, I checked the laptop screen. Tor seemed calmer than I'd ever seen him during the full moons. Although he crawled around on his hands and knees, and at times stood to walk flat-footed and clumsy like a bear, he never once rammed himself against the bedroom door. He did growl now and then and turn his head slowly and suspiciously from side to side. Around four in the afternoon he curled up on the floor and fell asleep. I allowed myself to hope that this time the bjarki moon would pass easily for him.

Fail! I'd forgotten how things changed at moonrise. The last of the sunset was fading when I heard the bjarki ramming himself against the bedroom door, a dull thud that echoed through the silent flat. Now and then he roared, as deep as a lion's roar but breathier. Another evening crawled by while he ached, and I felt helpless.

About two in the morning I did manage to fall sleep, but I woke again with the dawn. In the gray light I crawled out of bed and listened. The bjarki had fallen silent. I got dressed, and as I did, I glanced at the alchemical barometer. I saw the naked wild man, crouched and gnawing on his bone. Above and behind him in the sky shone a tiny golden spot, not big enough for the sun. Hope? I thought. But he doesn't see it. That's when I remembered the gold rune plaque.

I jogged down the hall to the living room and booted up the laptop. I started recording the nannycam signal and paused to watch the screen. Tor had taken off all his clothes. He crouched on hands and knees in the middle of the floor and swung his head from side to side as if he were a bear looking for prey. Now and then he raised his head and sniffed the air. On the dresser behind him the talisman glittered in the first light from the east-facing window. I ran to the bedroom door.

"Tor! Remember who you are! Can you hear me?"

Silence, not so much as a growl.

"Tor! The gold talisman! Find the talisman. It's behind you. Gold, Tor! Find the gold."

I heard a shuffling sound, nothing more. I realized that like an idiot I'd left the laptop in the living room. I ran back and picked it up, walked slowly, carefully, held it steady back to the bedroom door. I could see the bjarki sitting up on his hind legs—Tor's posture was so bear-like I couldn't think of it any other way—with his paws dangling in front of him.

"The gold, Tor! Find the gold!"

He stood and shuffled like a bear to the dresser, where the rune square hung from its leather thong. He peered at the gold plaque with his head lowered, then held out both hands and laid them like paws on either side of the rune-marked square. In the small image on the screen I couldn't see his face, but I heard him scream, a long drawn-out howl of agony.

"No, don't!" I was screaming myself. "Don't touch it! I was wrong!"

He ignored me. I sank to my knees and just managed to put the laptop safely onto the floor. My hands were shaking so badly I nearly dropped it. I could barely breathe, but I forced myself to look at the screen.

Tor had picked up the plaque in his hands—human hands with fingers that bent the way fingers were supposed to bend. He freed the leather thong from the drawer pulls and stood up—slowly, as if he hurt, but he stood like a man. He slipped the thong over his head and settled the plaque against his chest. When he turned around I could see that he was smiling. He walked over to the door and knelt to talk to me.

"Maya? Still there?"

"I sure am. Should I open the door?"

"No! I don't know how safe I am." He sounded exhausted. "The bear could come back. I just don't know."

"Okay. When you screamed, I thought oh my god I'd killed you."

"You heard the bear, not me. I'm going to work with this spell. Then we'll see if I can come out."

I took the laptop back to the coffee table and flopped onto the couch. Onscreen, I saw Tor sit down on the edge of our bed and study the plaque without taking it off. Since he hadn't bothered to get dressed, I could see the new bruises on his shoulders and upper arms from the bjarki's attempts to knock down the door. Now and then he paused to let the golden square lie against his chest so he could rub the sore muscles, but he always picked it up again. He'd pull the plaque out to the length of the leather thongs and turn it this way and that to read the runes in their spiral.

I fell asleep without meaning to, slumped back against the cushions. I woke to the sound of Tor chanting runes. Sunlight filled the room, and the air seemed oddly stale and hot. Onscreen I saw Tor, wearing a pair of jeans and nothing else but the gold square. He stood with his arms raised high in the rune shape of Elhaz, the fierce protector. One at a time he sang out the runes, but not in the futhark order. I assumed he'd memorized the writing on the plaque and was intoning it rune by rune.

Even through the muffling door his voice throbbed with

power. He fell silent, lowered his arms, and paused to take a few deep breaths. He raised his arms again and took a sideways step with one leg so that his body took the form of an X, Gebo, gift. He was invoking the power that the plaque had gifted him with. This time when he chanted, he spoke words. As they vibrated through the air, I felt I understood them—not literally, I could never have written out a translation—but on some wordless level I knew them. I remembered hearing them. Somewhere. Some time a very long time ago, ages ago, not in Germany, not in Denmark, somewhere older and stranger than that.

They sang a message to the gods, a statement that someone had fulfilled an oath. Somewhere, in that time long ago, they had meant the messenger's death—my death as a thrall, strangled, cut open, sent to Odin the hard way.

I wanted to run out of the room, run downstairs and outside, run screaming down the street, escape from hearing the words, flee the runes and his voice that burned me like a brand, but I forced myself to stay. Only cowards ran from truth. That thought became my anchor. I refused to give in to my fear, to my panic. It's now, I thought, not then.

Tor fell silent. I gasped for breath, exhausted. When I looked at my aching hands, I saw that my knuckles had reddened and were starting to swell. I needed élan. Cold sweat trickled down my back and between my breasts. Soon I'd be desperate for life force. Onscreen I saw Tor calmly picking up his tee shirt from the floor and putting it on. He pulled the golden square free of the shirt and settled it against his chest. Whatever he'd done had finished. I got up and staggered to the bedroom door.

"Maya!" he called out. "You can open the door."

"Okay." I heard my voice quaver like a crone's. "I'll get the keys."

When I opened the door I found him standing close by. He caught me by the shoulders and pulled me inside.

"You need élan. Come over to the window."

I let him lead me to the window, open to let cool air

filter through the screen. Tor pulled energy from the air and the sunlight, let it wash over both of us in waves, wonderful cooling waves of pure élan. Finally I could think and speak normally again.

"Is it over?" I said. "The bjarki?"

"Only in the daylight." He paused to kiss me on the forehead. "I think. As soon as the sun starts setting, you'll have to lock me in again. Then we'll see what happens."

"Do you know what the writing says?"

"No." He grinned at me. "But I know what it does. And that's what counts. As long as I can vibrate the runes, I don't need to know what the words are."

"Maybe they don't even mean anything. As words."

"That could be it." He laughed aloud. "No wonder I couldn't figure it out."

Tor made us both a meal as if the day were perfectly normal, but always I was aware of the gold square gleaming on his chest. Occasionally he'd stop whatever he was doing to lift it in both hands and hold it a little away from him.

"It's really heavy," he said, "and my neck aches. The thong bites in after a while."

"When it's safe for you to take it off, Brit can sew it onto a backing you can wear. A leather vest, maybe. She'll love working with magical gold."

"It might not be necessary. I'm going to try an experiment tonight."

"What?"

"You'll see. Don't worry about it."

Typical Tor. I bit back a useless snark.

"There's something I'm wondering about," he continued. "What drained your élan so fast? You should have had a reserve."

"It happened when I was listening to you chant."

"Shit! Look, before I go back into the lair, I'm going to put a circle around you. Not a painted one, I mean. You can walk around the flat and all that. But a barrier to make sure I'm not siphoning energy from you." He looked away, paused, caught by an idea. "This is all real interesting."

"Interesting. Only you would call it that."

He flashed me a grin. "I'm not sure what it all means. Yet. I'm going to see what I can find out."

When he came back upstairs, he was carrying a thin square of wood the same size as the gold plaque. He'd carved runes on it, front and back, that matched those on the plaque.

"I'm betting this will work," he told me. "I'll wear it to-night and see."

Toward sunset Tor turned restless. He paced back and forth in the living room, started to go downstairs, came right back up, walked around and around as the sun sank lower in the sky.

"The tide's changing," he said finally. "Let me ward you and feed you, and then you'd better lock me back in. I can feel it coming on."

More waiting, as the day darkened into evening and the full moon rose. Tor turned on a bedside lamp, so on the lap-top screen I could see him pacing back and forth with the wooden plaque on his chest. He stopped walking right beside the bed and spun around to face the corner of the room far-thest from the lamp. In the shadows something moved. Tor set his hands on his hips and roared a challenge.

The camera, the wireless connection, the laptop—the tech-nology failed to capture a creature that belonged to some other world. Tor I could see. I could pick out motion within the shadows, but the shape of whatever was moving never clarified. I could guess it was the cave bear. Tor kept turning in a tight circle as the wave of motion spiraled in slowly but always closer, closer. I heard Tor growl. Did something an-swer? It might have been only a noise from the street. I wanted it to be a distant car or a shout or a siren, anything normal. But I knew it was the bjarki growling to return the challenge.

The spiral tightened around Tor like the lash of a whip. Tor grabbed, swung a fist, grappled. In a blur of silver mist they wrestled, growled, swayed back and forth until they fell still wrestling onto the bed behind them. I clasped both hands over my mouth to keep from screaming as they fought, silent now, Tor and a mist-shape that at times vanished, at others strengthened until I could pick out a massive paw or the gleam of teeth.

On and on they fought. Tor disappeared in a billow of mist, then reappeared suspended on the smear of bear-shape like a wrestler pinning his opponent. Clasped together they rolled over and over and crashed into the end table and the lamp. It hit the floor hard and shattered. The light went out.

I did scream but in sheer frustration. I grabbed the keys from the mantel. What if the room caught fire? But the laptop screen showed no flames. I didn't smell any smoke. I clutched the keys so hard that they left marks on my palms, then shoved them into the pocket of my shorts, grabbed the laptop, and headed for the bedroom.

Even though my back stiffened up and started to ache, I sat by the bedroom door with the darkened laptop next to me. At first I heard muffled noises, the thump of something heavy hitting the floor, the creak of the wooden floor, the crash of a chair falling over. Tor growled, then roared. I heard no answer. The silence continued, on and on. I dozed off at intervals only to wake up with a spasm of tired muscles.

Finally light bloomed on the laptop screen and through the crack around the door. Tor had turned on the other bedside lamp. I staggered to my feet and stretched. Although I felt cramped and tense, I had a reserve of élan. The warding had worked.

"Tor?"

"You can open the door. It's nearly dawn."

I stopped recording and put the laptop on standby, then took off the safety chain and unlocked the door. Tor was sitting on the edge of the torn-apart bed and holding a wad of tissues pressed against the side of his face. I could smell blood on the air, a waft of primal élan that made me quiver with desire.

"What happened?" I said.

"Repercussion." He raised the blood-soaked tissues so I

could see the long cut across his cheek. "From her claw. She got one good swipe on me before I won."

I hesitated, stabbed by jealousy, even though I knew it was ridiculous. Tor saw it.

"Maya, she's a spirit, not even a real bear." He paused to press the tissue wad over the oozing cut again. "I won our fight. That's the first step toward getting her to serve me. She's going to be my fetch, my fylgja. If you get a fetch someday, he'll be male. Come on, you know what a fetch is."

The shaman's tame spirit, his friend and transport in the spirit world was always of the opposite sex. I did know that. I realized that I was staring at the blood on the tissues and made myself look away.

"We should go to the ER and get that stitched."

"No, I want it to scar." He grinned in a pure, boyish delight. "Kind of like those dueling trophies."

I should have known. Tor turned and threw the wad of tissues into the nearby waste basket. "I've got a styptic pencil in the bathroom. Time to stop the bleeding."

"Good idea."

"Unless you want to lick it clean."

I thought at first he was teasing, but he smiled, heavy-lidded, appraising me, liking what he saw.

"Tor, no, don't."

"Ah come on! You'll drain off the excess élan, and it'll stop." He patted the mattress next to him and smiled again. "You know you want to."

It was dangerous, what he was asking from me. I did think of just leaving the room, but the smell of blood, the overpowering scent of élan, perfume like roses and honey—I sat down next to him. He caught my face in both hands and kissed me. The élan swirled, sweet and strong, almost as sweet as the feel of his mouth on mine. When he let me go, I saw that the cut, horizontal across his cheek, had filled with fresh blood.

No, Maya, stop, don't—the words in my mind had no effect. I sat up straight, reached for him, and licked the cut. The taste of pure élan made me gasp aloud. He sighed in satisfaction and threw an arm around my waist to pull me closer. With his free hand he unzipped my shorts, reached under my shirt to my breasts and caressed them while I cleaned his wound like the animal in heat I felt myself to be. The flow of élan from the cut dwindled.

"It's stopped," I was shocked that I could still speak like a human being.

"Good. Come lie on top of me."

He let me go, rolled away and lay on his back and pulled down his jeans. I took off my shorts, dropped them on the floor, and did what he asked. The gold plaque lay between us, cold and pulsing with energy, but I barely noticed it once he entered me. I climaxed with a sob before he even moved. The feel of his body pressed against mine brought me so much pleasure that I fainted in a swirl of darkness.

White chill wrapped me round. I stood in the snow. Power swirled around me in pale blue flames . The cave bear, huge, her brown fur touched here and there with black, crouched in front of me and whimpered in defeat.

"Sow!" I said. "He's your master now."

She lowered her head to the ground.

"If you ever hurt him," I continued, "I'll hunt you down and destroy you."

She rolled on her back and whined while she waved her front paws like a terrified cub. The sky turned gold and fell around us in a shower of glittering frost.

I woke to find Tor sitting up, braced against the headboard, and holding me in his lap. My head rested on the warm, solid muscle and bone of his shoulder. When I lifted my head to look at him, he smiled, a thin, oddly tremulous smile, and his eyes narrowed in concern.

"Are you all right?" he said.

"Sure. I mean, I guess so." I stretched and yawned. "Sometimes it's so good with you that it's like being drunk."

I slid off his lap and sat up, cross-legged on the bed facing him. Sweat glistened on his shoulders, mottled with red and purple bruises. The sight turned me wide awake. I reached over and laid a gentle finger on the skin next to the worst one.

"I should get you some ice for those. And we've got some sports goop, too."

"No, just rest, okay? You went out like a light. Scared the shit out of me. Maya, you went limp!"

It occurred to me that I should be scared as well, but I felt too good, too relaxed and sated, to care. This must be what hard drugs are like, I thought. That thought did frighten me, and the fear was a sign that my intellect had come back online.

"It's the combination," I said, "the sex and the élan. Overload, I guess."

"Overloads are dangerous."

"But it feels so wonderful—"

"Yeah, for me, too, but too damn bad. Sweetheart, I never want to hurt you. Never." He frowned in thought. "Do you understand? You passed out in my arms, and I thought, shit! her heart's stopped."

My wonderful mood shattered like a glass thrown against a wall. I remembered my father, dying of heart trouble.

"I felt for your pulse," Tor went on. "It was there, but too damn slow. I was just trying to think of what to do when you came around."

"Okay. You can stop. I'm scared now, too."

Tor reached over and took my wrist, looked at the digital clock on the end table, and felt for my pulse. In a minute or so he smiled and let go of my hand.

"Back to normal."

We got out of bed. I was surprised that I had no trouble walking. Now that the fit had ended, I felt tired but perfectly normal. I picked up my shorts from the floor and put them on.

"Y'know," I said, "this was like the time we had sex when you were working a ritual, only stronger, because I didn't faint that time. This was worse."

"Worse is a good word." Tor winced and looked away. "We'll never do that again, either. Unless—"

"Unless what?"

"You match me in power someday."

"I'm working on it."

"Yeah." He smiled, a soft, gentle smile. "Finally."

I made Tor sit on the closed toilet lid so I could wash the cut out with warm water like a normal person. I slathered it with antibiotic ointment before I bandaged it.

"Are you sure you don't want to go to the ER?" I said.

"I don't need to. It's going to heal really fast." He grinned at me. "Now."

I turned away and began washing my hands in the bathroom sink. "If you keep cutting yourself like this," I said, "working magic, I mean, there's not going to be a lot of you left."

"Hey, I didn't do the cutting this time."

"Well, yeah, but I didn't realize that sorcery meant bleeding so much."

"Neither did I."

"What do you think is going to happen tonight? Will you have to fight her off again? Or is it all over?"

"I don't know. You'd better lock me in, just to make sure."

"Okay. I was hoping you'd be free now, from the bjarki and the moon change, and all that, I mean."

"Wouldn't it be pretty to think so? Or however that quote goes." He smiled but with a twist of his mouth. "One thing I do know is why Nils wanted this plaque. If he had it, he could've gotten some control over the varg. I don't know how much, because he physically transformed, and I don't, but it would have given him something to fight with."

Tor cleaned up the pieces of broken lamp, then spent most of the afternoon down in the ritual room. He took the laptop with him to study the recordings I'd made. He came back up to cook us an early dinner. By the time we finished eating, the sun hung low in the western sky. While I cleaned up the kitchen, Tor moved one of the leather armchairs around so he could face the eastern window. He sat down and waited, staring off to the east, for the sky to begin to darken. I walked into the living room to find him nearly asleep in the chair.

"Are you okay?" I said.

"Huh?" He paused to yawn. "Yeah, I am, but I'm not taking any chances. Lock me in now, but don't start recording till it gets dark. I'm going to put the other lamp on the dresser, out of the way if there's another fight."

Once again, I had nothing to do but wait. I called Cynthia and Brittany after I locked him in and told them the cautiously good news. At the last of the sunset I started the laptop recording. Tor lay fully dressed on our bed and slept, stretched out comfortably on his side. I was afraid to hope, but as the evening wore on, the bjarki stayed away, even when the moon shone directly into the bedroom window.

Just before midnight Tor woke up. He got out of bed, looked around him, shrugged, and grinned at the nannycam. I grabbed the keys and ran to the bedroom door to let him out.

"It's over," he said. "For this month at least." He laid a hand on the gold square and murmured something in a language I didn't know. "Just thanking the gods."

"I will, too. I feel like I should pour some mead onto an altar or something."

Tor laughed, caught me by the shoulders, and kissed me. "I'm going to take a shower. I'll try to keep the bandage on my face dry."

"Okay. I guess it's too early to celebrate, though."

"Yeah. Let's save that for next month—well, assuming I'm free of the transformation. I've got time to work on taming the fylgja."

"She isn't tamed?"

"Not in any useful sense, no. I don't think you can work with a fetch who's terrified of you. I'll have to make her into a friend."

I bristled.

"Just a friend," he said. "I may be weird, but I'm not into bestiality."

I felt myself blush. He kissed me and went to take his shower.

CHAPTER 9

Acrylic paints lack that wonderful buttery texture of oils, but they do dry really fast. Good thing, too, when I decided to work on my landscape painting at the house. I disliked the idea of the other students in our shared space watching me paint the image of Audo's body. Oh okay. I didn't want the snobs like Jason to see it. Eventually I'd have to show the work, but by then it would be finished, out of my control and my psyche both.

Since it refused to fit in the trunk of either car, retrieving the painting presented a problem. I vetoed tying it onto a roof. I'd put too much work into it to have it fly off on the freeway. Finally Tor solved the problem by calling Billy, who came over with the Land Rover. I went downstairs to join him.

"It's really cool of you to take time off work," I told him.

"Hey, it's okay," Billy said. "That's the pact. If I needed him, Tor would be right there." He smiled. "Faster than I can drive over, I betcha."

"Still, I totally appreciate it. Thank you."

"You're welcome. Do you want to go to IKEA once we get the painting home? Tor said something about you needing a work table and stuff like that."

"And an easel. We'll need to go to an art supply store for that. I can't take the one I have at school off campus."

"Okay. Where's Tor anyway?"

Tor answered the question by walking around the side of the house. "Sorry," he called out. "I left my phone upstairs and had to get it."

Billy was staring slack-mouthed at Tor's face. Tor grinned at him, then winced, because moving the muscles in his face pulled at the bandages.

"What in hell did you do to yourself this time?" Billy said.

"Nothing," Tor said. "A spirit bear did it for me."

Billy rolled his eyes heavenward. "Let's just go get what Maya needs," he said. "And there better not be any angry spirits at the art supply place."

Getting everything I wanted took a couple of trips. The size and weight of a real artist's easel, made out of solid redwood, not flimsy aluminum, shocked Billy and Tor. It took both of them to wrestle the flat pack into the Land Rover and then out again once we got it home. While they hauled the easel inside, I unloaded a couple of the lighter flat packs and leaned them up against the car.

"Shall I help you?" The voice came from right behind me.

I yelped and turned around to find the Frost Giant kid grinning at me.

"You came back?" I said.

"Yes. I wished to see you."

"Well, here I am. Still no elixir, though."

"That is too bad." He glanced around. "I have been sent to ask. Where is the vitki?"

"Inside with a friend of his, but they'll be right back."

He turned and looked at the front door just as it opened. Billy came out, stopped, and stared. "Whoa! Who the hell is that?"

"Ah, there is the friend! Now I shall go."

The kid vanished.

Billy trotted over to me, his normally I-live-in-front-of-my-computer pale face even paler. "Was there really someone here?"

"Yep," I said, "a Frost Giant. Just a young one, though."

"Jesus! Sometimes hanging out with Tor—the things you see can take years off a guy's life."

"What made you believe in his sorcery, anyway?"

"The things I saw that took years off my life." Billy gave me a grin, then hefted one of the flat packs. "Now we get to put all this stuff together. Tor's useless at that, by the way."

"Good thing I'm not."

Reinforcements arrived about ten minutes later when JJ and Aaron drove up in JJ's old gray heap, a Honda that had seen better days. Both of them had to hear about the bear spirit and Tor's cut face before we all got down to work. Aaron, a tall, skinny dude with a mop of curly brown hair, worked for a software company doing something arcane with security measures. He also, it turned out, loved three dimensional puzzles. Although his serious Asperger's kept him from understanding other people at times, IKEA directions presented no problems. He got the elaborate storage unit together faster than I thought possible and started on the work table. Billy and JJ assembled the easel while I finished the bookcase. Tor supervised by bringing down a cooler full of bottled beer.

We were standing around in my newly furnished studio when Tor's phone rang. He set his beer down on the work table and answered it. His eyes widened in surprise as the person on the other end identified himself.

"Thank you, sir," Tor said. "It's good of you to call."

Tor hurried out of the room and down the hall to the library to finish his conversation. Billy raised an eyebrow in JJ's direction.

JJ shrugged. "No idea, man."

While Tor continued talking in the other room, I unwrapped the protective padding from my canvas and set it on the easel. We had enough time to fetch the boxes of paints and other supplies from the Land Rover before Tor finally returned. He slipped his phone into his jeans pocket and picked up his bottle of beer.

"That was my faculty advisor," Tor said. "You guys remember him."

"The crusty old dude, yeah," Billy said.

"What was all that about?" JJ asked.

"My uncle's death. The cops were at Cal, checking out

my history. They wanted to know if I'm really a spoiled rich kid or some kind of drug dealer. They'd need a warrant to get into my bank records, and I guess they're not ready for a step like that."

"Fuck!" JJ shook his head in disbelief. "What is this? They think you killed him?"

"Oh yeah. I'm the one he tried to shoot. Pretty obvious candidate for the guy who might have shot back. Except he wasn't shot, of course. They don't know what killed him."

"Then why are they so fucking sure he was murdered?" Billy said.

"Because he was found dead in the middle of a parking lot miles from his apartment and his car. Can't be muggers, or they'd have cleaned out his wallet. He was carrying three hundred bucks in cash."

Aaron took off his glasses and wiped them on the hem of his tee shirt. He frowned, nodding to himself, as he thought things through. He looked up and put the glasses back on.

"Tor?" Aaron said. "Did you kill him?"

"No," Tor said. "To my eternal regret, I didn't."

"Do you know who did?"

Tor sighed. I knew he was thinking of his vow. "Yeah," Tor said. "I do."

Aaron gave him one of his horizontal straight-line smiles. "Who was it?"

"Hey!" Billy stepped forward and laid a gentle hand on Aaron's arm. "Enough."

"Hey yourself! I'm just curious."

An odd thought occurred to me—test out the truth. "I did," I said. "I killed him."

JJ muttered something I couldn't quite hear, then laughed under his breath. Billy grinned.

Aaron blinked at me. "Ah," he said eventually. "A joke."

"Don't let it bug you." Tor raised his beer bottle in my direction like a toast. "She's got a weird sense of humor."

"Aaron, look," JJ said. "What if the cops came around to ask us questions? Like, do we know who killed the wicked uncle? Suppose it's someone we know. Would you want to tell them the truth?"

"Oh!" Aaron beamed at him. "I get it. We don't want to know."

"Good man." JJ rummaged in the cooler. "Have another beer!"

"Thanks." Aaron took the bottle from him. "I could have a look at their site. See what they're thinking."

"Whoa!" Tor said. "That's dangerous, hacking into police files."

"Only dangerous if I get caught." Aaron paused for a swallow of beer. "And I won't."

"Up to you, dude," Tor said. "Sure, I want to know, but hey, these are the cops."

"Yeah. So?" Aaron paused for another horizontal grin. "I've got a polymorphic trojan all set up on an auxiliary box."

Billy choked on his beer, which I took as meaning he actually understood what Aaron had said. The rest of us tried to look as if we did. While Billy coughed, Aaron took out his smartphone and accessed the police department's public website.

"Can you get in?" Billy said.

"They've got all kinds of citizen access built right onto the site," Aaron said. "Email for all kinds of things. Port 25 will be up and running real soon now."

"Uh, look," Tor broke in. "I don't want you to get into any trouble."

"There won't be any trouble."

Aaron and Tor had a lot in common sometimes.

Although Tor offered to take everyone out to dinner, the guys begged off and left soon after. Tor saw them to their cars, then came back, lugging an old wooden kitchen chair. He placed it in a corner of the studio and sat down to watch me as I unpacked and stowed away my painting supplies.

"You didn't tell me," I said, "that the cops suspect you killed Nils."

"I figured you knew. I'm the logical choice. That's why

you could confess six times over, and they wouldn't believe you. They'd think you were trying to protect me out of a pure woman's devotion. All women are self-sacrificing angels, aren't you?"

"How much beer have you had, anyway?"

"Only one. I'm just naturally sentimental about pure womanhood."

"Oh yeah sure! I thought the cops were after Valdez and that other buddy of Roman's."

"I bet they're on the list, too. Right behind me. Or maybe tied for first."

I concentrated on loading jars of acrylic into drawers. Had my deep wound of guilt made me blind? Apparently so. I'd convinced myself that the police suspected me when all the time, it was Tor they were after. At the worst, in their eyes I'd be a clue leading back to him. They might wonder, for instance, if Nils had assaulted me and Tor wanted revenge. Another ugly thought clawed at my mind.

"What if they want a swab of my DNA?" I said. "You know, from my cheek. Because of that bite."

"They won't. I made sure of that."

I spun around to stare at him. He smiled blandly back. "Tor—"

"I cast an aversion spell over you. And a couple of wards. Do you remember when they barged in to interrogate Roman at the hospital? They never even looked your way. If I keep refining the spell, they might even forget who you are. That's what I'm working toward."

"I—" I groped for words. "I guess I should thank you. But—"

Tor got up, smiling, and walked over to me. "I keep telling you, Maya, I'm a barbarian. I don't give a shit about due process of law. You're mine, and that comes first with me. I intend to keep you safe. No matter what it takes. Okay?"

"Not if it lands you in jail instead of me."

"It won't. I might have helped him along his way when I broke his wrist, but I didn't kill him. I wish I had."

"Tor, how can you say that?"

"Because it's true."

"Because I'd be off the hook that way?"

"That, too, but basically, because I hated his guts."

He was standing with his thumbs tucked into his leather belt, his head thrown a little back, watching me with a small smile. Barbarian. Oh yes, I saw it, all right. I saw something else, that the cold, lawless side of him attracted me sexually even as it frightened me. Halfway between Björn and Audo, I thought. For a moment he seemed to be waiting for me to make a comment; then he shrugged. He laid his hands on either side of my face and kissed me open-mouthed.

"Okay?" he said.

"Okay."

I felt more frightened than reassured, but he kissed me again before I could say anything more. Élan oozed from the cut on his cheek. He smelled like sweat and beer, a raw male scent that turned me into the female animal in heat. I reached up and pulled him down for another kiss. His hands slid down to my buttocks, and he pressed me against him.

"Let's go upstairs," he whispered.

We never made it that far. In a corner of the library room was a sagging old couch, narrow, awkward, but good enough because it was close to hand. I stepped out of my jeans and panties and flopped down on the cushions. I had to keep one foot on the floor to leave room for him to kneel between my legs. He slid his jeans halfway down, far enough, because neither of us could wait any longer. A few thrusts, and I climaxed, sobbing under him, just as he came.

He rolled off to kneel beside the couch and rest his upper body against me. I stroked his hair and listened as his breathing slowed back to a normal rhythm. With a sharp sigh he lifted his head, smiled at me, and stood up, wincing a little.

"Shit, my back!" he said. "This is worse than the back seat of a car."

"I know what you mean."

"Oh yeah? How do you know?"

"Huh! How do *you* know? I don't suppose we've got any tissues."

He pulled off his tee shirt and delicately dropped it onto my stomach. "Might as well use that."

I cleaned up while he pulled up his jeans. We made ourselves just decent enough to get upstairs, where we showered and changed our clothes. Once we were respectable again, we went out for dinner like normal people.

One of Tor's favorite restaurants lived in an old Victorian house on Berkeley's Gourmet Row. No, not Chez Panisse, although this place owed a lot to them as a model. When we arrived without reservations, the hostess seated us immediately at a primo table in a bay window, which told me how much money Tor must have spent there in the past. White linen, nice china, comfortable chairs, and a view of a garden—perfectly lovely until Tor looked around the dining room and muttered "oh shit!" under his breath.

I followed his glance and saw a couple seated at a table across the room in an alcove. The young woman was gorgeous, tall, with auburn hair, perfect features, perfect makeup, modest kelly green dress—real silk as far as I could tell. The man, some thirty years older, had gray hair, streaked with a little red, and wore a gray business suit. She glanced our way, noticed us, and did a classic double-take.

"Old girlfriend?" I said.

"Yeah." Tor picked up the menu.

"That her dad?"

"Yeah." He opened the menu and raised it to hide his face.

I took the hint, shut up, and opened my own. When we ordered, the waiter took the menus away and left Tor with no place to hide. While we ate our first couple of courses, I noticed the O.G. across the room glancing our way now and then while she and her dad worked their way through the wine list with their meal. For a change, Tor restricted himself to one glass of white wine, which told me he anticipated a Scene, so I did the same.

The Scene, however, arrived in the women's restroom. To

reach it I had to pass by the O.G.'s table. I'd just gotten inside the clean, well-lit anteroom when she followed me in. I could smell the wine practically oozing from her pores.

"So," she said, "you're Tor's latest, are you? Lucky old you!"

I felt like slapping her, but a girl fight in a public toilet struck me as a totally awful way to spend an evening. I smiled and said nothing.

She set her hands on her hips and glared at me. "Is he still a major nutcase?"

I had to say something. "I wouldn't call him that."

"You will. Trust me, you will! He looks so good at first, doesn't he? But just wait till he starts talking about the runes and all that crap."

By then I really had to pee. I darted into one of the stalls and locked the door. I was hoping she'd just go away, but when I finished and came out again, she was still standing by the marble-topped vanity.

"What is it you really want to say?" I said. "Did he dump you?"

Her turn to stay silent. I washed up while she watched me. I got a couple of paper towels from a wicker basket and began drying my hands.

"Well, what is it?" I said. "Why did you follow me in here?"

"I don't know." Her mouth trembled. "I think I wanted to warn you. Sorry."

"Warn me or cause trouble for him?"

That made her cry. Since I didn't know what else to do, I threw the towels into the waste bin and grabbed a handful of tissues from the box on the vanity. When I offered her the wad, she took it and dabbed at her tears.

"Did he dump you?" I said again.

"No." Her voice sounded thick with wine and frustration both. "I dumped him. I had to, I just had to. But it hurt."

"Did you really love him?"

"No. Well, kind of. A crush, I guess. I never really liked sex, y'know, until—" She blushed so deeply that her dusting of freckles showed through her make-up. "But god, he's crazy!

All that sorcery crap. Have you heard his rant yet?"

"Uh, yes. It sounds real to me."

"You believe it?"

"Yeah."

"Then it's lucky you guys found each other." She clutched the tissues tighter and stared at me. "Where did you meet him? In a therapy group?"

Before I could answer, she turned and fled with a clatter of high heels on the tile floor. The door slammed behind her. I waited for a minute or two before I left the restroom. By then she was sitting with her dad again and wiping her smeared eye make-up on a white linen napkin. Tor had moved his chair and place setting around so he could sit with his back toward her. When I sat back down, he stared at his empty plate.

"Well, that was interesting," I said.

Tor raised his head and looked at me. "It ended pretty badly. The time I spent with her, I mean."

"I gathered that."

He winced.

"Y'know," I said, "you're not as big a monster as you think you are, if that bothers you."

"Thanks. I guess. I felt shamed. That I didn't handle it better."

"Shamed?" I stared at him.

He shrugged the question away. "I don't want to talk about it."

"Fair enough."

I hadn't told him about my previous boyfriends, either. I concentrated on cleaning up the perfect wine sauce with the last few bites of my pork medallions. I did notice that the O.G. and her father were getting up to leave. When I re-layed the news, Tor turned tense, but they swept by us and out without saying anything. He relaxed with a long sigh of relief and ordered more wine.

When we returned home, I changed into my painting jeans and an old tee shirt and went downstairs to gloat over my new studio. I hadn't planned on working in the artificial light, but studying the landscape canvas made me wonder where I was going to place the image of the corpse. Acrylic provides a good surface for the indecisive. I picked up a stick of natural charcoal and sketched in the shape. Fail! I wiped it off with a rag and tried another placement. Still wrong. I removed the sketch, then put the rag and the charcoal down on the work table.

Wait till morning, I decided, but I lingered, staring at the canvas. Where on the long sweep of snow had Mia found him? The memory image had become faint and fuzzy in my mind. I retained a word memory, the knowledge of what I'd remembered, rather than a clear picture. Where exactly had he been lying? I concentrated on the faint image, tried to clarify it, augment it so I could find the proper spot.

I felt a chill and crossed my arms over my chest so I could rub them. That damn air conditioning again, I thought. Tor kept it up high no matter how big the electric bill was. A cold breeze lifted my hair away from my face. I looked over my shoulder at the vent for the heat and air conditioning—down at floor level, and closed. I turned back and found that the painting, the frame and the easel, that is, had disappeared. I shivered, because I was standing in snow up to mid-calf with the long slope rising before me. Dawn touched the distant peaks with pink light.

I was watching a woman struggling to run uphill. She wore a long brown skirt and a sweater and high boots, no jacket, no scarf, and no hat over her tousled blonde bob. The snow clotted the hem of her skirt, clutched at it as if it were trying to slow her down, to stop her insane climb in the freezing weather. Mia. I knew what she was going to find. I tried to call out and warn her, but the wind blew my words away. I could feel the élan of Niflheim swirling around me and breathed deep. It strengthened me, but it also called to me. *We are Isa incarnate*, it whispered. *Escape to the ice. Leave your life and lover behind. The wraiths are waiting where you belong.*

"No!"

I spun around. I could see a narrow space like a door

that led back into the studio. I turned and ran for it, dashed through and nearly rammed myself into the work table in the process. The room felt warm and real. The landscape was only a painting. But my feet and ankles were soaked with snow melt. I sat down on the floor before I fell down and shivered, but not from cold.

Footsteps came pounding down the hall. Tor rushed into the room. I looked up gape-mouthed. Words had deserted me.

"The nisse came and got me," Tor said. "What happened? Wait—what? How did you get so wet?"

"Snow." I pointed at the painting. "It swallowed me. Or something. I went inside it."

Tor whistled under his breath. He glanced around the studio, grabbed the charcoal stick from the work table, and walked up to the easel. With the charcoal he drew a pair of runes on the sky of the painting: Sowilo and Othala.

"Try to go into it now," he said. "I bet you can't. I've marked it as the sun's odal land."

I got up and stood staring into the painting, made myself remember Mia's run through the clinging snow. I could remember the cold—my wet ankles and calves took care of that—but I stayed where I was.

"Thanks." Dumb thing to say, but I had no energy for eloquence. "I need to discuss this with Liv."

"Well, you could tell me about it first."

"She's the one who knows about image magic. Obviously you don't, or you would have warned me this could happen."

"Hey! Why are you so pissed off?"

"You wanted me to develop my talents." I felt like hitting something, someone, anything. "Well, I did. Thanks a lot! How am I supposed to paint if this is going to keep happening?"

"It's not going to keep happening." Tor smiled in full arrogance mode. "You've got me to—"

"Fat lot of good that'll do me."

He kept on smiling. I picked up the paint rag and threw it at his face. He ducked, and it draped over his shoulder. He picked it off, tossed it back onto the table, and made a serious mistake.

"Maya," he said, "be reasonable."

"Oh go to hell!"

I strode past him, and as I went out of the door, I flicked off the lights and left him in the dark.

"Hey! What?"

I slammed the door, too, and nearly whacked him with it because he was right behind me. As I headed for the stairs, I heard him following. I ran up the stairs, but with his longer legs he caught me in the living room. By then I was panting for breath and feeling more than a little stupid. We sat down facing each other on the couch.

"Okay," Tor said, "what is all this?"

"I told you. I feel like you pushed me into something I can't handle."

"You can learn to handle it. All I was trying to say is I'd show you how to get control of it."

"It's the fucking arrogant way you say it."

He winced.

"Hah!" I said. "You've heard that before, haven't you? From your old girlfriends."

He crossed his arms over his chest and looked into the empty fireplace.

"Besides, if it wasn't for the nisse, you'd never have known," I said. "And maybe I'd have been stuck there."

"I already knew something was wrong." Tor kept his voice level. "It merely told me where to look."

Thanks to his vow, I knew he was telling the truth.

"Besides," he continued, "you got out by yourself, didn't you?"

"Well, yeah." The importance of my escape finally dawned on me. "I did. I really did."

"Okay." He uncrossed his arms, but he gave me one of his smug smiles. "You want to know why you're so angry?"

"I know damn well why I'm angry."

He went on as if he hadn't heard me. "You summoned a

lot of magical energy. And you must have absorbed a lot of élan from the snow. But you didn't earth it out once you got back. Because you don't know how."

I considered hissing and snarling at him. Yet I could feel the extra energy simmering in my blood, seeking an outlet—rage, magic, whatever. Any outlet would do.

"Okay, Mr. Mighty Sorcerer," I said. "How exactly do I do that?"

"There are ritual gestures you need to do when you finish a magical operation." He grinned, but in the way I loved, with his cute dimple and all. "But I can think of something even better."

"I'd rather you showed me the ritual."

"You're sure?" He slid over next to me and slipped an arm around my shoulders. "Tell me to stop, and I'll let you go and teach you the gestures." He bent his head and nuzzled the side of my neck. "Just say no." He laid a hand on my breast.

'No' refused to leave my mouth. He kissed me and sealed it in.

After we finished making love, Tor fell asleep. I got up, dressed, and went into the Burne-Jones bedroom to fetch my laptop. On the alchemical barometer, a pair of doves flew in a clear sky, surrounded by a ring of butterflies.

"Doves are totally aggressive birds, despite the bill and coo," I said. "Or is that your point?"

The desk remained silent, probably out of fear of incriminating itself. I returned to the living room couch and settled in to write a long email to Liv. I'd just sent it off when I heard a wolf howling: Tor's ringtone. I hurried into the bedroom and saw him sitting up crosslegged on the bed with the phone.

"That's real strange," Tor was saying. "I'm glad you told me." He paused to listen. "Yeah, you bet I'll try to figure this out. Be careful, will you? Don't go out at night alone." He listened for a moment more, then clicked off.

"What?" I said.

"That was Billy. He looked out of his bedroom window and saw a Frost Giant standing on the lawn, staring at him.

He opened the window and yelled at him, like a jerk. The jotunn disappeared. This time."

"Oh my god! Billy doesn't live alone, does he?"

"No, he shares a house with a couple of other guys. But there's not a lot the three of them can do against a twelve foot high dude with a battle axe."

"Twelve feet?"

"He had to stoop to see in the window." Tor laid the phone down on the nightstand. "I'd better get dressed. Get downstairs. I need to cast the runes."

Tor said nothing about the reading once he'd finished. I picked up the vibe that I shouldn't ask. First thing next morning, though, and fortunately it was a Saturday, Tor called Billy. While I finished my breakfast, they squabbled back and forth. Billy wanted to drive over to our house, while Tor insisted that he stay inside at his place until Tor could get there. Eventually Tor won.

"I'm going to jump over," he told me. "That'll scare any giants shitless if they're watching. A display of vitki power."

"Are you going to draw runes and staves on the house?"

"Yes. And on Billy." He grinned at me. "You're catching on."

"Don't cut yourself again, will you? It's so icky."

Tor rolled his eyes and refused to answer. I went downstairs with him while he assembled his weapons, as he called them: the rune knife, the special paint, and some Sharpies, because their ink wouldn't wash off easily, for drawing runes on Billy.

"You shouldn't use that kind of ink on skin," I said. "It's dangerous to humans."

"Angry giants would be worse."

I couldn't argue with that.

"What are you going to do while I'm gone?" Tor said.

"Work on my senior project."

"Sounds good. I'll be back as soon as I can. I might have Billy with me, I might not. Depends on how sensible he's willing to be."

Tor kissed me goodbye, then jogged outside to the back yard. I watched him through the sliding glass doors in the library room. First he drew a sprawling equal armed cross with a piece of chalk on the patch of cracking concrete at one side. He slung his backpack over one shoulder and took three precise steps that brought him on top of the symbol. At the point where the arms crossed, he vanished.

I went to my studio and considered the landscape sitting on my easel. I needed to add Audo's dead body, the last important compositional element. Besides the white slope and the distant peaks, I'd added the dark masses of forest to either side of the snow, but I'd done the trees as figures from a German Expressionist silent film, distorted shapes, leaning inward, toothed and jagged forms, as though Life longed to despoil the purity of Death. At the moment the whole thing really did look too much like a still from a Disney movie, but the corpse would fix that.

I hoped, anyway. I made sketches on paper, then transferred the best of them to the right location, a slight hollow partway up the slope, close enough to the hypothetical viewer to allow me to add detail to the form. I did an underpainting in pale blue to tie the corpse in with the snowy background, which I'd also underpainted to produce faint spectral shadows. Before I went any further, the underpainting had to dry. I stepped back and considered the overall composition.

I'd placed the body correctly, but did it look like him? I can't articulate why, but making a portrait of that final moment mattered. I remembered him as lying on his back, one arm flung out to the side, the other cradling an empty whiskey bottle to his chest. Did I have it right? I tried to tell myself it didn't matter, but I wanted the painting to be perfect.

I picked up the paint rag and wiped out the runes Tor had drawn on the sky. Immediately I felt the cold air rush out from the snowscape. I dropped the rag and took a step forward. Once again, I was standing in the snow, knee-deep this time. Élan swirled around me, succored me, gave me the strength to stand in the freezing cold even though I was wearing a pair of white shorts, an old tee shirt, and nothing more.

I heard someone down the slope cry out: Mia, babbling in German. I understood nothing but her tone of voice, so angry, reproachful that he'd died without her. Like a drift of snow carried on the wind I floated downhill until I stood among the snow wraiths who had come to watch. Although some of the wraiths glanced my way, no one objected to my presence at my previous death. Yes, I'd drawn Audo's pose correctly. That was my main concern as I stood and observed my former self ready herself for suicide. Around me the wraiths murmured and wrote their crystal voices on the air. The she-wraith stepped forward and knelt by Mia as she lay down next to her dead love.

Far down the hill men shouted. The villagers were coming. I turned and looked back the way I'd come and thought of the studio, thought of Tor, as well, and the way I loved him. The tunnel-door opened to lead me back. I slogged uphill through the snow, reached the gateway, and hurried inside to my studio room. In front of the easel, a scatter of snow lay melting on the floor. I could just make out a shadow-image of the actual, physical painting hovering in the tunnel mouth. I grabbed the charcoal from the table and drew Sowilo and Othala in the sky that somehow was also a surface.

The air turned warm around me. The snowscape snapped back to existing only as acrylic paint on canvas. Despite the élan I'd gathered, my legs were blue and shaky with cold. I rubbed them, then hobbled out and headed down the hall. By the time I reached the stairs, the feeling had returned to my skin and muscles. I made a mental note to dress properly if I ever needed to go into the snow again. If I got wet, or if the snow touched bare skin, I'd feel the cold just like anyone else. My twisted DNA could only protect me so far.

I put on my sweatpants and one of Tor's flannel shirts. He'd left some coffee in the carafe. I warmed it up in the microwave and sat at the breakfast bar to drink it. Once the aching cold left my body, it dawned on me that I might have stumbled on a way to get the élan I needed, even if I couldn't summon it the way that Tor did.

I took my coffee into the living room, where I'd left a sketchbook and a box of Conté sticks on the coffee table. I concentrated on the memory of the day my dad had taken me and Roman out of school to go to the snow. I summoned a clear image of a pine tree, its branches loaded with snow, that grew near a white drift over rocks. As soon as I sketched in a jagged line to represent the trees farther up the hill, I felt cool air and smelled the rich honey and roses scent of élan.

For a few minutes I breathed deep and luxuriated in the energy oozing from the drawing. How to turn it off? I found a piece of charcoal in my box of implements and drew Sowilo and Othala in the sky. The scent vanished and took the spray of cold air with it. Worked like a charm, I thought, and then realized I had indeed just worked a charm. Once my success would have creeped me out, but this particular magic meant too much for me to get all drama queen over it.

Since I'd finally warmed up, I changed into my old jeans and a dry tee shirt, then practically ran down the stairs to my studio room. I found a canvas board small enough to carry in my backpack and did a colored drawing in acrylics of the snowscape I'd previously sketched. A thick coat of gloss medium covered a patch of sky, so I could draw and wipe off the runes as many times as I needed to stop or release the magic. People with breathing difficulties have to travel with cumbersome oxygen tanks. I was lucky enough to have what I needed come in a convenient package. Eventually, maybe, I'd be able to conjure élan from the natural world like Tor did. In the meantime, I no longer needed to ask him for it. I no longer needed to steal it, either, from the people around me.

For the first time in my life, I was free.

I wept in a flood of tears, but out of joy.

CHAPTER 10

I can't figure out why they'd spy on Billy," Tor said. "Unless they wondered if he's another vitki."

Tor had returned late that Saturday afternoon. It had taken him hours, he told me, to carve and paint all the necessary runes on Billy's rented house. The roommates had objected until Billy promised to reimburse their shares of the cleaning deposit. When the landlord saw the damage, and you know he would, sooner or later, he was going to raise hell.

"The place is filthy anyway," Tor told me. "I don't know why they're worried. They're not going to get one single buck back when they move. Anyway, I drew a protective rune helm on Billy, and I hope he doesn't wash it off. He's got a hot date tonight, he told me. I made him take his shower before I started decorating his back."

"If things get interesting, I wonder what she'll think of the runes?"

"That's what's worrying him." Tor looked briefly sour. "I told him, body art's a trend. Run with it. But anyway, I've been gone a long time. You must need élan by now."

"No, actually, I don't. I've figured out how to get it for myself."

Tor blinked a couple of times. "Already?"

"Well, it's kind of a kludge, but it works."

He sat up straighter, his neck rigid, his head tilted a little back, and his face became utterly expressionless—just for a few seconds. He smiled and said, "Yeah? I mean, hey, that's great!"

I didn't believe his enthusiasm for a minute. "I'll show you if you'd like."

"Sure. I mean, that's really wonderful." His smile turned as fake as a Halloween mask.

"Tor! What's wrong?"

"Nothing."

"Oh come on!"

He sighed and looked away. "Okay, sure, I'm disappointed. I really get off on feeding you. You always look so happy."

"You can keep on doing it if you want to. Your way is lots faster, and I enjoy it, too. It's kind of like you're kissing me."

"You're just saying that to make me feel better."

What would have been a whine from someone else was only another dodge. At that point I realized that I was seeing through a new kind of illusion. I was afraid to call him on it.

"No, I'm not! I told you, the trick I figured out is clumsy. Slow. It just means I can feed myself if you're gone or doing something you can't stop. Y'know, emergencies."

"Okay." He finally smiled for real. "And I can teach you how to harvest it from the air. Well, if you still want me to."

"Of course I do."

I kissed him, then got up to fetch the colored drawing for my demo. When I finished, he spent a couple of minutes studying the drawing. I studied him and saw in his unguarded expression a welter of feelings, hard to untangle, but one stood out. I gathered my courage.

"Tor?" I said. "I love you. You don't have to use the élan thing to make sure I stay with you."

He raised his head and looked at me, his eyes wide, his lips half-parted.

"That's it, isn't it? Control?"

"Yeah." He handed me the drawing and stood up. "I'm going downstairs."

He stomped off before I could think of what else to say. I put the drawing away. I was just wondering if I should follow him down when he returned.

"I'm sorry," Tor said. "You did something really cool, and

I acted like a jerk."

"Do you really think it's cool?"

"Of course I do."

"Okay. Thank you."

He held out his arms, and I hurried to his embrace. Neither of us mentioned the issue again.

Sunday morning Billy called to tell Tor two things, that he hadn't seen any more Frost Giants, and that the girlfriend loved the rune art. He was thinking of getting a tattoo, and would Tor draw him up a couple of designs?

"Of course I will," Tor told me. "If he's going to keep hanging out with me, he probably needs some kind of permanent ward. Aaron and JJ, too. And you."

"I can't stand needles. It makes me sick to just think about it."

"I could draw them on you."

"No, can't you make me another pendant? An anti-giant rune stave?"

"That'd work. Okay, but if and only if you promise me you'll wear it whenever you leave the house."

"Don't worry! I'll promise you, swear on anything you want."

We went downstairs together, Tor to design the wards, and me to work on the problem of representing snow wraiths in paint. I tried Maxfield Parrish's technique of using a turquoise blue underpainting. Under white, I figured, it would reproduce the icy glow and oddly fluid sense of solidity I'd seen. On a small canvas I laid in a ground of dead grass yellow, modeled to indicate the terrain, added an underpainting of dilute thalo blue, and built up the snow field from there. Then came the turquoise underpainting and finally, for the snow wraith herself, white with icy shadows. She most definitely did not look like a Halloween decoration. Thanks to the related blues of the underpaintings, she looked of the snow yet separate from the snow, a being, not an illusion.

Tor knocked on my door. "I've finished the talisman."

I opened the door and waved him in. He handed me

a smooth round of oak carved with a bindrune: a reversed Thurisaz, the rune signifying the jötnar, guarded round with Tiwaz and Elhaz. He took a leather thong out of his shirt pocket, threaded it through the roundel, then tied the ends together. When I slipped it over my head, it hung just below my collar bone.

"Perfect," I said. "Thank you."

"Remember, wear it whenever you leave the house. I've done the designs for the guys. I'm going to call them and see if we can get together at the tattoo parlor on Monday. I don't want to waste any time with giants hanging around." Tor was looking over the studio as he talked. "What's that on your easel? Can I see?"

"Sure. It's kind of a portrait."

He studied the she-wraith for several minutes. First he stepped back to get a long view, then moved closer to study the details of her face, the pale blue lips and eyes, and her hands with their ice chip nails.

"Whoa!" he said. "That's really good. And frightening. I wouldn't trust a word she says, if she appears to you again."

"She kept her word to Mia."

He raised an eyebrow in my direction. When I told him about Mia's death, he listened with the same serious attention he'd paid to the portrait.

"You need to go farther back if you're going to understand this," Tor said when I was finished. "How you got connected to the wraiths in the first place."

"Farther back into my past lives, you mean?"

"Yeah. That. Start with Magda and see if you can go beyond her. Backwards, I mean. And remember that the Nazis tried to wipe out the Romany tribes, too."

He'd given me just the boost I needed. She'd been a Romany girl, Magda, sold by her father against all of her tribes' traditions and laws because he'd fallen into a desperate alcoholism. I drew like a madwoman. I started with her affair with Kristjan, then tried working backwards to her childhood. In a week I'd filled a large sketchbook with pieces of a life that was at least mostly Magda's. As I drew, it hardly seemed important how accurate, measured against some objective reality, the images were. They held meaning for me and, I was willing to bet, would have been meaningful to her.

During that week I hardly touched my senior project, although I did realize that I could use some of the Romany imagery for it. While I worked upstairs, Tor worked down below on taming the cave bear spirit. After their battle, she needed coaxing, he told me, but he felt her presence close by.

"I can't follow her out, is the problem," he told me. "She belongs to another world, one of the eight beyond Midgard. If I can tame her, she'll be my guide and take me there, but until I do, she can always hide from me."

Now and then, as I sat drawing in the living room, I heard him chanting galdrar. The deep vibration of his voice, reaching me from a distance, made me imagine ancient shamans sending their messages to the spirit world. I started to sketch one of them, based on some illos I'd seen of modern shamans in Siberia, but the image made me so uneasy I stopped. Something evil had happened to me, not out on the steppes of Siberia, but in the northlands of Europe, where they chanted as Tor was chanting, invoking runes. The only other thing I remembered in connection with this possible memory was the feel of leather thongs biting into my wrists.

I had just started a new sketchbook when I saw an image of a different past life: a dark, dirty doorway in some city, maybe in the 18th century, maybe Paris. As I drew it, I realized it led to upstairs rooms where I lived with my parents. I tried every trick I knew, but I never got another image that fit with that one, only a memory of burning with fever. I must have died shortly after.

Over the next few weeks, I filled that second sketchbook with pieces of imagery, some of them solid scenes, like a birch tree by a spring, some of them incomprehensible patterns of light and shadow. In between these extremes were fragments, such as a crude wooden cup, a frog sitting on a wet stone, a man's hand missing a couple of fingers, a slice of dark bread on a cracked plate. They could have come from anywhere and any time. All of them indicated poverty, a hard life somewhere in the countryside. No wealthy noble ladies or famous artists for me! My soul must have lived like the vast majority of people have always lived—on the edge of civilization, dying young, working hard to grow enough food to keep working.

When Tor asked, I showed him the images. He agreed about the hard lives.

"Me, too," he said. "I always hoped I'd been part of the Varangian Guard in Constantinople, or sailed with Leif Ericson, but no such luck. A couple of lives farming and herding cattle, and some in a warband, and then I was a wanna-be Viking killed on his first raid. After that it was merchant families all the way to Kristjan."

"Nothing glamorous. Me either."

"But y'know, you might have had an incredible talent for art in one of those lives. You would never have had the chance to develop it."

"Sad but true, yeah. You must have had some contact with rune magic."

"Everybody did. In the old days, magic wasn't shoved off to the side of life. It wasn't a big secret, not until the Christians got control, anyway. Then it hid in the dark, but now we can work in the sunlight again."

We. Not just him, but me, included in that we. I thought of the Old Girlfriend, and her nasty crack about Tor and me belonging together. She was right enough.

"I guess I must have some contact with some kind of magic, too. Tarot cards, probably, if I was a Romany child. But I'm sure not getting anything more about snow wraiths."

"Keep working at it. They must have known you from somewhere." He frowned, thinking. "It could have been pretty far back as we measure time. The wights—all the different kinds—live in worlds that we'd consider timeless. I've got no idea how they judge time or if they even do."

"The snow wraith who knew me, y'know? He did tell Mia he was meeting her again. And he said, 'at last', too."

"Which shows some idea of ordering events, yeah. And a sense of duration. Who knows how precise either one of those is, though?"

A big help—not. Still, it gave me a line of thought, a slender thread that might, if I followed it carefully enough, lead me back into the past.

We also went to the City to visit my brother in the hospital a number of times during those weeks. Finally, on a Tuesday morning, Brittany called me with the news we'd been expecting. Roman had healed to the point where the hospital needed to move him into a VA rehabilitation facility. The only place that had an opening was in Palo Alto. Tor and I drove in that afternoon for a conference with Dr. Mellars. I was relieved by how good Roman looked. He sat up normally in bed, and his eyes were alert and clear. Mellars came straight out with his opinion.

"I'm not worried about you regaining muscle strength," Mellars said to Roman. "It's the morphine that's going to be the problem, isn't it? Getting you clean and then off drugs for good?"

Roman winced and nodded a yes.

"I know the therapy group you've been in," Mellars said. "It's a good one, but there's a limit to what they can do. Do you really want to clean up, Cantescu?"

"Sure." But Roman kept looking down at the blankets on his bed, not at any of us. "For Brit's sake if nothing else."

"Idea," Tor said. "What about a private rehab facility, like that Sonoma ranch? The one that thinks it's Betty Ford North."

"Wonderful idea," Mellars said. "But he doesn't have any insurance. Do you know what that place costs?"

"Yeah, actually, I do. I can pick up the tab." Tor turned to Brittany. "You won't be able to visit him there, not at first."

"I can live with that if it helps him." Brit was watching Roman. "Can you stick with it?"

Roman raised his head to give her a crooked smile. He was shaking, I realized, an uncontrollable tremor in his hands and around his mouth.

"It won't be easy," Mellars said. "But you're a Marine at heart, damn it. You've got the guts, if you want to go for this."

"You saved Maya's life," Tor put in. "I owe you."

Roman caught my glance. I mouthed the word "please."

"Okay," he said. "I've lived through worse things."

"Good." Tor turned to Mellars. "Let's get the paperwork done. You'll need to call for the referral."

"Come to my office. I've finished my hospital rounds, and I've got some time."

They left, talking quietly of official decisions. Brittany perched on the edge of the bed and took Roman's hand. He smiled at her, but he went on trembling. None of us spoke until Tor came back. He had a handful of papers for Roman to sign and a second handful for Brittany to read. As the three of them discussed the move, I realized that by going into the therapy program, Roman was basically signing his freedom away. He'd be as much out of his own control as he'd been when he'd enlisted in the Marines. I could only hope he'd stick it out. Settling everything took a couple of hours, partly because Roman would have to travel in an ambulance. The VA, or so a hospital admin person told us, would pick up the tab for that.

Once Tor had settled everything, I gave Roman a hug, the first time I could hug him without worrying about the wound on his back.

"You can do this," I said.

"Sounds like I'll have plenty of help." Roman took a deep breath. "What the hell, it sure beats Iraq." He turned to look at Tor. "Hey. Thanks."

"Welcome," Tor said. "I mean it. I owe you."

They shook hands, and we left. On the drive home, a question nagged at me. I waited until we'd gotten clear of the bridge traffic to ask it.

"Tor, how did you know how much this rehab place costs?"

"A while ago I paid someone else's fees."

I waited. He never told me more.

Family matters, especially Halvar's various legacies,

remained very much a part of Tor's present. A couple of days later, Joel sent him email to say that he was coming west to settle up a last few details of his father's will. He was hoping "to get together, maybe at that Indian restaurant where I ran into you."

"Can you face him, Maya?" Tor said.

"Sure, out in public like that." I hoped I was speaking the truth.

"I found some things I need to give him. Stuck in one of Halvar's journals. Some pictures of Joel as a kid with—I guess—his mom. The old bastard gloated over having another grandson."

"I guess he wasn't all bad, huh?"

"Maybe. Who knows what plans he had for us? Me and Joel, I mean. Spare parts for his old age? Could be." Tor paused to bring up the lunar calendar on his laptop. "Okay, Joel's visit. He'll get here before the full moon, so we can have dinner."

"You're still worried about the moon? Do you think you'll turn into the bjarki again?"

"I'm hoping I won't, but let's plan for the worst."

That afternoon Tor put a deposit down on my engagement ring. I would have been perfectly happy with something from a franchise jeweler in the mall, but Tor heaped scorn on that idea. He took me to a shop down in Berkeley, a narrow slice of a store between two larger ones, where he knew the craftsman personally. The sign painted on the glass door read simply "Diego's Jewelry." The place looked empty when we walked in—nothing on the recycled wood paneled walls, one glass case doubling as a counter down at the far end. A curtain hung over an opening behind the case. A man with black hair just touched with gray at the temples twitched the curtain aside, saw us, and came out smiling.

"Haven't seen you in a while, Tor," he said.

"I've been busy finding the right girl. This is Maya, and she's got some ideas for our wedding rings."

"Well! Congratulations to both of you!"

When I handed over my sketches, Diego laid them on the counter so he and Tor could study them. I looked over the merchandise in the glass case below the counter—some nice silver work pins, a few gold pendants, some strands of turquoise hishi, a lot of empty black velvet trays. I got the distinct impression that most of Diego's work came from commissions.

"I like these," Tor said. "Open-ended."

"No one owns anyone, huh?" Diego said.

"That's what I had in mind, yeah," I said.

I'd designed the wedding rings as spirals of gold, two twists around the finger so they'd be secure but not symbols of captivity. I did compromise on the engagement ring, though, and made that a regular band, because of the diamond. Tor insisted on a diamond, and I didn't want anything that expensive slipping off my hand. It would fit below the wedding rings once we were married. The stone's mount would overlap the bottom twist of the spiral and tie the two rings together.

"I'll need at least two weeks for the engagement ring," Diego said, "because I have to find the right stone. I'm not going to mount just any old diamond. This is an important wedding."

"Yeah," Tor said with a smile. "It sure is."

Diego took our sizes, then brought out a contract form. The quoted price for all three rings nearly made me gasp, but Tor kept smiling and handed over his credit card.

"Tell me something," Tor said. "I'm looking for a chunk of white stone I can shape into an animal figurine. It needs to fit into my closed hand. Do you know a good place to buy something like that?"

"Depends. How good a sculptor are you?"

"I don't know. I've never tried it before."

Diego rolled his eyes. "Then don't buy anything expensive. Practice on Ivory soap. Cutting stone isn't like wood carving."

"That's what I was afraid of."

"Do you have to start from scratch? I've got a tray of Native American sculptures in the back. Some Navajo alabaster pieces, and then some Zuni work by a guy who studied with

Leland Boone."

Tor went very still, and his eyes stared out at nothing. Diego smiled a little.

"Anything call to you?" Diego said.

"Yeah. You've got a bear back there. Want to bring her out?"

Diego did just that, and some of her friends for good measure, beautiful little animal sculptures, some in marble, some in striped native stone. The cinnamon-brown bear, as sleek and stylized as a Bufano sculpture, stood about three inches high. Tied to her back were a tiny turquoise arrowhead and a coral bead. Tor picked her up and closed his hand around her.

"Mine," Tor said quietly. "Name your price."

"Two hundred."

"Put it on the card."

You don't haggle over magical objects. I read that somewhere, and I was seeing how true it was. Diego took the other fetishes into his back room and returned with a small cardboard box and tissue paper. Tor wrapped the bear in the tissue but spurned the box. He put the sculpture into his shirt pocket and buttoned the flap over her. Jealousy stabbed me. Why was he buying something for the sow right in the middle of getting our wedding rings? I realized that I had a feud of my own underway.

As I was driving us home, Tor's phone did its howling wolf number. He answered it and made arrangements to meet someone at our house.

"That was Aaron," Tor told me. "He's on his way over to give me some printout, because he wanted to wipe the data off his box as soon as possible, and he didn't want to put it on mine."

"Oh my god! He really did manage to hack into the police department."

"He called it easy pickings."

Since Aaron couldn't drive, JJ brought him over. They only stayed a few minutes, just long enough for Aaron to hand over an inch thick stack of paper. JJ kept looking around him as if he expected cops to come bursting out of the walls.

"I feel like an accessory to a crime," JJ said.

"You are." Tor gave him a grin. "And thank you."

After they left, Tor and I settled down in the living room to read Lieutenant Hu's write-ups on the case and various relevant emails. Tor started, then handed me pages as he finished them.

The core of it: Tor began as suspect number one, all right, with Valdez a close second. At first Hu and his team had suspected drug dealing, thanks to Roman's habit. As the investigation proceeded, Hu decided that neither Tor nor Valdez could be implicated in drug trafficking, which led to a question of motive. In the early reports, I was Cantescu, perhaps what—not who, but what—the men were fighting over. By the later emails I'd become "the girlfriend". The last few never mentioned me at all, not even as a prize in the fight between uncle and nephew.

Tor's aversion spells were working.

What bothered Hu and his superiors the most was the lack of a provable cause of death. In their currently favored theory, an unknown woman had driven with Nils to the parking lot, where he'd assaulted her. She bit him and escaped, taking the car, and he then had a heart attack of some irregular type and died on his own. Hu felt frustrated that the medical examiners could find none of the usual traces fatal heart attacks leave in their victims' bodies. If only Nils' heart had displayed a burst aorta or some other damage, the police could just sign off and be done with it. Budget cuts had brought the Oakland police force to an all-time low. They had too many clear-cut murders clogging their caseload as it was.

"This all looks promising," Tor remarked when we'd finished. "Still worried?"

"No, not about the police arresting me. I just hope they don't come after you because they've got to arrest someone. If Nils had been a poor black guy, I don't think I'd worry at all."

"But he was white and wealthy, and he's got ex-wives back east who are probably pissed about losing their alimony. I bet

Hu's getting some pressure from somewhere." Tor paused to gather up the papers. "I'll shred these."

"Good idea. Y'know, there's one more thing that bothers me. Nils grabbed me after we had dinner in the restaurant in that strip mall. You paid for our meal with a credit card. Hu talked to all kinds of people in the businesses there, looking for witnesses. But the restaurant staff couldn't tell him anything."

Tor gave me a smug and sunny smile. Why did I bother to ask?

"It's just a real good thing you don't have criminal tendencies," I said.

"My dad made sure of that. I've got some sense of honor, y'know."

I held my thumb and forefinger about an inch apart. "Yeah. That much."

Tor laughed and headed downstairs to shred the papers. I picked up my sketchbook and began looking through it in the hopes that one of the images I'd recorded would expand itself into a memory. In case one did, I took a black Conté stick from my box of drawing supplies and got ready to trap the memory in the book. Through the heater vent I heard the whine and growl of the shredder. Eventually, it fell silent, and Tor began chanting again. The sound reminded me of my father, chanting late at night while I lay in bed and listened through the thin walls of our various apartments. I found it oddly soothing. I nestled a little further into the soft cushions of the leather sofa and drowsed.

I came to myself with a convulsive shudder and realized that I'd done a drawing in a trance state. In the center of the page lay the outline of a cave bear like the ones I'd seen in my art history class—big broad head, long muzzle, and hunched, powerful shoulders as it prowled on all fours. I also realized that Tor had stopped chanting. I could hear him coming up the stairs, in fact. He walked into the living room and gave me an odd look.

"Are you okay?" he said.

"Yeah, I guess. I kind of nodded off, but I drew something

anyway."

He came over, glanced at the drawing, and swore under his breath.

"What's wrong?" I said.

"Nothing wrong, just weird. I was calling to the bear spirit. I could feel her coming closer, but she disappeared. Suddenly she vanished like something had frightened her. I think you almost caught her."

"I didn't mean to."

"I know that, but she doesn't. It's a good thing you used black. She's brown, and that might have pinned her to the page."

"Tor, that doesn't make any sense."

"None of this stuff does." He grinned at me, then let the grin fade. "Did you plan on going into trance?"

"No. It just happened."

"That's not good. You should tell Liv about this."

"Don't worry, I will for sure."

As things turned out, we had a lot more to tell Liv about than my brief trance. Tor had planned on doing a ritual that evening over the bear fetish he'd bought. He wanted to charge it with power, then link it to himself. He was hoping that doing so would attract the bear spirit to this substitute for a body. If she could contact our world through the fetish, she might leave his body alone during the full moons. Since I seemed to have some affinity for her, he asked me to come down and watch.

"Not participate," he said. "Just watch. You might see something I'm missing, some kind of flaw in the way I approach her."

"Okay. Should I bring my drawing materials?"

"No, I think just observing would be best."

At sunset we went downstairs to the ritual room. Tor put on his usual shabby blue hoodie, but instead of the white shorts, he word a pair of red sweatpants, the color that the lore associated with vitkar. I put on my ritual shirt while he scattered handfuls of dry grass from our back yard, laced with blueberries he'd bought at the supermarket, around the edge of the crossed circle.

"They say cave bears lived on mostly plant material," Tor said. "So I thought I'd try these."

He lit four candles, but he placed them well away from the scatters of dry grass. Finally he brought out the bear fetish and placed it at the point where the arms of the cross met. He knelt behind it and gazed off to the north for a moment, then rose with a nod of his head. I sat down outside at the west, cross-legged to make sure that none of me touched the circle. He turned to face the east. We were ready to begin.

Tor raised his arms above his head in the rune of Elhaz and took a deep breath. Before he could chant a single word I felt a presence enter the room from the north. Tor turned to face her as the bear spirit manifested. She appeared as no more than a trace of shimmering silver mist in the air, an outline much like the one I'd drawn, but I could see the articulation of her shoulders and hips as she crawled forward. Very faintly, like a sigh on a distant wind, she whimpered and stopped moving.

Tor spoke in a soothing murmur of what sounded to me like Old Norse. She crawled forward again and laid the tip of her nose on the fetish. Slowly, a bare inch at a time, Tor lowered his arms. Her silvery form began to solidify into wisps that formed a cloud-image of a bear's head and a more substantial braid of mist along her spine. Slowly again, as slowly as he could manage, Tor knelt to look into the pools of shadow that marked where eyes should have been.

For a long time they communed while the candles burned down and gave me a way to keep track of time. Fifteen minutes, I estimated, then another fifteen—neither Tor nor the bear moved, neither made a sound. My right leg began to cramp. I ignored it for as long as I could, but the pain turned into a sharp fang, biting deep in my leg. Very slowly I moved my hand, keeping my arm close to my body, until I could reach the cramp and rub it. I heard the tiny sound of fingers on flesh.

So did the bear. She whipped her silvery head around

and noticed me for the first time. With a howl of terror she vanished.

"Shit," Tor said. "It's you she's frightened of, not just your imaging power, I mean, but you."

"I'm sorry. I had to move." I stretched out my leg and rubbed it hard to ease the pain. "Sitting like that—"

"It's okay. I've learned something really important." He stood up and stretched his back. "I'm kind of cramped myself. Y'know, she came here to warn me about something."

"Me, probably."

"No, though she couldn't tell me what the threat was. But she wants to be my fylgja. I can tell that. She just doesn't want you to hurt her."

"If she stops trying to take you over every month, I'll be glad to make peace." I got to my feet—slowly, because my leg still felt sore.

"Okay, I'll tell her that, next time she appears. But that warning. She showed me ice, snow sliding over rocks. Your wraiths, maybe."

"If she thinks I'm a snow wraith, no wonder she's afraid of me. I might force her to hibernate."

"Very true." He smiled at me. "You're catching on to all this, Maya."

So much for my attempt to lighten the mood with a little joke.

Tor closed down the ritual space before we changed into our ordinary clothes. When we went upstairs, I wrote Liv a long email while he cooked dinner. I had no idea when she'd read it, of course, but it turned out that she'd received a different kind of message. We were still in bed the next morning when the wolf howls of Tor's ringtone woke us. He sat up and grabbed the phone. I glanced at the clock on the end table: just six a.m.

"It's Liv," Tor said and switched into Icelandic for a couple of exchanges. He returned to English. "You need to hear this, Maya. Liv had one hell of a dream last night. When she got up, she drove into town and picked up your email. Let me put the phone on speaker."

I sat close to him so I could hear both sides of the conversation, though hers was hard to make out at moments.

"You two are generating so much power between you," she said, "that you're getting phenomena. This is dangerous."

"Yeah," Tor said. "I kind of know that."

"Look, brother of mine, get off your high horse! This is important."

They squabbled for a while in a way that reminded me of how Roman and I used to snarl at each other. I suspect they enjoyed it. We did.

"Be that as it may," Liv said eventually, "Maya can't go on slipping into trance at the drop of a hat. Why aren't you teaching her how to control it?"

"I'm going to. It just happened yesterday—"

"No, it happened before, over the picture of that German guy. Maya, are you there?"

"Yes." I leaned close to the phone. "You're right."

Tor muttered something in Icelandic that sounded nasty. She ignored it.

"Trouble is coming," Liv said. "In the dream a bear appeared to tell me that. A huge thing, like one of those Paleolithic creatures. Does that image—"

"The bear?" Tor snapped. "Very important, yes."

"And then I saw a woman made of snow. She told me that Maya needed to hear from me."

"True so far, yeah."

"Tor, this doesn't involve the jötnar, does it?"

"Well, yeah."

"Damn good thing I drove into town! Thank god the roads are still open! I'm thinking I should come visit you."

"I can handle it on my own."

They lapsed into Icelandic again, and this time the squabbling sounded serious. Finally Tor shrugged and spoke in English.

"If you really want to come, then come," he said. "Besides, everything must have moved indoors by now. The kids are probably driving you nuts. Don't bring them, please."

The time of year had arrived when in the far north the sun barely rose all day.

"I won't," Liv said. "It'll do their father good to deal with them. It depends on when I can get a flight, and if it can take off. We've had snow already, of course."

More squabbling, genial this time, until they finally signed off. Tor laid the phone back down, then turned to me. "Never tell my sister this," Tor said, "but I'm glad she's on the way. I'm beginning to think we could use some reinforcements."

That scared me.

Tor made coffee, but as soon as he'd drunk a cup, he took a refill downstairs so he could study the runes staves. I ate a piece of toast with my coffee, thought of eating more, and decided against it. I wandered into the living room and looked at the Chinese vases and the jade mountain on the bookshelf. The jade glowed from within; the carved trees seemed to tremble in a wind. The flowers on the vases seemed to float against the perfect white porcelain. When I looked away, I saw everything abnormally clearly in the morning light, the colors vivid, the details so sharply defined that even the soft cushions of the furniture appeared carved from stone.

Power, Liv said. Too much power. I felt it flowing all around me.

I needed to calm down. I took deep breaths, then decided that a nice soothing shower would help. As soon as I turned the water on, the sound of it, water rushing like rain, beating against the wall, broke through a barrier in my mind. I felt peculiarly light, as if I could leap into the air and float on the sun beams coming in the bathroom window. I knew, suddenly and completely, what had eluded me for so long. I turned the water off and ran back into the living room to write and draw the memories of that long-ago life before the tide went out, and they drained away.

My mother and I lived on a little island way out in a stretch of boggy land in the place they call East Anglia now, but we had no name for the land, my mother and I. We owned a hut and a little leather boat and some knives and fire flints. We ate fish, eels, and water birds along with watercress and green herbs. She taught me how to make my way through the bogs and creeks without being sucked under by the mud. I knew the ways long before I learned to speak, not that I ever learned to speak well.

Now and then, men came into our watery world to catch eels. We hid from them. When I asked her why, she said, "The priests will kill you if they catch us." She refused to tell me more.

One cold spring she caught a fever and lay gasping for air on her bed of rushes. I made a fire and cooked a broth of water bird. As I fed her, she talked between sips, a few words at time.

"Your father. You have a father."

"All things do. The birds and the salmon."

She smiled at me. "He's not an ordinary man."

"Not an eel hunter?'

"Not that, and not like them at all."

"Am I a bird, then?"

"No, no. He looks like a man." Her mouth worked as she fought for words. "His eyes will tell you."

I stared. The words made no sense to me, because eyes cannot speak, and in that life, metaphor lay beyond me.

She sighed and laid a cold hand on my arm. "Such big eyes, and him so pale."

"I understand now."

"Snow. Magic. Try to find him."

She gasped once more and died. I put down the bowl of broth and howled with grief, on and on for some long while. I covered her with our scraps of blankets and spent the night shivering beside her.

In the morning I took our knives and what food there was and put them in the boat. I paddled to the solid ground and set off on foot to do what she'd asked. I don't know how old I was, but something under twelve years of age, a skinny scrap of a girl, filthy and smelly from the bog until the first hard rain came and washed me clean. I thought I'd catch the fever from the rain and die, but it spared me.

I don't remember how long I traveled or how I survived. I do remember my first sight of the sea, the dark water stretching toward sunrise and the foam, white on the pebbled beach. I sat down on a clump of coarse grass and stared at the sea for most of a morning. While I watched, ships came with striped sails and dragon's heads on the prows—not that I knew any of those words then. I only learned what to call the ships later, after the men in iron shirts seized me, after we sailed back across the sea to their homeland, where I became a farm thrall. What the work was like I do not know. The memories of an ordinary way of life have faded after so long a time.

I do remember the burning of the farmstead, although I've lost the knowledge of why the enemies came to burn it. When the howling men broke down the gate, I ran without thinking into the stable. I heard the fighting and the screams of women. I smelled the smoke of the burning longhouse. Four enemies came into the stable to take out the cows and horses before they set fire there as well. One man, red faced and snarling, saw me and strode over to seize me, but I grabbed a two-pronged hayfork and thrust it deep into his groin. He screamed and staggered and fell. His blood ran between his legs like red piss.

He raised himself on one elbow and moaned, whimpered, begged the others for aid. The leader looked at the wound and shrugged. No one helped him.

"Die like a man, you coward!" one warrior snarled.

The bleeding man fell back and began to weep. Two men turned away. The leader walked over to me. I set my back against the wall and raised the pitchfork. He was tall, heavy-set and laden with chain mail, twice my size easily, reeking with sweat and the smell of fresh blood. He pointed his sword at me.

"What's your name, girl?"

I hissed. I could not speak well at the best of times, and all that came out then was a hiss like that of a huge cat.

"Let her go," he said to his fellows. "She's cursed."

They nodded and returned to leading out the cows and the plow horses. I slipped out of the back door of the stable and left the farmstead before the looters saw me go. I took the pitchfork with me.

I don't remember anything else, not even how I died. I think the man who spared me was Tor, or, I mean, the man whose soul later became Tor. In my heart I know that my soul became tangled with those of the wraiths for the very first time in that life, because that mysterious father had to be a wight, one of the snow creatures, who had somehow se-duced my mother. No doubt the priest in her village thought he was a demon and I was a demon child. The village priests in those days were almost as ignorant as the folk they served.

Did I ever find my father? No, not then, not for a thou-sand years, but as I lay down to die on that mountain in Austria, he found me. When my soul left Mia's body, he was there to greet me. In my grief and confusion, I chose to be his daughter again. Eventually, in San Francisco, his human form supplied the body for my soul to indwell, but his soul somehow influenced our DNA and left it twisted.

Was it a good choice on my part? No, but I made it freely, and I'll live it out.

CHAPTER 11

Joel Halvarsson arrived in the Bay Area on the second Wednesday in November, but official business kept him so busy that we didn't see him till Saturday, the last day of his trip. Tor arranged to meet him at the Indian restaurant at seven o'clock.

"You can always have a bad cold," Tor told me. "I'll make your excuses for you when I see him."

"No, I want to go." I could act like a grown-up murderer, I decided, even though the decision bothered me. Was I growing so callous that I could accept what I'd done? "I want to hear what he's got to say."

"Okay, if you're sure."

"If Joel loved his dad, it'd be different. I couldn't face him then."

"Huh! You don't need to worry about that."

Before we left the house, Tor received a text from Liv. She and her husband had nearly reached the island's one international airport, a long way from the farm. Her husband, she said, would get some sleep in a hotel before he drove back. "Storm on the way," she texted, "hope it waits till I'm gone, and Helgi's safely home." I hoped so, too, fervently, on both counts.

When we arrived at the crowded restaurant, Joel was already seated at a table in the back of the big room. He stood up as we joined him and shook hands with Tor—gingerly, as if he worried that Tor might be electrified.

"Good to see you, Maya," he said, but he sounded troubled.

My guilt sprang to life and stabbed me. Did he suspect something, after all? We all sat down and studied menus. I noticed Joel giving Tor the occasional sideways glance. Tor noticed, too.

"Have you seen the police since you've been out?" Tor said.

"Yeah. A long and lousy chat with Lieutenant Hu."

"Did they tell you they suspect me of killing your father?"

Joel winced and shut the menu with a snap. "Yeah," he said. "Did you?"

"No. I'll swear that on anything you want."

Joel smiled, the first normal smile I'd seen him give that evening. "I believe you. Never thought otherwise, but once the police get talking, you wonder." He shrugged his shoulders. "Why would you kill him? It didn't make any sense. He's the one who hated you, not the other way around."

"Exactly. It's my guess that they don't know who in hell killed him, or even if he really was murdered. They've got to blame someone."

The waiter appeared. We all ordered, somewhat randomly. Tor and Joel pitched into their beers the moment they arrived. I contented myself with ice water and worked on the plate of samosas while they continued talking.

"The police have some ideas," Joel said, "about motive. Drugs, mostly. I know he did snort coke now and then. He ran with a pretty fast crowd back home. They had too much money that took a hell of a lot of stress to make."

"Yeah, the cops mentioned drugs to me, too. It's because of Maya's brother, though, the guy Nils shot when he missed me. Roman has a drug problem. A big one."

Joel winced again and looked at me. "I didn't realize he was your brother. Shit! I mean, sorry."

"The language doesn't bother me," I said. "I live with Tor's mouth."

Joel managed another smile. "Okay, but hey. Look, I'm really sorry about the shooting. Crap, that sounds lame! Allow me to apologize for my father's crime? Nah, that's worse."

"You don't have to say anything." I managed to force out the words through a wall of guilt. "Roman's going to be okay."

"That's what counts, yeah. Still." Joel looked away, and he'd gone a little pale around the mouth. "I always knew Dad had problems. I never dreamed how deep they ran. I mean, like, he was just my weird dad, and he'd always been that way. Y'know?"

"Yeah," Tor said. "When you're a kid, you accept things."

"But when you grow up, you learn more. His second wife— I keep in touch because of her kids. They're my half-brother and sister. She never told me until Dad was killed that he used to hit her. That's why she left him. He never did that to my mother. I dunno about the third one—she was the kind of dingbat who might have put up with it."

"No kids there?" I forced myself to join the conversation.

"No, luckily," Joel said. "Say, Maya? If your brother needs some kind of fancy rehab, let me chip in, will you? I make good money, and I'd like to pick up part of the tab."

I was sincerely touched. "Well, thank you," I said. "He's in therapy now for the drugs, but Tor—" I glanced Tor's way.

"I'm taking care of it," Tor said. "The reason Roman got hit was he was protecting Maya. Covered her from enemy fire, just like in the Marines." He gave Joel a brief smile. "But if you want to help, we can discuss it when the final bills come in."

"Okay. Good idea." Joel raised his beer glass and clinked it against Tor's.

Nils really could have killed me that day in San Francisco. I could have been shot instead of Roman. I'd shoved that terrifying fact out of my mind. *Self-defense.* And he knocked one of his wives around. The guilt began to ease, but it lingered. *It's not your place to judge and execute him. Yeah, he was scum. That doesn't mean you get to punish him.* Abruptly I realized that both guys were looking at me.

"Fazing out?" Tor smiled at me.

"Just thinking. It's all so sad."

"Yeah," Joel said. "It is that."

Waiters arrived with our meals and baskets of naan. The evening turned as normal as it could ever be. Between bites, the cousins talked about football, the Jets and the Raiders, mostly. As I watched them laughing, pretending to argue over their two loser teams, I realized that they would have been friends had they been raised together. I wondered if they could patch up a relationship now, with Nils' death lying between them.

We'd almost finished eating when Tor abruptly snarled, but at himself.

"Shit!" he said. "I forgot to bring those pictures. Hey, Joel, do you have time to come back to the house? I found one of Grandfather Halvar's journals with a whole lot of family pictures in it. He wrote it in English, mostly, and I thought you'd like to have it."

"Say, thanks! I would, sure." He glanced at his watch. "But I can't stay long."

By the time we all got back to the house, the evening was growing late. Joel had just time to admire our flat, in particular the Ming vases and the jade sculpture. When Tor brought out the leather-bound journal, he opened it to a picture of Joel as a blond toddler on a grassy lawn. Under it the old man had written "handsome lad and very smart." Halvar's writing was small, cramped, and backward-slanting. I bet a graphologist would have had a field day with it.

"I barely remember Grandad from when I was a kid," Joel said. "When he moved to New York we had lunch a couple of times, but he was even weirder than Dad. So I never got to know him well as an adult."

"You're lucky," Tor said. "Take it from me. Real lucky."

"Okay." Joel checked his watch. "You'll have to tell me more in email."

Tor wrapped the journal up in archival quality tissue paper and slipped it into a heavy manila envelope. Joel took it, and we walked him out to his car. In the clear night sky above us, the first quarter moon shone among scraps of fog. To the far west the sky hung silver and close.

"I hope your plane takes off okay," I said.

"Should be clear at the airport for a while yet," Tor said.

"Let's hope, huh? Hey, thanks for these photos!" Joel switched the packet to his left hand. "Our grandfather was one weird dude, but y'know, it's cool to know he did care about us."

When Tor shook hands with him, I saw an odd expression pass over Tor's face. For a moment, a flicker of a moment, his mouth hung slack and his eyes seemed glazed.

"What time does your plane take off?" Tor said.

"Midnight," Joel said. "Why?"

"That'll be pretty much the last flight of the day, and the airport, it'll be nearly deserted."

"Yeah. What—"

"Be careful, that's all. Be real careful when you get to the airport."

Joel stared at him. He was probably thinking that Tor was as crazy as his father.

"Just a feeling." Tor took a step back. "I can't even explain it, but I get this kind of feeling now and then."

"Well, uh, thanks." Joel forced out a smile. "Thanks for dinner." He turned and hurried off. Neither of us said anything until he'd driven away.

"You felt something when you touched him, didn't you? When you shook hands," I said.

"Yeah, I don't know why, but he's in danger. I know I sounded like an idiot. I had to warn him. It would've broken every vow I've ever made to let an innocent man walk off without even a fucking warning. Okay?"

"Well, sure, I didn't—"

"Sorry. I didn't mean to snap at you." He ran both hands through his hair and shivered. "I shouldn't have let him drive off like that."

"Would he have listened if you'd tried to explain?"

"No. It would have just made him leave faster."

As we walked around the house to the side door, I saw a pale shape, barely visible, moving on the hillside. Tor had seen it, too. One of the outside alarms muttered, then fell silent.

"Get inside," Tor snapped. "Fast!"

I rushed through the door, and he followed. He slammed and locked the door, then hurried upstairs right behind me. I ran to the kitchen window and looked out, but the movement on the hill had stopped. The alarms stayed quiet. Tor called the security system people anyway. He hung on the phone for a few minutes while they checked their recording equipment.

"Nothing?" Tor said. "Okay. It must have been a stray dog, then. Some kind of animal, anyway."

In a moment he said goodbye and hung up the landline.

"Do you really think it was a dog?" I said.

"I hope so." Tor frowned, thinking. "The alarm turned off so fast that it's likely."

"But what about Joel? Do you think you should go to the airport? You can just jump there, can't you?"

"And leave you here alone?"

I caught my breath with a gulp. "There's the security system—"

"If someone's already prowling around, will the cops get here fast enough? What if the prowler's a vitki just waiting for me to be somewhere else? Look, I like Joel. It's a shitty choice I've got to make, but I'm not risking you." He paused, then nodded as he made a decision. "I'm going to go outside and cast a few wards. But I won't be more than three feet away from the door."

"Okay. I've got to admit I'm scared."

After he warded the house, Tor did a long complicated rune stave reading centering on Joel. When he came back upstairs, he said one word to me, "bad", before he went into the kitchen and got himself a bottle of beer. Neither of us felt like going to bed. Tor sent Liv email to bring her up to date. We tried to read. At 11 o'clock I insisted on catching the late local news on my laptop. The story had broken: "Mugging in Oakland Airport! Was it a kidnapping? Details after these messages."

The details started off with a description of someone who

had to be Joel. Apparently he'd returned his rental car and taken the shuttle van from the lot. He'd just gotten off in front of the terminal when two men appeared. One grabbed his suitcase; the other grabbed Joel. At this point the eyewitnesses became totally confused. Several agreed that the assailants were "as tall as basketball players, huge guys."

"They must have shoved him into a car," one woman said. "There were a lot of cars pulling up, letting off passengers, you know, picking people up. That must have been it, because then they were gone."

"Yeah," her husband said. "It all happened so fast"

The final witness, racist though he maybe was, delivered the clincher. "They were real tall," he said, "but they weren't black. I've never seen white guys that tall."

The phone in Tor's pocket howled like a wolf. "That'll be Lieutenant Hu," Tor said and answered the call.

It was, and he was at our front door. Tor went down to let him in, and I turned off the laptop. Hu, dressed in jeans, a business shirt, and a sports coat, came alone this time. He'd been home—I heard him tell Tor as they came upstairs—but checked with "the office" when he heard the news on TV. Hu and Tor stood in the middle of the living room. I felt like screaming at them to sit down. I don't know why. Instead I huddled in an armchair and said nothing. Since the lieutenant never glanced my way, I could assume that the aversion spells had taken hold.

"Saw that your lights were on," Hu said to Tor. "Thought I'd stop by. Do you know about your cousin's disappearance?"

"I just saw it on the late news. Do you have any leads?"

"Not yet. That's what I'm hoping to get from you. Look, Thorlaksson. I don't know how close you and your cousin are, but if he was one of my relatives, I'd want to cooperate with the police."

Tor had masked his face with the nerd illusion. He played into it by nodding as if he was considering what Hu had told him.

"I'll tell you what I think," Tor said eventually, "but I

could be wrong."

"Try me," Hu said.

"Okay. When Joel was leaving, we were standing outside by his car. I handed him a package about so big–" Tor gestured with his hands, "–that contained family pictures and a journal that belonged to our grandfather. I'm willing to bet that someone was up on the hill behind our house and saw it. Thought it was something entirely different. After Joel left, I noticed something moving up on the hill. My security system blipped just as I was going back into the house. I called in, but at the time, I thought it was maybe a stray dog. You can check that with the security company."

"I will, yeah. Something different, huh? Drugs?"

"You know what Joel's father was like. Didn't the urinalysis find traces of cocaine?"

"Good point, yeah."

"I'll swear to you that Joel's as honest as you could want. Do his father's old associates know that?"

"It's a thought." Hu considered him for a long cold moment. "I don't suppose you know who these associates are."

"If I did, I'd tell you. But I'm willing to bet you've already got a damn good idea."

Hu allowed himself a very thin, very brief smile. "You might not be wrong about that. We've been doing some digging."

"I heard about my mother's testimony."

"She would have told you, sure." Hu seemed to be considering something, himself, but I had no idea if he was really thinking or just pretending to hesitate. "Look, that bite mark on your uncle's arm. It was made either by a small woman or an older child. Our DNA man talked publicly about the peculiar results of his analysis. Did you hear that on the news?"

"Yeah, I sure did. There was something strange about the DNA he got from the saliva."

"Right. Well, there are a lot of population groups in Asia who haven't been scientifically typed. Some of them sell their surplus daughters to scumbag traders." Hu looked furious at the thought. He collected himself and continued. "Your mother's suspicions about sex trafficking—we're always on the lookout for that in the Bay Area. Do you think Halvarsson was the kind of man who'd involve himself in the trade? Or maybe just buy one of the products now and then?"

"The latter, sure. Maybe one of the girls fought back and bit him?"

"It's a possibility."

"Well, considering he tried to shoot me, I don't have a real high opinion of him. I do know that three women divorced him."

"Your cousin told us that his father physically abused the second wife. I'm taking that into consideration." Once again Hu hesitated, then fired his surprise. "Is there a chance that the assailants might have mistaken Joel Halvarsson for you?"

"We sure look alike, don't we? I'm worth a hell of a lot of money. Do crooks kidnap people for ransom these days? Or is that only in old movies?"

"Generally, only in the movies." Hu allowed himself a twist of his mouth that most likely he meant as a smile. "But there could be exceptions."

"Okay. As far as I know, Uncle Nils is the only person who hated me enough to have me disposed of. He tried to do it himself, after all."

"Yeah, he sure did."

"Can I ask you something?" Tor arranged his best dumb nerd look, slightly open-mouthed, all wide eyes. "Have they ever discovered what killed Nils? I can't find anything about that in the online news."

"That's because we don't know. Yet. Wait a minute! Didn't you tell me that your father died of leukemia?"

"He did, yes."

"And he and your uncle were brothers." Hu considered Tor for a long minute, then came to some decision. "The medical examiner told me that your uncle's blood supply was abnormally low. What there was had too few red corpuscles. Pernicious anemia at the least, he said."

My stomach clenched. I forced myself to sit stock-still.

"That sounds real bad," Tor said. "Do you think it would have affected his heart? Made it weak or something."

"Maybe. Maybe not. Well, thanks, Thorlaksson. I might be calling on you again."

"Any time. Look, I want my cousin found."

Hu raised an eyebrow in his direction. "I believe you," he said at last. "We'll do our best."

Tor showed him out, then came running up the stairs two at a time. He was grinning as he strode into the living room.

"What's so funny?" I said.

"The idea that Hu will maybe pin Nils' death on the same disease the bastard gave my father." Tor wiped the smile away. "Not that it's really funny at all. Wyrd. Karma. I told you, these things come back around to the person who does them."

"Like to me someday? I was afraid I was going to hurl when Hu started talking about blood supply and like that."

"You had the right to defend yourself."

"I've come to see that. But do I have the right to hide what happened?"

"Will they believe you if you tell them the truth?"

He had me there. "No. Not in a million years."

"Okay then." Tor flopped into the other armchair and stretched his legs out in front of him. "I made sure to ward the guys, but I never thought they'd go after Joel. He probably would have freaked if I wanted to draw runes on him, anyway."

"They? Who's the they who went after Joel?"

"The rime jötnar, of course. I wonder if they thought he was me."

"They're terrified of you."

"True. I bet they wanted a hostage. Get the upper hand that way."

"A what? You mean they want to trade Joel for the gold plaque?"

"That's my theory, yeah. Well, if I'm right, it's not going to work. I told them no, they couldn't have the goddamn plaque, and I will not go back on my word." Tor crossed his arms over his chest and stuck his chin out. "If I do, it'll only cause more trouble later."

"Oh yeah? And what are they going to do with Joel, then? I bet they don't just let him go."

"They'll probably threaten to kill him. In some unpleasant way."

"Tor, you can't let that happen. You've copied the inscription. You even made a rubbing of it. You know what it does now. Why not let them have the chunk of gold, if the rotten plaque means so much to them?"

"It's the principle of the thing. When I shouted at that kid in our driveway, I meant what I said, and I said what I meant."

I'd had enough of his heroic posturing. "And an elephant's faithful one hundred per cent. Right, Horton?"

"Maya, damn it!"

"Well, if you want principles, for crying out loud, he's your kinsman. Your fathers were brothers. If you let him die, you'll be dishonored."

Reading the old sagas had just paid off big-time. Tor opened his mouth to speak, stopped, hesitated, then sighed and uncrossed his militant arms. He let his hands sag onto his thighs and sighed again.

"Okay, you win," he said. "I'll have to think about this. There's got to be a way out of the dilemma. It's the classic cleft stick."

"I don't even see why it's cleft."

"I know you don't, but I do." Tor stood up and smiled at me. "And that's what counts. I'm going downstairs. I'd better put the plaque in the safe."

If I'd had the stupid thing within reach at that moment, I would have heaved it at his back. As it was, I sat and steamed for a couple of minutes before I got control of myself. I got out my phone and texted Liv. "Situation worse. Jötunn s--- hit the fan." She answered, "Reached airport. Plane not loading on schedule, but hope, they say. No storm yet."

I offered up a prayer to the Aesir that the Icelandic weather would hold until her plane was safely on its way. They seemed like the right ones to ask.

When Tor came back upstairs, he looked oddly calm, not smiling, not frowning, just calm in a way that I found terrifying.

"You've made up your mind about something, haven't you?" I said.

"Oh, yeah." He sat down, but he took an armchair rather than sit next to me on the couch as he usually did. "Don't worry about Joel. I'll make sure nothing happens to him."

My terror turned into ordinary anxiety.

"Something I need you to remember," Tor said. "Don't ask me why, because it might not matter. But I put my ski parka on the old couch in the library room. Remember that. It's on the couch."

"All right. But I—"

"Hush!" He held up one hand. "This is one of those times when words have power. We can't discuss anything that matters."

I really did wonder if the stress had sent him over the edge into insanity. He looked at me so calmly, a little sadly, maybe, but too self-possessed, too serene to be crazy—unless that unnatural calm was the symptom.

"Okay," I said. "What can we talk about?"

"You could surf for news on my laptop. Just in case the police found something useful."

I'd just booted it up when I heard a car pull into our driveway. I put the machine into stand-by.

"That'll be the guys," Tor said. "I called them when I was downstairs. They know what's happening already, so we don't have to tell them again. Come on. I'm going to do a summoning. Why hang around and wait for the fucking jötnar to show up?"

The autumn night was cool enough that I grabbed a sweater. Billy, JJ, and Aaron met us outside on the driveway. In dead silence we walked around the house to the back yard.

"You stay here," Tor said. "In the south."

I took the place in front with the three guys behind me in a horizontal row. Tor stood in the middle of the lawn and faced east. He began to chant softly, his voice a growl in the night, as he scribed runes in the air. Like the hand of a clock, he kept turning. Each turned scribed more runes until he'd complete a glowing gold circle about six feet above the ground. Tor raised both arms in the air and called out three words. I saw, some fifteen feet above the ground, a silvery dome appear, marked with fiery red runes. As Tor continued to chant, the edge of the dome began to drip pale light. The drips became a flow of bluish light and turned into a shimmering wall that slowly, a foot or so at a time, spread around the circle. The flow of light turned green and slipped further until it reached the ground.

Once again, Tor faced the north. He chanted a galdr while he made a peculiar rubbing motion with his right hand. A door appeared in the wall of light.

"The dome should hide everything," Tor said, "from the neighborhood."

"Let's hope," JJ said. "We don't want the cops swarming in here."

"Or the alarm system going off," Aaron said. "I'm kind of surprised it hasn't. Lot of energy flowing around."

The door in the wall sprang open. The air trembled, thickened, became a pale bluish fog that brought with it a chill wind. The door widened slightly as four figures stepped through into our world from Jötunheim. An enormous flood of élan swept through with them. I soaked up as much as I could gather. The two male jötnar were easily twelve feet tall, huge men, heavily muscled, with white hair that flowed around their pale faces. One carried a flaming torch; the other, a battle axe with a long wooden handle and double-bitted blade. He held it casually in one hand, where it looked no bigger than the axe Tor kept for firewood.

With his other massive hand the axe-wielder pushed Joel forward, then snarled as he forced him to his knees. In comparison to Joel's head, the axe appeared huge. In the flickering torch light Joel looked as pale as the giants, but his mouth was set in a grim line of fury, not fear. His left eye was swollen and bruised. They'd bound his hands in front of him.

The fourth person was a woman who looked delicate next to the men but who stood somewhere over seven feet tall. Although her skin appeared pale, her hair was blonde, worn in a crown of braids. In one hand she held a knife that glowed with runes along the blade—the etinwife, I realized, who had magic of her own.

"So!" the axeman said. "Give us our gold. We give you your kinsman."

"No," Tor said. "I told you no, and I meant no."

"Then your kinsman dies."

He swung up the axe, but Tor sang out a galdr. The axeman froze in place, axe raised, and tried to speak. He gabbled. Foaming spittle ran from his mouth into his beard. The woman sang out a few runes of her own. He lowered the axe but stayed silent. Tor grinned, narrow-eyed, and nodded in satisfaction. Here, wherever we were between worlds, his galdrar had more power than I'd ever seen him summon before.

"Joel, get up," Tor said. "Never grovel before scum."

The axeman snarled but never moved as Joel got to his feet. Joel trembled, but only slightly, and his face betrayed no feeling at all.

"Here's my offer," Tor said. "My kinsman goes free. I take his place."

The woman and the torchbearer both spoke at once in their language. I knew none of it, of course, but they sounded utterly confused. From behind me I heard Billy mutter, "What the fuck?" I glanced back and noticed that Aaron had his smartphone out. He was concentrating on taking photos of the giants. I had the insane thought that he was going to post them on Facebook.

The axeman finally spoke. "Why?" he said. "I trust not this."

"A vitki never goes back on his word," Tor said. "I told you no, I won't give you the gold. If I'm the hostage, then giving you the gold is someone else's decision."

The woman laughed in an oddly pleasant way. She spoke to the axeman, who nodded.

"Clever," he said. "You will promise, yes, not to harm us?"

"I swear I won't harm you, your kin, your steading, your thralls, or your livestock unless you attack me."

"I swear no attack on you by me, my kin, my warband, my dogs, or my thralls. Very well. We take the bargain." He pushed Joel forward. "Go."

Joel strode forward to join Billy and JJ, then staggered so badly I feared he'd faint. JJ threw an arm around his shoulders and steadied him.

"Woman!" Tor turned to me. "It's cold in their country. I need my parka."

"I'll fetch it." I said.

I ran inside, ran to the library room, and grabbed the parka from the couch. I had the muddled thought that I should just fetch the gold plaque right then, but I couldn't think beyond that one impulse. Later I'd realize that Tor had cast some kind of spell to ensure that I wouldn't demand he give it to me. At the time I just ran back with the parka. He'd stashed something in each of the interior pockets: his rune knife, a leather sack of staves, and the carved stone bear.

When I got back outside I saw that Tor had taken a few steps forward. He stood poised between two worlds, ours and that of the jötnar. When I handed him the parka, I said, "Why are you doing this?"

He grinned at me. "It's the cave bear's own country." He dropped his voice to a whisper. "Don't give them the gold."

"Fuck you! That's my decision now."

Tor started to speak, but the etinwife snapped out, "We must go! The galdr weakens."

"We return tomorrow night," the axeman said. "Give us the gold. We give you the vitki."

Tor laughed and put on the parka. He took a couple of steps forward, turned to face us all, and swung his arm in a circle. Overhead the dome cracked. The blue fog swirled around the yard as the giants and their hostage vanished. Tor's voice sang out one last time.

"Joel, your dad really was a werewolf. Wanted you to know—."

Joel sagged in JJ's arms and fainted. Billy sprang forward to grab him, and in the confusion, I never saw the dome disappear and the fog dissipate. When I looked again, the yard had returned to normal—except the patch of grass glittered with frost. I stared at it as it melted away.

"Maya!" JJ's voice cut through my confusion. "Are you okay?"

"No, but that doesn't matter. Let's get inside."

By then Joel lay on the ground, awake but totally dazed. Billy knelt beside him. He took a Swiss Army knife out of his jeans pocket and began cutting through the thongs around Joel's wrists. JJ and Aaron stood watching.

"How can you guys act so totally cool?" My voice shook beyond my power to steady it.

"We've seen worse," JJ said. "Back when Tor was still learning—shit, man! When he fucked up, it was spectacular."

As if this wasn't, I thought to myself. A fuck-up, that is.

"Besides, it's simple," Aaron said. "Maya gives them the gold thingy, and Tor comes back. Right?"

The men were all smiling at me. I shook my head. "Wrong," I said. "Because the cruddy thing is in the safe, and I don't have the combination."

The smiles disappeared fast. Joel groaned and sat up, rubbing his wrists. "Please," Joel said, "tell me this is all a drug experience."

"I only wish I could," I said. "C'mon, guys, let's get inside before the neighbors notice something. Okay?"

While Billy and JJ helped Joel up the stairs to the flat, Aaron and I went to look over the safe. Built right into the wall, it measured four feet on a side, solid steel, probably, with some kind of fancy plating on the front as well. The combination lock looked like state of the art—three little wheels of numbers, stacked one inside the other and set above a steel handle.

"I was hoping for something digital," Aaron said. "I could've cracked that."

"Do they make digital safes?"

Aaron shrugged and continued studying the lock. He gave it a couple of experimental turns. I could hear nothing, no useful clicks like in the TV shows.

"Nitroglycerine," I said. "That's the only thing I can think of."

"Right, and blow up the whole house." Aaron scowled at me. "Last chance. Let me have Tor's laptop. Maybe he recorded the combo somewhere."

The laptop sat on the coffee table in the living room. When we got upstairs, Aaron grabbed it and took it over to the breakfast bar to work. The other two guys were drinking beer on the couch, while Joel slumped in an armchair and pressed a plastic bag full of ice cubes to his swollen eye. I snagged a dish towel from the kitchen.

"Wrap the ice in this." I handed him the towel. His wrists were bruised and chafed red from the thongs. "It'll be more comfortable."

"Thanks. Tor tried to warn me, didn't he? When I was leaving. Did I listen to him? Oh no! Dumb as a bucket of mud, that's me. I thought he was nuts."

"I can understand why." I sat down in the other armchair. "He takes people that way sometimes."

"Maya?" He leaned forward to look right at me. "Was Dad really a werewolf?"

"'Fraid so. He bit Tor, as a matter of fact."

"But Tor changes into a bear, not a wolf," Billy put in. "Only once a month, though."

"The talents come from Grandfather Halvar," I said. "Your cousin Liv has magic, too, but she's not a were-creature."

For a moment I thought Joel was going to faint again. He slumped to one side, but only to set the ice pack down on the floor. When he straightened up, he had the same grimly furious look on his face that he'd shown when the giants forced him to kneel.

"Are you telling me," Joel said, "that I belong to a family of sorcerers?"

"Exactly that, yeah."

Joel glanced at Billy and JJ for a second opinion.

"She's right," Billy said.

"You bet," JJ said.

"Shit." Joel retrieved the ice pack. "Well. Just shit." He leaned back in the chair.

We all waited for him to say more, but he stared with his good eye at the ceiling in silence. We gave up and let him brood in peace.

"Hey, Aaron," Billy said. "Any luck?"

"No." Aaron looked up from the screen. "But there are a ton of files on here in other languages."

Billy groaned and pried himself off the couch. "We should be looking for a string of numbers."

"Yeah, but who knows if he used numerals or wrote them out?" Aaron took off his glasses and wiped them on the hem of his tee shirt. "I guess Old Norse had numbers."

"Of course it did! I mean, everybody had numbers, even the Egyptians. I bet we can find them online."

"And next they say," JJ murmured. "Look, historical babes!"

I managed a smile at that.

About an hour later my phone rang in the backpack by my feet. Liv—she had a couple of minutes before her plane left the gate.

"They'll be making us shut off real soon," Liv said. "I tried to text Tor. Is his phone offline?"

"No," I said. "He is. He's in Jötunheim."

"God in heaven help us! The idiot! What's he doing there?"

"It's too complicated to explain right now."

In the background I could hear a stewardess' voice droning in Icelandic. I assumed she was repeating the usual safety instructions.

"Look," Liv went on, "they've cancelled the direct flight

to SFO. I'm heading for New York. I'll be in touch. Gotta turn off."

The connection went dead. I put my phone back in my backpack and slung the backpack onto the coffee table. JJ was watching me expectantly.

"Liv's coming. Tor's sister, y'know?" I said. "I just don't know exactly when because of weather delays."

"I'll pick her up at the airport," JJ said. "I've met her, and I won't be Tee Aying tomorrow."

"Doing what?"

"Leading student sessions as a TA. How exploited grad students earn their seminars."

"Right. I knew that. Sorry. I'm all to pieces." I took a deep breath. "I could strangle him."

"I'll help." JJ shot me a grin. "If we could only get that damn safe open!"

While Aaron and Billy worked over every sector on the hard drive, JJ and I searched through all the papers on Tor's business desk, the place where he paid and filed things like bills and tax statements. None of us ever found the combination. Around four in the morning we all agreed that the job was hopeless. The combination existed only in Tor's brain, and that was in Jötunheim with the rest of him.

"When they come back tomorrow," Billy said, "make Tor give you the combination. Or if you can't pry it out of him, I bet Liv can. Liv's awesome."

"Good," I said. "I'm so glad she's on the way."

I cooked everyone breakfast while the guys planned strategy. Joel came out of his funk long enough to eat.

"Do you have someone picking you up at the airport?" JJ said. "In New York, I mean."

"No, I left the car in the long-term lot. Good thing, huh? I don't want to call the police right away and tell them I'm okay. I mean, shit, they'll ask me who attacked me. What am I gonna say?"

"Nothing, that's what," JJ said. "Lay low until we get Tor back."

"I'll call into work and tell them I'm taking an extra day, maybe two," Joel said. "They know that I had a lot of crap to do out here. If they've seen the news story, I'll just say it wasn't me."

"You can get some sleep in the spare bedroom." I said. "I'll get some clothes out of it first. JJ, I hope Liv phones in soon. You can take Tor's car to pick her up."

"Hey, a chance to drive that baby? It's worth the trip."

We'd just finished eating when Liv texted me from New York. She'd been through Customs and found a flight that would take her direct to the Oakland airport. It was scheduled to land at three p.m. our time. I texted her that JJ would be there to meet her.

"I'll go home and grab some sleep," JJ said. "I'll be back by one o'clock to pick up the car."

Before Billy and Aaron left, Aaron showed us the photos. He loaded them on Tor's laptop, a couple of clear shots of the giants, both with and without Joel, and then a couple that showed what lay behind the giants, the front of a roughly built house with an animal pen of some kind next to it. Joel stared at each one for several minutes. Now and then he shook his head in disbelief.

"Not guys in costume?" Joel said. "Like in New Orleans for the Mardi Gras?"

"Nope," Aaron said. "I took these so we'd all know it was real."

Joel sighed in defeat. "I can tell you what the inside of the house was like. Right out of the Viking movies. Straw on the floor, and all these big guys sitting around on benches and drinking. Stank to high heaven. Pigs and dogs lying by the fire. Fucking big dogs, too, and hairy gray pigs. Jeez, I hope Tor's gonna be all right."

"They'll keep their word." I put all the confidence I didn't feel into that statement. "They're etins, not thursar."

"Whatever," Billy said. "They'll be back tonight, and we'll find out if they will or not."

CHAPTER 12

In the dream, Tor stood in a room with green walls. Every time he tried to walk out the door, the cave bear blocked his way. Although I couldn't hear him, I saw his mouth moving as he tried to reason with her. She lowered her head and refused to move. From the way he waved his hands, I could tell he was trying to cast galdrar. He looked first frightened, then angry when they had no effect. The bear tossed her head back and growled so loudly that I heard her, an angry droning whine.

I woke up after too few hours of sleep. The whine turned out to be the gardener next door and his leaf blower. I felt muzzy, exhausted, and angry at Tor for being so damn stubborn. I reminded myself that his family had drilled him in his archaic view of manhood from the time he'd been a toddler. The reminder left the anger untouched. I also regretted telling him about my ability to evoke élan for myself. I was willing to bet that he never would have gone off to Jötunheim if he'd thought I'd fall ill without him. I was angry, yeah, but not irrational about it.

After I fed myself with élan, I took a shower in the bathroom off the master bedroom to avoid waking Joel. I got dressed, then went into the kitchen and started coffee. I was just pouring myself a cup when a shower of gravel hit the kitchen window. I looked out and saw the young Frost Giant standing in the back yard. I opened the window and called down to him.

"What are you doing here?"

"Please come talk. I have news to tell you. Please!"

His voice sounded so urgent that I hurried down the stairs and outside. As he walked up to meet me in the driveway, I felt an odd sensation just above my collar bone. The bind-rune pendant Tor made was glowing and twitching against my skin. I laid a hand over it to calm it as the kid walked up.

"Here I am," I said. "What's the news?"

"Tonight they will try to cheat you. My father and his men, I mean. They will take the gold, but they cannot give you the vitki back. The bear came and got him. He is not with us anymore."

"The bear—a huge bear with a long face?"

"Yes. Never have I seen such a bear! She killed two of our dogs. She broke the door to the shed and let the vitki out. No one could stop her. She made him leave, so they left."

"She made him leave? How?"

"She grabbed him by his blue coat with her mouth and dragged him. He did get free once, but she grabbed him again, and that time he went with her. We feared she would kill him, but no one could move until they were gone."

"Did the vitki cast a spell?"

"Oh yes, and no one could move or speak until they were gone into the forest." His eyes grew very wide. "He is a man of great power, my grandmother says."

The boy appeared so genuinely frightened that I was inclined to trust him, but as Tor was fond of saying, you never know with giants.

"Why have you come to warn me?"

He blushed scarlet. "I did not wish to see you cheated. I—I like you."

"I see. Well, I like you, too, and you've just been a very good friend to me. Would you like some elixir? I have some upstairs."

"I would very much, but I cannot go into the house. The runes, they keep me out."

"That's okay. You wait here, and I'll drop the bottles out

of the window. You catch them so they don't break."

He grinned so broadly, so innocently, that I figured he'd told me the truth with his warning. I hurried back upstairs. When I dropped the plastic bottles of cola down to him, one at a time, he caught them in his huge hands. I leaned out of the window.

"Don't open those right away! See how the elixir's foaming? Wait till it stops."

He glanced at the bottles. "I see this, yes. I do as you say."

"One more thing. I have a message for your folk. I cannot give you the gold unless they give me the vitki. The gold is in a magic box with a powerful lock spell on it. I cannot open it. Only the vitki can open it."

He laughed aloud. "Very good," he said. "This will teach them not to cheat."

The Frost Giant kid and his bottles of cola vanished in a shimmer of silver mist. I spent maybe thirty seconds feeling smug about inventing that magic lock spell until the meaning of his message sank in. Tor was off somewhere with the cave bear spirit. Would she let him find his way home? Another sodden thought: in Jötunheim Tor's sorcery worked in a spectacular way. He could produce manifestations in their version of the physical world, not mere divinations or the etheric visions of his rituals. Why hadn't he just come back once he was free? Maybe he didn't want to.

"Liv," I said aloud, "I hope your plane's on time."

I fetched my laptop from my backpack, opened the journal files, and began compiling bits and pieces that seemed relevant, descriptions of Tor's magics and some of my own, so that Liv would have more information. When I came to my notes about my trip into the Wilderkaiser snows, I got an insane idea. I tried to talk myself out of it. In that other world the cave bear had a physical presence. She'd already killed two dogs. She might kill me if I came after her prize. On the other hand, I terrified her. I also knew that Tor would do his best to protect me from her. I was mad at him, and maybe crazy as well, but I never doubted that he loved me.

Once again, I'd fallen into the trap of thinking that someone else, Liv in this case, would solve my problem. But I could
solve it myself. If I did, if I brought Tor home all by myself,
like a big girl, I would have gained a victory for myself, not
merely for him.

How could I get there—Aaron's photos. I booted up Tor's
laptop and brought up the pictures of the giants' steading.
I left a note for Joel on the refrigerator door, telling him to
shout down the heater vent in the living room when he woke
up, then gathered up both laptops and took them down to
my studio. While I studied the photos, I printed out the com-
pilation from my journal.

The day before, I'd stretched and primed a new canvas
for my senior project. I grabbed a stick of charcoal, stood in
front of the easel, and thought about the summoning ritual.
In my mind I could see faint images of the farmstead behind
the figures, but I'd been concentrating so hard on Tor that
I'd never focused on the details. Fortunately Aaron's snaps,
taken with his absolutely state of the art smartphone, had
captured most of what I needed. I worked between memory
and photos and laid in a rough drawing. When I finished, I
stepped back and considered underpaintings to increase the
feeling of depth.

"Maya?" Distorted and hollow, Joel's voice came down
the heater vent. "There's a Frost Giant in the driveway."

"Oh great! Help yourself to coffee. I'll see what he wants."

I wiped my charcoal-dusty hands on my jeans and hurried
to the side door. Instead of a 'he', the etinwife stood a few feet
away and looked around, squinting against the bright sunlight. I could see streaks of gray in her crown of blond braids.
Her eyes were blue, very human eyes. I opened the door and
called out a hello, but I stayed half inside the doorway, just
in case. She, however, smiled in a perfectly friendly manner
and handed me Joel's suitcase.

The pendant inside my shirt gave out a shriek of rage. She
jumped back, and I squealed. We looked at each and laughed.

"Sorry," I said. "The vitki made me a ward. It takes itself

seriously."

"That's likely all to the good." She still possessed the trace of a British accent from up Yorkshire way. "My grandson told me about the lock spell. I thought I'd have a try at dispelling it, if you agreed."

"I only wish you could." I set the suitcase down inside before I continued. "I called it that so he'd understand, but it's actually a combination lock on a safe, and only the vitki knows the combination. Do you remember what that is?"

"Oh yes. Well, that is a difficulty, then! I can do naught about that." She sighed and shook her head. "The men have made a right mess of this, haven't they? I told them to let the damned thing go, the galdr gold, that is, but of course they wouldn't listen."

"My vitki wouldn't listen to me, either."

"I'm not surprised to hear that."

I hesitated, but she looked so genuinely weary of the feud, and it was so decent of her to bring Joel's stuff back, that I decided I could trust her—at least a little.

"Can I ask you a question?" I said.

"Of course. Whether I'll answer—" She smiled in sincere good humor.

"Could any of your people use a telephone?"

Her eyes widened, and she laughed, a startled bark.

"Heavens, no!" she said. "I can't imagine how I could even explain what one is. And their fingers wouldn't fit in the little holes on the dial."

She must have gone off to Jötunheim before touch-tone phones were invented, much less cell phones. Still, their fingers would have trouble even with the push button kind of phone.

"Then I wonder if someone else is looking for your gold," I said. "They may have just wanted something else from my vitki and his cousin, but it might have been clues to the gold."

"A right mess, indeed!" She groaned aloud. "Well, dear, I hope your man can find his way home again. The others have gone off to look for him, you see, and I'm afraid of what they'll do if they find him. That bear killed two of their best dogs."

She gave me a sad smile and disappeared.

I shrieked louder than the ward in a mixture of anger, fear, and frustration. Cave bears and angry Frost Giants both! I nearly dropped the idea of going after him right then, but I refused to be a widow before I was married. Footsteps trotted down the stairs behind me. I turned around to see Joel, coffee mug in hand, standing about halfway down.

"Are you okay?" he said. "I heard you yell."

"Yes, I am." I stepped back inside and closed the door. "She was just trying to help."

"She was the most human of the lot, yeah. She stopped them from kicking me around." He gulped down a mouthful of coffee. "I hope to god that Tor's going to be okay. Everyone was talking about his sister. Do you think she can do something?"

"Probably. Help yourself to food if you're hungry. I've got work to do down here. Oh, and the etinwife brought your stuff back."

He took the suitcase and went back upstairs. For the rest of the morning, I painted like a mad fiend. I'd never slapped paint on canvas so fast before, and I probably won't ever do it again, but I felt the urgency like a fire in my hands. The landscape, the dark forest behind the rough wood house, the muddy yard in the foreground—the forms built up fast, still blocky and unrefined by the time JJ arrived at one o'clock. We went into the library room downstairs while I gave him the car keys and the printout for Liv.

"I might not be here when you get back," I said.

"You're not going after him, are you?"

"Of course I am, if I can get there. Tell Liv where I'm gone, okay?"

He looked at me narrow-eyed, started to speak, then just shook his head.

"He's really in trouble." I decided to give him only the essence of the story. "He's escaped from the giants, and they're after him."

"Jesus! Do you know how to shoot? Tor's got a couple of

hunting rifles around here somewhere."

"I've never touched a gun in my life. I'd probably shoot my own foot off. Besides, I couldn't stand to–" I caught myself. "Couldn't stand to do what? Kill someone else?"

Ice. Isa. I know what it means, to feel like you've turned to ice. JJ was watching me with a twisted little smile, sad-eyed, sympathetic.

"I don't know how you did it," JJ said. "But from what I know of Nils, good for you!"

"How did you–" Fear froze in my throat.

"Oh come on, you're not white, either. You know what it's like, always watching for clues, always on your guard around them, checking out the faces, the postures, the tone of voice. It gets to be a habit. Every time someone mentions Nils, you flinch, you look away, you bite your lower lip. I don't suppose the others noticed. Aaron's got his problems, and Billy, he doesn't need to notice."

"Yeah." I forced it out. "Okay."

"And then you confessed. Some joke, huh? I saw Tor recoil like you'd slugged him. I knew then."

"No one ever said you were stupid."

JJ grinned at me. "But about those guns." He turned away and began gazing around the library room. "I think they're in a closet down here."

"I don't care."

"Okay, you can't and won't use one, but Tor will if you find him. He's a good shot. And I wouldn't be surprised if he could kill someone without thinking twice."

"That's why I don't want to take him a gun. Look, if he shoots a couple of giants, do you think the rest of them will ever leave us alone? Blood feuds used to be considered entertainment, y'know."

JJ whistled under his breath. "Good point. Okay. No gun."

"Besides, if I can find him, he can bring us right home. I mean, like in two minutes."

"If he's escaped, why isn't he back already? Are you sure he's not some place where you can't get him out?"

"Not sure, no, but I'm betting I know what's stopping him. There's no time to explain. It's all in that printout. You can read it while you're waiting for Liv's plane."

"I will, okay, but Maya, for god's sake, Tor wouldn't want you to run this kind of risk."

"Then the bastard should have just given them what they wanted when he had the chance. You better leave. I've got to finish painting the gate."

"The—oh. That kind of gate."

"Yeah. Go!"

He went.

I returned to fiend mode and finished what I could do on the painting. I felt the power gathering, trembling behind some kind of barrier, as if it wanted to break through but could find no breach. From my other experiences with painted gates, I figured it lacked important details. With the charcoal I drew the Mannaz rune, to symbolize Midgard, and Othala on the sky to hold the power in check. I knelt by the heater vent and yelled for Joel. He came trotting down the stairs and joined me in the studio. He'd shaved, showered, and changed his clothes. Cleaned up, he looked so much like Tor that it wrung my heart.

"Tell me what's wrong with this painting," I said. "It has to be accurate."

"More magic?"

"You bet. I need details."

"Okay." He took a deep breath as if he needed to steady his nerves. "Over the front door, a pair of antlers, the biggest pair of antlers I've ever seen. Irish elk, probably."

I slapped those on with a fine brush and felt the painting strain at its barrier. Joel kept talking, I kept painting. At about two o'clock he ran out of additions. Didn't matter. I could feel the image struggling to be free.

"Okay," I said. "I've got to get some stuff together before I go through. Let's go back upstairs."

"Go? What are you—oh never mind! I'll hold the fort here until JJ gets back with Cousin Liv."

In a closet I found Tor's backpack, larger than mine, and filled it. I scavenged through the kitchen cupboards and packed a lot of food. I added some miscellaneous stuff I figured I might need, like matches. I saved room, though, for the crucial equipment, that is, my art supplies—the box of Conté and pastels, my biggest sketchbook, a couple of X-acto knives in case I had to carve runes or cut Tor free of leather bindings. I rolled up a couple of fleece blankets and tied them on the outside. I dressed in sweatpants over my jeans and my beaten-up but warm winter parka over a couple of shirts. The backpack went on top, heavy but bearable.

I said goodbye to Joel, who'd gone back to looking stunned in an armchair. Although I considered waiting for Liv's arrival, every minute I spent in safety might mean more danger for Tor. I went downstairs before my nerve failed and hurried into my studio. The canvas on the easel swelled to greet me, then subsided behind its chain of runes. I grabbed a paint rag from the work table and wiped Mannaz and Othala away.

Cold wind laced with élan swept over me. The warding pendant throbbed against my skin. I walked forward, stepped through, then turned to look back at an open landscape of fields and pasture. My studio room had dwindled to a tiny image caught in the bare branches of a tree. Overhead the sky hung slate-gray and swirling. I turned to see the giants' ramshackle steading about thirty yards away. The wooden house, vaguely A-frame, sat in a big yard behind a fence made of pieces of tree trunk and dead branches, randomly smeared with mud. I heard pigs squealing and smelled a thick ugly stench. In the animal pen off to the left a tall woman wearing mostly rags was emptying buckets into a trough. She never looked my way.

The bear had dragged Tor into the forest, which loomed a good distance behind the house. I headed for the trees, but I made a wide circle around the steading. As I passed it, a dog barked for a moment, then fell silent. Although I could see windows on the sagging walls of the rough wooden house, shutters covered them. Nothing moved among the garbage heaps and dunghills standing around in back near the cow barn, either. Once I got a good distance from the steading, the stench eased up, and I could smell snow coming on the wind.

The forest began suddenly behind a row of cut stumps and dead leaves, trampled into the ground. I hurried into cover and paused to look around. In the gray daylight I saw the trees clearly for the first time. I guessed that they were oaks, some European species, anyway, tall and crowned with spreads of bare branches. A few dead leaves clung stubbornly to twigs. On the ground, a litter of fallen leaves, brown and faded orange, clustered on the leeward side of the trunks and collected among the stunted shrubs and browning ferns—bracken, I think it's called—in little hollows. When I stepped on something that crunched, I squatted down and found acorns. Oaks, then, for sure.

Here and there stood trees of a totally different kind: huge conifers, bristling with bright green needles, dotted with red berries, or at least, with things that looked like berries to my California eyes. A few must have been a hundred feet tall, but none of them were shaped like the kind of pines I was used to, Christmas trees and the like. These conifers grew in untidy lumps and heaps. On the largest ones, their lower branches hung tent-like almost to the ground.

I picked my way through the forest until I could be sure I was hidden from the steading. In a clearing where gray boulders poked through dying ferns I stopped and swung the backpack off my shoulders. I propped it up against a rock and crouched down next to it. On the far side of the clearing stood more of the conifers, these short with trunks that looked like bundled logs. I finally remembered the name: yew. Eihaz was their rune.

In an oak that stood among the yews, movement caught my attention. I looked up and saw two ravens perched on a swaying bare branch.

"Do you know where the vitki is?" I said.

They cocked their heads to one side and considered me. I

waited. With a sudden caw they flew off. The branch bobbed from their leaving, then shivered to a stop. Otherwise, nothing moved, nothing made a sound around me. I'm a total city girl, but I remembered reading somewhere that forests fell quiet when there were predators around. Maybe I was the predator. Maybe something worse was.

I marked in my mind the direction in which the ravens had flown before I opened the backpack. I got out my sketchbook and a stick of charcoal. I had a number of pictures of Tor in that book, but I was looking for one in particular, a study that I'd done while he lay asleep and naked on our bed. I remembered aching with emotion while I'd drawn it, and as I'd hoped, there in the élan-soaked other world it seemed vibrant, solid, almost alive. I drew Tiwaz on the corner of the page.

"Where is he?" I breathed the question rather than spoke it. "Tyr, help me!"

On the paper the blank background developed smudges, faint marks and thin lines. The ravens returned, settling on a lower branch. They bobbed their heads at me and squawked. Odin's birds, I thought, not Tyr's. As far as I knew, Tyr had no particular bird associated with him, so maybe these were on loan. They flew off in the same direction as before. It was, I suppose, the only hint I was going to get. I started to close the sketchbook but caught my breath with a gulp. In the background of the drawing, among the smudges and marks, stood the outlines of not one but two cave bears, face to face.

"You sow!" My voice sounded more like a growl than human speech.

I flipped to a blank page in my book and began to draw. First, her outline, then her eyes—I could see them, suddenly, staring at me in terror. I grabbed brown Conté and began to fill her in, her humped shoulders, her powerful legs and claws. Inspiration! I snatched a black stick and drew a chain around her front legs.

I heard her shriek and roar with my physical ears. She was at some distance from me, off in the direction that the raven flight had indicated, but even though her voice sounded faint, I felt her rage and terror. I drew a collar on her neck and heard her snarl and chuff. A chain linked to the collar—another roar. I stood up and roared in answer, snarled and hissed as if I were one of the tiger spirits in my mother's folk tales. Silence was the only reply I received. I knelt again and attached the collar chain to the links around her feet.

"There, you sow! Let my man go!"

When I turned the pages of the sketchbook back to the original drawing of Tor, the outlines of the two cave bears had vanished. The smudges and marks in the background had formed themselves into a rough view of a cave on what might have been a hillside. It gave absolutely no clues as to where the cave might be. I also had no idea if the bear really was helpless or what form Tor might be in. Maybe the moon was already full, here in Jötunheim. When I looked up, the darkening sky told me only that night was coming on. The flood of élan mingled with the smell of coming snow. I could survive the cold, but what would snow do to Tor, assuming he was human? He had his parka, but he'd been wearing jeans, not heavy pants, when I'd last seen him.

I started to close the sketchbook but paused. For the briefest of moments, the Tor in the drawing opened his eyes and looked at me. I could swear I'd seen it, but it happened so fast that it might only have been wishful thinking. I kept staring at the page while the light darkened around me. The drawing stayed only a drawing.

I stood up, put away the art supplies, and got out the flashlight. I'd remembered to bring some extra batteries, too. When I flicked it on, it worked. I'd wondered if it would, here in some strange world beyond Midgard. I turned it off and slipped it into the interior zipper pocket of my parka where it would be handy for emergencies in the night. I put on the backpack again and headed off in the direction that the ravens had indicated.

Trying to walk in a reasonably straight line through an unfamiliar forest at twilight turned out to be impossible, at least for me. After maybe a quarter mile I gave up. I found an enormous oak, bare of leaves like the others, that had branches hanging low enough for me to climb. After a struggle, I managed to get up into them. The backpack hindered me, not just the weight, but its nasty habit of hooking itself on little branches. Finally, after a lot of swearing and a few tears of frustration, I reached the tree's crotch and managed to find a semi-secure sort of perch. I hung the backpack on a branch and sat astride another, one thick enough to nearly be a horizontal trunk, with my back braced against the main trunk. With the leaves gone, the oak provided no shelter, but I was off the ground and out of the reach of any wandering animals that might smell the food I carried.

The ravens returned, a flock of them, this time, led by an enormous bird who looked somehow familiar. I'd seen the matriarch of a raven group before, and I could have sworn I was seeing her again.

"Can you guys fly between the worlds?" I said.

She bobbed her head and danced a little on the branch.

"Do you know where Tor is? The vitki who helped you this summer?"

She turned her head away and stared off in the direction that the birds had previously indicated.

"Over there, huh?"

She squawked one sharp angry note. Look, I told myself. What is she looking at? After a dangerous scramble I managed to get to my feet on the super-thick branch. I clung to the trunk and stared into the darkness. Not all that far away, maybe a quarter of a mile, I spotted a tiny glow among the trees: fire. Jötnar, maybe, or Tor? A gamble, but I instinctively felt the ravens wouldn't betray me.

"Thank you."

She cawed, and the flock flew off again, a swirl of black against a leaden sky, heavy with twilight, that had fallen closer to the ground. By the time I managed to get myself and the backpack safely out of the tree, a blue gloaming had turned the light to fog, or so it seemed, thick, difficult to see through. When I looked up through the bare branches, I saw the ravens circling. They flew to a tree some yards on and settled. When I caught up with them, they flew again, a little farther, this time. They led me once more, but I followed stumbling in near darkness. When I tried to pick out their black shapes against the sky, I failed. While I looked up, I felt something wet and cold touch my face. A brief scatter of snow flakes, the first early warning of the storm to come, fell, then died away.

By then, however, I could smell a trace of woodsmoke in the chilly air. I got out the flashlight, kept my arm by my side, and flicked it on just long enough to gauge the ground ahead. Treacherous with tree roots, rocks, piles of leaves—I decided that trying to walk without light was as great a risk as signaling my presence. I kept the light low, however, when I walked on. The smell of smoke grew stronger. Another smell joined it—animal, greasy, strong. For a moment I panicked. I thought I'd gone round in a circle, as lost people do, and reached the farmstead again.

I flicked off the flashlight. In the darkness, the utter darkness of wild country on a night without stars, my eyes refused to focus. I said "the hell with it," turned the flashlight back on, and raised it to illuminate the path ahead. No farmstead, but the swollen shape of a tall mound, not really a hill, loomed out of the night. It matched what I'd seen appear on my drawing of Tor. I strode toward it. Piled up stones, huge stones, roughly shaped, formed the mound, which rose some twenty feet above my head. Grass, dead in the chill, and bright green mosses grew over and in the cracks between them. I swung the flashlight back and forth to get some idea of its size: nearly a football field, so just under a hundred yards. I walked along its length to its nose, then paused. Smoke and the animal smell grew thicker.

Bear, I thought. I bet that's what that stink is. The sow. Maybe Tor, too.

As I rounded the end of the mound, the smell of smoke abruptly vanished. I would have turned back if I hadn't remembered Halvar dousing Tor's fire. I was willing to bet that in this world, all of Tor's magics had become not just more powerful, but literal. He could command the Kennaz rune, and Kennaz would command the fire. I walked on past the short end of the mound, then turned down the long side. Apparently Tor could do nothing about the smell of bear. I sent a beam of light along the ground ahead of me.

"Tor," I called out, "Frost Giants don't have flashlights."

I heard him laugh and call my name. All the anger I harbored transformed like alchemy into relief and love and even a few tears.

CHAPTER 13

About halfway down the side of the stone mound, firelight blossomed into a spill of gold. I could see an opening and Tor silhouetted against it. Even though I felt exhausted, I hurried along as fast as I could. The backpack seemed to weigh a hundred pounds on my sore shoulders. Tor jogged out to meet me, helped me take it off, and then caught me by the shoulders for a kiss. He was stubbled and dirty and smelled like bear, but his mouth had never felt so good on mine.

The snow had begun to fall in earnest. Since he wore only a tee shirt and his jeans, I could feel him shivering. He grabbed the backpack, and we hurried into the shelter, a rough chamber, not quite square, with mossy walls of crudely cut stones—the green room of my earlier dream. Near the entrance Tor had laid his fire to let the smoke billow outside. I noticed a pile of dead wood nearby, ready against the night. His torn and filthy parka sat next to it. An opening on the far side of the room led deeper into the mound.

Between the fire and that opening lay a heap of brown fur and malice. The cave bear lay on her side in an odd posture. She'd tucked her front legs up by her chest and rested her head on them. When she saw me, she snarled and tried to raise her head. She could only get it a few inches off the floor. Her paws jerked along with her head when she tried to raise it further. She howled in pain.

"Maya," Tor said, "what did you do to her?"

"What makes you think I did anything?" I shrugged out

of my parka. Thanks to the fire the room was warm. "I've brought food."

"Great, but what did you do to her?"

"Why do you care? She trapped you here, didn't she?" I knelt down and began to rummage in the backpack. "Now she can't stop you from going home."

He said nothing. I looked up. "Well, didn't she?"

"Yeah." Tor sat down next to me. "How did you know that?"

"I dreamed it. And then one of my drawings showed me the pair of you. You really did transform this time, didn't you?"

He winced. In the fire a branch burned through with a shower of sparks. He twisted around, grabbed another branch, and laid it on the fire. I refrained from asking him just what he'd done as the bjarki, alone with this ardent female.

"I can't leave her here like this." Tor looked at the bear. "She'll starve to death."

"Tough."

"Shit, I never thought you could be this cold."

"You said you want me to be your equal, didn't you?" I handed him a chocolate power bar.

"I— Am I really that bad?"

"Yeah, actually. You are."

Tor shrugged and unwrapped the bar. At the scent the bear whimpered and turned pathetic eyes his way.

"Don't," I said. "Chocolate's bad for animals."

He scowled, then tossed the wrapping into the fire and bit into the bar. I found another one and opened it. Tor wolfed his down. I handed him crackers and a chunk of cheese. He stuffed those in, too, while I ate my powerbar. I brought out two bottles of mineral water and handed him one. While we ate, the bear kept watching me with her dark squinty eyes. Once she lifted a lip to show fang. I snarled at her, and she flinched.

"Come on," Tor said. "What did you do?"

"First, you tell me what she did to you. Then I'll decide if I tell you or not."

"She thought she was rescuing me. Trying to do a good thing."

"Oh, yeah, sure!"

Tor had a long drink of water. "Some guys," he said, "are so stupid that they think they'd like it if women fought over them. Maybe if both women were human. Fully human, that is. Unlike some."

"I could just go home and leave you here."

"Now you're being stupid."

He was right, or I would have snarled again.

"What did she do?" I repeated. "Tell me!"

"Okay, okay." He paused, thinking, for a minute or so. "When we got to the giants' steading, they started arguing about what to do with me. I couldn't understand much of what they said. I got the idea that some of them wanted to tie me up, but the leader thought that was a lousy way to treat a hostage. He was right. The inside of their longhouse is like a barn, mostly open. No chambers, just a few stalls on one side and a big loft upstairs. So they handed me a pair of greasy blankets, marched me outside, and locked me in a shed. Lots of straw on the floor and not much else. They left one poor bastard outside on guard.

"I'd been planning on leaving and looking for the bear, so this arrangement suited me fine. I never swore I wouldn't escape, y'know. I was figuring out what runes to cast when the bear found me. I heard a lot of yelling, and then dogs barking. As far as I can tell, the dogs smelled her first—"

"She does stink to high heaven."

Tor ignored me and continued. "The dogs came rushing outside, and the men must have followed. I heard a lot of yelling and barking. Something heavy crashed into the shed door and broke it off its hinges. She stuck her head in. I was so shocked I couldn't move for a minute. So she grabbed me by the arm and pulled me out." He pointed at the parka. "One sleeve's never going to be the same."

It had been shredded, yeah, from what I could see of it.

"Anyway," Tor said, "I stumbled over a dead dog. The

mob of giants all had axes, it looked like, so I cast a galdr that froze them and took off for the woods. She followed me, and a damn good thing. I tripped over something and fell hard. She grabbed me and somehow or other got me onto her back. My memory's blurry on that point. I hit my head when I fell. Anyway, I ended up riding her like a horse. Just like the shamans in the books. She brought me here."

"How sweet. A love nest?"

Tor finished the water in the bottle. "What's eating you? Do you really think I'd fuck a bear? Is that it?"

"Yeah, actually. It is."

"Well, I didn't. We're just friends, and she knows that."

"Hah! They go into heat in the fall. I read that on the Internet."

Tor rolled his eyes heavenward. "I told you I'm not poly, didn't I? Even if I was, it wouldn't be with animals. What do you think I am, a pervert?"

"When you're a bjarki, it wouldn't be perverted, would it?"

"That doesn't matter! I'm still aware that I'm a man, even in bear form." He glared at me. "You know I can't lie about myself."

"I do know. Okay, I believe you. But I bet she—"

"It doesn't matter what she wants. I'm the vitki. She's the fylgja." His voice snapped with authority, with command. "She had to learn that lesson this afternoon. Before you got here, I mean. She trapped me by bringing me to this chamber. She must have known about the wards in place here, and they were powerful ones. When I tried to chant a galdr, I got no response. This death mound sucked up the power of the runes. I was stunned when the power snapped back in my face. Couldn't think for a long time."

"Death mound?"

"It's a burial mound, yeah. I could feel the ghosts moving." He pointed to the opening that led deeper in. "It's filled with bones in there, all sorted out."

"You went in there?"

"Oh yeah. I needed to know what I was facing. Nothing

much, it turned out. Leg bones in one pile, arm bones in another, skulls heaped up together on a stone altar. Rotting baskets full of smaller pieces. The chamber we're in was a temple to the people buried here. The ghosts told me that. Ancestor worship. Someone set those wards against rune magic in here because they thought it would disturb the ghosts. I think. That's just speculation on my part."

Outside the wind had picked up. It whistled around the mound and made me yelp and shudder. I stared down the dark tunnel that led to the place of bones. Tor laughed at me.

"Don't worry," he said. "Eventually I sealed it off, cleaned the place up astrally. But anyway, when we first got here, every time I tried to leave, the bear would block my way. Physically, that is—she stood across the doorway. I tried talking to her. Ordered her to move. She never growled or threatened. She just stayed where she was."

"That's a lot of ugly bear fat to shove aside, yeah."

He ignored my nasty crack. "I kept testing the wards. They didn't prevent really primitive magics, like the priests here would have used. So I transformed." He smiled, just faintly. "I became a cave bear. I can really transform, here. I became the bjarki. It hurt like hell, but once I did it, I was bigger than she was. So she couldn't stop me. She didn't even try, just crept aside when I growled. Once I got outside, I could work. I changed back to human and cast galdrar against the wards until they shattered."

"How did she take that?"

"She was furious. I thought I'd have to transform again to fight her off, but all at once she crumpled. Fell to the ground, writhed, barely managed to crawl back in here. That was your doing. Right?"

It was an accusation, not a guess. "I suppose so," I said. "Why didn't you just come home then?"

"For a very simple reason. Sweetheart, I was worn out. I came back in and got dressed and fell asleep. I hadn't eaten anything since yesterday, remember. When I woke up, I cast the staves. Help was coming, they told me. I expanded the reading, and it seemed pretty clear that you were the help they meant. I didn't want to play hide and seek across the worlds. Y'know, I leave, you can't find me. I come back, but you've left, and so on."

"Oh my god, yeah, that would have been horrible."

"Besides, I couldn't leave her like this." He gestured at the bear. "She knows now who's in charge. Both of us, that's who. Not just me, but you, too." He gave me a soulful look. "Maya, please, tell me what you did."

"You finally said the magic word."

"What?"

"Please." I reached into the backpack and took out the sketchbook. "But if I release her, is she going to try to savage me?"

"Not with me here, she won't." Tor rose to a kneel and turned to look in the bear's direction. He caught her gaze, then spoke in Old Norse for a couple of quick sentences. She moaned and scrabbled with her front paws. The motion made her head jerk alarmingly. "She'll behave," he said to me. "She knows she'll die if she remains stuck like this."

"How can she die? I thought she was only a spirit bear."

"We happen to be in the spirit world. Or haven't you figured that out yet?"

I was shocked enough to stare open-mouthed. "It feels real to me," I said at last.

"It is real, just not in the way ours is. Real after another manner, the occultists would say." Tor paused to pull the backpack over to him. "Its atoms are built of another kind of energy, basically. Matter's only an illusion, anyway, even in our world. It's just a real stubborn one back home."

He found a candy bar and sat back on his heels to strip off the wrapping. I flipped through the sketchbook while I tried to assimilate what he'd just said. I found the page with my drawing of the chained bear, tore it out of the book, and held it out. The bear whimpered and writhed in such pain that I began to feel sorry for her. Tor wiped the chocolate off his fingers onto his jeans and took the drawing. The bear fell silent.

"Shit," he said. "No wonder! I don't suppose you can just erase those chains."

"It's Conté. It doesn't erase."

"Okay." He got up, then squatted by his parka. He felt in the pockets and brought out his rune knife. "Let's see how delicate I can be."

Tor laid the backpack flat on the ground and used it as a table of sorts. He set down the drawing, chanted a galdr, and held the rune knife up. A shimmer of runes flashed along the blade, Jera, Berkano, and Ánsuz. Carefully, slowly, he brought the knife down and with the tip cut through the paper and the drawing of the chain that bound her head to her forepaws. With a jerk of her head she whimpered. She raised her head and shook it, swung it from side to side, lowered it, raised it again, but all the while she was staring at Tor in what I took as adoration.

He was studying the drawing and never noticed. I'd drawn the chain around her front paws when she—the bear in the drawing, that is—had been holding them a little apart. Tor had just enough space to cut the chain without nicking her actual feet. Once again she whimpered, but again, she could finally move freely. When she scrambled up, she showed me her teeth. I snatched the drawing from Tor and held it up. She closed her mouth and backed up fast.

Tor growled under his breath and snapped his fingers. She lay down again, but on her stomach, this time, and rested her head on her front paws to watch him.

"She's totally yours, isn't she?" I said.

"Now, yeah. I don't know what to do about the collar."

"It's loose enough so it won't choke her."

"Yeah, but it'll chafe. Catch on branches, too, in the forest."

I was tempted to say "tough" again, but I held my tongue. Now and then the bear would look my way and whine, just softly under her breath, in what sounded like fear. I felt cruel for hurting her and a little guilty. Not very guilty, but enough to make me lighten up. I'd dominated her, and now she knew who was boss. I saw no reason to push things farther.

"Let's see how tight the collar is," I said.

I took the backpack and found the fruit I'd packed. When I held up an apple, the bear sniffed the air and turned her head in my direction.

"If I give her this, will she take my hand off like Fenrir did?"

"No, of course not. She knows you're my mate."

Still, I took no chances. I laid the apple down a couple of feet in front of her. "There you go." I moved back. "That's for you."

She raised herself up, stretched out her neck, and snagged the apple. She crunched it a couple of times in her massive jaws and swallowed with no trouble. Tor found another apple and held it out. She nipped it with her front teeth and took it safely out of his hand.

"Whoa!" I said. "She really is tame."

"Yeah. She's finally learned. She won't try to trap me again. Not here, not at home at the full moon. No more bjarki for me."

"Oh my god! That's wonderful. Do you mean you're free of it?" I wanted to shout and dance in triumph, but he held up a hand for silence and chilled my mood.

"Maybe or maybe not," he said. "Remember what I told you, that night, way back when I offered you a job? There's always a catch. Every full moon I'm going to be vulnerable because of the virus. I might have to fight off every spirit who smells the power leak and takes their chance to attack. I just don't know yet."

I felt sick with disappointment. "You can't tame all of them."

"That's where the bear comes in. She'll fight them off. To protect me." He smiled briefly. "Unless she can't for some reason."

Unless, he meant, she was caught by the collar somewhere in the spirit world or chafed raw and too angry to have anything to do with us.

"Okay, I understand." I picked up the drawing again and

studied it. "If you cut through the collar, will it cut her, too?

"That's what I'm afraid of. Repercussion."

"Will the wound heal okay?"

"I don't know. Sometimes magical damage doesn't. Look what happened to that guy in the Grail legends. The Fisher King."

"That's who I was thinking of, all right. Let's see. Maybe if I weaken it she can throw it off."

I'd drawn the collar as a simple band of some indeterminate substance, just a pair of roughly parallel lines wrapping around her neck. I got my drawing materials out of the backpack. First I used an X-acto knife to remove as much of the Conté forming the collar as I could. Since I'd been so angry when I was drawing, the clay and wax base of the sticks had gone on thickly enough for me to lift some of the black lines off. The pigment, however, remained, a dark stain on the paper. I put the knife back and took out a stick of brown Conté.

"Let's make it leather." I glanced at Tor's belt to get the texture right, then added color and a little stippling. "And sort of torn."

The cuts Tor had made on the paper had mysteriously healed. In the drawing, the bear's paws were free, and a length of chain dangled broken from her collar. At the place where the iron links touched the leather, I drew a deep tear, as if the weight of the chain had been too much for the collar itself. I looked up and noticed the bear watching me.

"Scratch," I said. "Scratch at your neck."

Tor repeated the words in Old Norse. I demonstrated by scratching at my own neck with my fingers closed into a paw. The bear hesitated, looking back and forth between us, then followed suit. I heard the chain fall onto the floor, a definite, real, undeniable jingle and clank even though I could see nothing lying on the stone. She tossed her head back and chuffed in what I hoped was delight. On the drawing the collar had disappeared. Ice slid down my back, the spirit ice that signaled powerful magics, and these were mine.

"There," I said. "She's free."

"Thank you. And I'm free with her."

"It's all good, then?" I smiled at him. "So you won't care if I give the Frost Giants their gold back."

"Hey! Unfair!"

"Oh come on! I risk my life to come find you, I help your bear girlfriend, and you won't even open the safe for me when we get home?"

"Why do you care if they have it?"

"So they'll leave us alone. Tor, c'mon! Do you want to fight with them for the next fifty years? They're too stupid to stop trying to get it back. I don't want to start our life together in the middle of a feud with Frost Giants."

Tor opened his mouth, shut it again, glared at me, and crossed his arms over his chest. "We'll discuss it when we get home."

"How middle class of you."

"Maya, damn it!"

"If we can get home." I looked past the fire. "It's a real storm out there."

The firelight penetrated the night just far enough for us to see snow falling, thick, silent, fast, like ropes let down from heaven.

"Can you cast a gate in here?" I said.

"No, there's not enough room for a ritual circle. You need space to clear off other influences, to make a neutral ground. I don't think I can do that with all three of us crammed in here. Where's the image gate you made?"

"Hanging in a tree near the giants' steading. It was the only way in I had, the image of their awful farm. We don't want to go back there, even when the storm's over."

"I guess we'll just have to spend the night here." Tor grinned and slid over next to me.

"Keep your hands to yourself! I'm not going to make love with you where that bear can watch."

"She won't care."

"So what? I will."

"I can make her turn over and stare at the wall."

"Yuck! Not good enough!"

"Now who's being middle class?"

"There are limits even with artists. Besides, we'd better stay on our guard. The Frost Giants are looking for you. The etinwife told me that."

His grin vanished. "They won't be able to find us in this storm, but yeah, we need to leave as soon as we can. Once we're home, I'll renew the wards around our house. I'm tired of them strolling down the driveway like they own the place."

"Once we give them back their gold, they won't have any reason to hang around."

"Once we—I haven't agreed to open the safe yet."

I smiled and fluttered my eyelashes. He sighed.

"I suppose I will, sooner or later," he said. "Yeah, the gold does attract them. Like dead meat and flies."

I found a blank page in my sketchbook and picked up a piece of charcoal.

"Could you build up the fire a little?" I said. "I could use more light."

"Okay. What are you going to draw?"

"Home."

He smiled, a slow, sly grin. "Think it'll work?"

"I don't know. I've never used paper and pastels for this before, just paints and canvas."

I started by making an image of the front of our house, but it stayed stubbornly dead, a sketch only. I turned the page and thought about my studio. I'd set up the room myself, I'd created both art and magic in it, and I could see it so clearly in my mind, its simple furniture in particle board brown, its gray walls. My easel stood where I'd left it and held the painted gate into Jötunheim. The window—I put in a view of the back yard. As I worked on the colored drawing, I felt the power flow.

Tor got up and began to gather our possessions together, the backpack, our parkas. His faith in my magic gave me faith in myself. I put in detail after detail, the drawer I'd left half-open, the jars of acrylic on the work table. The paper seemed to swell and billow under my fingers like the sail of a ship.

"What rune should I draw on it?" I said. "Othala might hold us here."

"Try Mannaz."

Tor began to chant a galdr. As soon as I drew the rune, the image floated off the paper. It drifted to a chamber wall and hovered in the air as it grew larger and larger. I grabbed the sketchbook and the box of my drawing stuff and stood up. The bear scrambled to her feet and growled. She took one step toward the gate, but when I hissed and snarled at her, she backed off.

"He'll bring you through when he needs you," I said.

Tor let the chant fade away and spoke to the bear in Old Norse. She whimpered, but she lay down on the opposite side of the chamber, near the dying fire. Tor and I exchanged one glance, then strode forward together. As the gate enveloped us, I felt a cold touch of nausea like rocketing downhill in a rolling coaster. I took one more step, and the sensation vanished.

"You left the lights on," Tor said.

We were standing in the middle of my studio. So my art tends toward illustration, does it? All that "unnecessary" detail, huh? Illustration has its uses.

I glanced out of the window. Night had fallen here in Oakland, too. Right in front of us stood my easel with the painting of the Frost Giants' steading. That image glowed and throbbed with life, but the image I'd drawn in the mossy chamber had returned to the paper. I set my sketchbook and box of supplies down on the work table. Tor crowed with laughter, dropped the stuff he carried, and grabbed a charcoal stick. When he drew swift runes on the painted sky, the canvas returned to being a canvas with a hurried, sloppy farmscape in acrylics on its surface. He threw his arms around me and kissed me before I could say a word.

I took another kiss, then pushed him away. "You're opening the safe," I said. "Right now."

"What is this? Don't you trust me?"

"Of course I don't, but that's not the issue. We don't

know when they're going to give up looking for you there and come looking for you here. I want to have the gold so I can hand it over."

"Shit, I hate to admit this. Yeah, you're right. But!" He held up a hand and glared at me. "It's your decision, not mine."

"Fine. I'll take the responsibility."

I lingered in the studio while Tor went into the other room to work the combination of the safe. He came back in a couple of minutes with the shoebox. I opened it to make sure that the plaque was in it, then made him leave the room while I hid it in a drawer. We gathered up the backpack and parka and walked down the hall to the library room just as a car pulled up in the driveway. Someone got out and slammed the car door.

"I bet that's the cops," Tor said.

Sure enough! The doorbell rang. We heard someone hurrying down the stairs from the upper flat and waited in the darkened room until we heard Lieutenant Hu's voice.

"Uh, good evening, ma'am. I just wanted a few words with Mr. Thorlaksson."

"Not here just now." A fake Nordic accent colored Liv's speech. She must have practiced it for hours. "I am sister. You are?"

We heard Hu sigh. I could imagine his martyred look at facing another damned Icelandic speaker.

"Liv?" Tor called out. "I'm here. Just came in the back door."

We hurried to the stairwell and a much relieved Lieutenant Hu. Since she was a bare inch shorter than Tor, blonde and blue-eyed Liv towered over the cop. She was wearing jeans and a pale pink shirt with short sleeves that showed off her nicely muscled arms. A farmwoman, I thought, and she looked it, from her honey-colored bobbed hair to her heavy walking shoes.

"Sorry I'm not cleaned up," Tor said to the lieutenant.

"Yeah," I put in. "We spent the night camping over at Stinson."

"Huh," Liv said, still with her fake accent. "You both stink, yes. Old fish."

Hu's look of martyrdom intensified. "Just wanted to tell you some news," he said. "The medical examiner agrees that a pre-leukemia condition likely contributed to your uncle's death. We're still not sure what happened, but it looks more and more like some degree of manslaughter rather than murder. Probably involuntary. Maybe even death by misadventure."

"That's good to know," Tor said. "Any news of my cousin?"

"Not yet, no, but don't worry. We're working on it."

Hu muttered good-bye and retreated from the smell of bear. The three of us waited until we heard him drive away. "Liv," I said, "Pleased meet you. Literally."

We all laughed, then hurried upstairs. Joel was waiting for us in the living room.

"Jesus," he said. "What did you two do? Roll in carrion?"

"Close enough," Tor said. "Me and Maya had better clean up. Then we need to figure out what you're going to tell the cops."

"Say what?" Joel blinked at him, then smiled with a wry twist of his mouth. "How I escaped from the drug dealers, you mean."

"Exactly that, yeah." Tor grinned at him. "Welcome to our side of the family. I think you're going to fit right in."

CHAPTER 14

When they'd grabbed Joel at the airport, the giants had bruised him pretty badly without even meaning to. He'd made the mistake of struggling with them once they'd gotten him to Jötunheim and earned a few more bruises in the process before the etinwife intervened. Swollen red-like-meat and bluish purple patches marked his arms, his back, and the side of his torso, where someone had kicked him. It looked to me like they'd just missed breaking one of his ribs.

"They all hurt like hell," Joel remarked, "but they'll come in handy now. Where do you think Dad's druggie friends threw me out of the car?"

"Not far from here there's a nature preserve," Tor said. "I'll bring up Google maps and show you. You must have wandered around up there all day."

"After hiding for hours in the underbrush to make sure they didn't come back. Uh, is there any underbrush?"

After the two of them spent some study time with Tor's laptop, Joel changed back into his dirty clothes. Liv got some dirt and leaves from the back yard and rubbed them into his hair while Tor called the police to tell them that his missing cousin had just staggered up to the door. The police wanted them down at the local station immediately.

After they left, Liv and I sat at the breakfast bar. I gobbled the leftovers from the dinner she'd cooked for herself and Joel while we exchanged the stories of our recent travels. Her voice had returned to its California norm.

"I thought my trip was harried," Liv said. "Nothing compared to yours."

"Once I got control of the spirit bear, it wasn't that bad."

"You say that so calmly!"

"Calm? No! I just haven't processed it all yet, what happened, where we were."

"It could take a couple of days, yeah, and then it'll hit you."

I got up and checked my hands, which had finally stopped shaking. I found a package of cookies and made a pot of fresh coffee. While we waited for it to drip through, Liv took out her cellphone and showed me pictures of her children. After the things Tor had said about them, I was surprised to find them not only perfectly human-looking, but very handsome, three year old fraternal twins, a boy and a girl, Reyr and Sonja. Both had dark eyes like their uncle's and very pale hair. There was a particularly cute snapshot of them riding a shaggy pony.

"Tor and I were both that blonde when we were that small," Liv said. "But our hair darkened as we aged. Theirs will too, probably."

"They're three already? You must have married young."

"When I was nineteen, yes. I talked my father into letting me go back to Iceland to college, but I hated school, just hated it. I met Helgi, and that was that."

Someone pounded on the front door, slow, measured knocks like the drum of fate. Liv put down her smartphone with a sigh. "The police again?"

"Worse, I bet," I said. "I wondered when they'd come here to look for us."

Tor's laptop was sitting on the breakfast bar where Aaron had left it. I booted it up and accessed the security cam. A pair of scruffy-looking Frost Giants appeared in the gray scale image. They wore filthy tunics, leather leggings, and wolf skins draped over their shoulders. Against their height, the skins looked like scarves. The giants carried battle axes and glared at the door as if they were calculating how many blows it would take to shatter it.

"Oh my god!" I said. "I'll call the security company."

"No, don't!" Liv ran into the living room and threw open the front window. She leaned out and yelled at the giants in Old Norse. I joined her at the window in time to see one of them shaking a fist in her direction. Liv flung up her hands and chanted a galdr. The jötnar duo screamed and vanished–too late.

"There!" Liv said. "I cursed them."

"You don't mean just swearing at them, right?"

"Right. Not a huge curse. The boils should go down in a day or two."

"I'm glad you're here." I laid a hand on my chest to reassure my pounding heart. "They could have so smashed that door in."

"As soon as Tor admitted he was feuding with giants, I knew I had to come. He *is* my brother, after all. But you've really got to give them that talisman back."

"Don't worry. I intend to, but that pair weren't the right guys to give it to."

"For sure. Tor needs to do a summoning and get the etin-wife to come over. Judging from the printout you left me, she's the only one of them with a whole brain in her head."

Just to make sure I had the rotten thing well hidden, I went downstairs and retrieved the shoebox with the gold plaque from the drawer. I stowed it on the high shelf in the wardrobe in the Burne-Jones bedroom and threw a jacket over it to hide it further. By then it was getting on to nine o'clock. I sank into an armchair while Liv brought us each a cup of fresh coffee. I sipped mine and thanked her.

"I hope the guys get back soon," I said. "I'm starting to worry. What if the giants get hold of them on the road?"

"One of us would know it if that had happened. I bet the police are just being sticklers for protocol."

It took me a moment to assimilate what she'd said: one of us would know it. We both had powerful talents beyond the normal. If danger threatened her brother, my lover, we'd know.

"Yes." I felt my life settle into its new direction like a plane reaching cruising altitude. "You're right."

Tor and Joel returned some twenty minutes later. After they made the formal police report, Tor told us, they'd had to wait at the local station until Lieutenant Hu could arrive to "discuss" what had happened.

"To grill us, of course," Tor said. "But by then, our family lawyer had gotten there, too. Hu had to pull in his horns. Liv, Mr. Rasmussen says hello. I mentioned you were here. Anyway, we're done with the cops. It's going to be okay. They're closing the book on Nils' death by misadventure. Joel's case might drag on for a little while, but Joel, you were really convincing."

"Thanks. With a dad like mine, I learned to lie early. It comes in handy in the business world, too."

Tor started to say more, but Liv held up a hand to stop him.

"While you were gone," Liv said, "a pair of jötnar arrived at the front door. Carrying big axes. I scared them off, but Torvald, this is serious. You have got to do a summoning before they come back with a warband."

Joel turned pale.

"Shit!" Tor said. "Yeah, you're right, but I'm wiped out. I won't be able to control the structures if I don't sleep first."

Liv fixed him with a glare. "Are you sure you just don't want to give up the gold?"

Tor said something nasty-sounding in Icelandic. When she replied in kind, I stepped in.

"It's my decision now," I said. "About the gold, I mean. Not his. And Liv, Tor and I are both totally exhausted. Do you really think they'll come back tonight? They know that there's two vitkar in the house now."

"Only two?" Liv smiled at me. "I'd say three vitkar."

My first reaction: she can't mean me. My second reaction: what else am I?

"Thanks," I said. "Three."

Liv turned to her brother. "Can we do a casting?"

"Good idea," Tor said, then muttered under his breath. "For a change."

Liv ignored the comment. Joel had taken to staring at the ceiling again. Adjusting to the truth about his family was going to be a long, slow process.

Tor retrieved the red pouch of rune staves from his parka and took a white linen napkin from the kitchen cupboard. He and Liv sat on the floor at opposite ends of the coffee table and spread out the chips of wood between them. Liv drew three, then flipped them over one at a time: Fehu, Thurisaz, Wunjo, but this time, Wunjo stood upright for a perfect outcome. She drew two more and set them either side of Wunjo: Elhaz and Gebo, protection and gift. Once again the siblings mixed up the staves. This time Tor drew Raidho, Eiwaz, and Tiwaz—wagon and yew, movement forward, protected under Tyr's judgment.

"We're safe enough for now," Tor said.

Liv nodded her agreement. "I'm tired, too. It's been a very long day. But tomorrow, Torvald Einar—"

Joel groaned under his breath and stood up. "Tomorrow is another day," he announced. "Liv, you take the bedroom. I'll take the couch."

I smiled thanks his way. I too was dreading another squabble in a language I didn't understand.

In the end, the etinwife settled the feud. We all slept till about noon. While Tor and Liv collaborated on cooking a massive brunch in the kitchen, and Joel made a string of calls on his smartphone, I went into the Burne-Jones bedroom to consult the alchemical barometer. Under a golden sun, a red lion snoozed on a rock by an ocean. I took that as a good sign. While I stared at it, I felt another mind touch mine: come down to the back garden. Only one person I knew would have called our scruffy yard a back garden.

I retrieved the shoebox with the plaque from the wardrobe and sneaked down the hall to the stairwell. Everyone remained too busy to notice me. I hurried downstairs and out. The etinwife sat perched on the stone wall, and her grandson, dressed in proper jötunn clothes of baggy homespun pants and a linen tunic, stood beside her. They smiled and waved as I walked over to them.

"Here you go." I handed the kid the shoebox. "You get to be the hero who brings the treasure back."

"Very nice gesture," the etinwife said to me, then smiled his way. "Your granddad will like that."

He grinned at me and opened the box. Gold flashed as the sunlight hit the surface of the plaque. For some moments he and his grandmother studied their treasure. "It is so beautiful," he said at last. "We thank you."

"Yes, we do indeed," the etinwife said. "Ours again at last!"

"How did you lose it?" I said.

"A vitki stole it from my husband." She frowned at the memory. "He looked much like your man and his kinsman, but older."

"I bet it was my man's grandfather. All he thought about was money."

"It could very well be." She smiled at me. "He had spells that would draw gold toward him, and this was the only piece of gold my husband had."

"The greedy old bastard! I'm so glad you've got it back."

From the kitchen window upstairs I heard Tor howl in—not exactly rage. Annoyance, maybe.

"We'd best go," the etinwife said. "You've got a bit of work ahead of you." She winked at me. "Men!"

"Yes," I said. "But don't worry. I can handle him."

A silver mist fell upon them like rain. When it cleared, they'd vanished. More than one feud had ended. They had their gold, and I'd stopped fighting with myself over who I was.

I sauntered back to the house and Tor. My new life had begun.

Historical Note

Otto Rahn (1904-1939) was a German medievalist, mountaineer, and officer in the Ahnenerbe SS. Although it's currently fashionable to claim he was the model for the Lucasfilm movie about Indiana Jones, such is hardly the case. His theories about the Grail had nothing to do with the legendary cup of Joseph of Arimathea. Rather, they depended on a close reading of Chrétien de Troyes' Grail poems and Rahn's studies of the Cathar heresy in Provence. His book, CRUSADE AGAINST THE GRAIL (KREUZZUG GEGEN DEN GRAL in the original German) set forth the theory that the Grail was originally a "stone from heaven," a meteorite and a Cathar sacred artifact.

Writing fiction is a strange process. I had no intention, when I started to fill in Maya's past life as a young Nazi, of bringing any real persons into her story beyond the obvious references to Hitler and Himmler. Rahn somehow shoved his way out of my subconscious mind and into the book. Until I included him, I suffered from "writer's block" on this particular project. Once I gave in, the words flowed again. What particularly caught my attention were the mysteries surrounding his death.

He did indeed commit suicide after a stint as a guard at Dachau, and the motive by all accounts was that Himmler had found out about his sexuality. He never could have passed the "racial purity" test, either. However, there was also a persistent rumour that Rahn had gotten himself engaged to some unknown woman just before his suicide and that Himmler was delighted by this. Other sources deny it. Such ambiguities leave seductive openings for novelists.

Was Rahn a dedicated Nazi? I doubt it very much. As Maya says in my fiction, if the SS wanted to recruit you, you couldn't just say no. Before he killed himself, Rahn told a friend that he could no longer live in the country Germany had become. The translator of his two books, Christopher Jones, sums it up nicely when he remarks that Rahn made the mistake of thinking his enemies were his friends. I have to agree.

CRUSADE AGAINST THE GRAIL: The Struggle between the Cathars, the Templars, and the Church of Rome, by Otto Rahn, trans. Christopher Jones © 2006, Inner Traditions.

LUCIFER'S COURT: A Heretic's Journey in Search of the Light Bringers, by Otto Rahn, trans. Christopher Jones © 2008, Inner Traditions.

CPSIA information can be obtained at www.ICGtesting.com
Printed in the USA
BVOW08s2016140816

459016BV00001B/27/P

9 781940 121024